D0240218

MEDICI
Ascendancy

Matteo Strukul

Translated from the Italian
by Richard McKenna

First published in Italian as *I Medici. Una dinastia al potere*
in 2016 by Newton Compton
First published in the UK in 2019 by Head of Zeus Ltd

9 7 5 3 1 2 4 6 8

A catalogue record for this book is available from the British Library.

ISBN (HB): 9781786692092
ISBN (XTPB): 9781786692108
ISBN (E): 9781786692085

Typeset by Silicon Chips
Cover design by Patrick Knowles

Cover image: *The Journey of the Magi to Bethlehem*, c. 1460.
Fresco by Benozzo Gozzoli © Bridgeman Images

Printed and bound in Great Britain by
CPI Group (UK) Ltd, Croydon CR0 4YY

Head of Zeus Ltd
First Floor East
5–8 Hardwick Street
London EC1R 4RG
WWW.HEADOFZEUS.COM

To Silvia

February 1429

1

Santa Maria Del Fiore

Cosimo raised his eyes to a sky that was as blue as lapis lazuli dust. It made his head spin, so he quickly brought his gaze back down to his surroundings. Around him were the masons, some mixing lime with the pale sand of the Arno River to prepare the mortar while others perched on the partition walls, eating a quick breakfast. They worked exhausting shifts, often spending whole weeks up here and sleeping among the wooden scaffolding, bricks, slabs of marble and rubble.

Almost two hundred feet above the ground.

Seen from up here, the city both entranced and unnerved him. Placing his feet carefully, Cosimo slipped between the beams of the scaffolding, its edges like the sharp black teeth of some mythological creature, and made his way slowly to the base of the dome, which was under construction. The architects and master builders called it 'the drum'. He glanced down at the piazza below, where, with wide-eyed wonder, the people of Florence were finally witnessing the completion of Santa Maria del Fiore cathedral. Wool carders, tradesmen, butchers, farmers, prostitutes, publicans and wayfarers, all seeming to mouth a silent prayer of thanks that Filippo Brunelleschi's design was nearing completion. The dome for which they'd waited so long was taking shape, and it looked as though it would be that eccentric, balding goldsmith with the bad teeth and the surly demeanour who would accomplish it.

Cosimo could see Brunelleschi now, drifting like a lost soul between the piles of building materials and stacks of bricks, his expression seemingly absent but surely in fact engrossed in who knew what calculations. His eyes were so pale and clear that they resembled chips of sparkling alabaster set on his pallid skin, which was stained with all manner of paints and building materials.

The clanging of hammers roused Cosimo from his daydreaming: the metalsmiths were at work, and shouted orders and instructions echoed through the air. Cosimo took a deep breath and then looked downwards towards the base of the octagonal structure. The gigantic hoist Brunelleschi had designed turned endlessly as, guided by a young lad, the two chained oxen trudged calmly in silent circles, working the cogs and gears of the winch drum which was capable of hauling heavy stones up to impossible heights.

Brunelleschi had devised some truly amazing machines. He had designed them himself; then he'd called in the very best craftsmen and driven his workers mercilessly, and the arsenal of mechanical wonders he had rapidly assembled allowed him to lift and set slabs of marble, sections of wooden scaffolding and dozens of sacks of sand and mortar precisely in place.

Cosimo was overjoyed to see how well the work was proceeding. Before Brunelleschi, no one had managed to design a dome capable of spanning the vast 118-foot-wide octagonal drum, but not only had Brunelleschi managed it, he had somehow contrived to do it without visible supports. His design had none of the external buttresses or wooden centring that Neri di Fioravanti had proposed, and it had left the commissioning Opera del Duomo committee open-mouthed with amazement.

Brunelleschi was either a madman or a genius, perhaps even both. And the Medici – and Cosimo, above all – had wedded themselves to the man's crazed brilliance. He smiled at the audacity of it and reflected upon what the cathedral might eventually come to mean, not only for his city but also for himself. To judge from what was happening up there, he had every right to feel ecstatic as he looked at that ever-growing construction site. It was like some crazed Tower of Babel of scaffolding and planks, which played host to a multitude of workmen: wheelwrights, rope makers, bricklayers, plasterers, carpenters and ironmongers, food vendors, wine sellers, and even a cook equipped with an oven for baking bread to serve to the men. Labourers were climbing up the wooden scaffolding while others worked on wicker platforms perched on the surrounding rooftops like birds' nests as though they had enlisted a flock of storks to help them complete the titanic project.

'So what do you think, Messer Cosimo?' asked a quiet, firm voice.

Cosimo spun round and found himself face to face with Filippo. A gaunt man with frenzied eyes, Filippo was clad in a red tunic and nothing else. Full of a mixture of pride and hostility, his evasive gaze spoke of his rebellious, sometimes violent nature, but it softened when he met men he considered noble.

Cosimo did not know if he was numbered among these, but he was undoubtedly the firstborn son of Giovanni de' Medici, the family patriarch who had generously financed the construction and had provided crucial support for Brunelleschi's involvement in the project.

'Magnificent, Filippo, magnificent,' he said, his eyes glowing with wonder. 'I did not expect to see such progress.'

'We are still far from finishing; I want to be clear about that. The most important thing, *messer*, is that you allow me to work.'

'As long as the Medici are among the principal patrons, you have nothing to fear. On that you have my word, Filippo. We started this together, and together we will finish it.'

Brunelleschi nodded.

'I shall attempt to complete the cupola in accordance with classical canon, as planned.'

'I don't doubt it, my friend.'

While he was talking to Cosimo, Filippo's eyes darted everywhere: first to the builders preparing mortar and laying the bricks one by one, next towards the source of the blacksmiths' constant hammering and finally to the carts carrying bags of mortar down in the square. In his left hand he grasped a parchment containing one of many preparatory designs and in his right he held a chisel. Cosimo wondered what plans he had for *that*.

But that was Brunelleschi for you.

And as abruptly as he had appeared, Brunelleschi gave him a nod of farewell and disappeared between the beams and scaffolding of the dome, swallowed up by that colossal, restless enterprise buzzing with activity. Cosimo was left staring at the imposing wooden arches while shouts announced the hoisting of yet another load.

Suddenly, he heard a voice from behind him call his name.

'Cosimo!'

Holding on to the scaffolding, he turned and saw his brother Lorenzo approaching. Before he even had the chance to greet him, Lorenzo cut him short.

'It's our father, Cosimo. Our father is dying.'

2

The Death of Giovanni de' Medici

As soon as Cosimo entered the room, his wife Contessina came up to him, her beautiful dark eyes red from weeping. She was clad in a simple black robe and a fine gossamer veil.

'Cosimo...' she murmured. She could say nothing more – all her energies were focused on holding back her tears. She wanted to stay strong for her beloved husband. He put his arms around her and embraced her, but after a moment she freed herself.

'Go to him now,' she said. 'He's waiting to see you.'

Cosimo turned to Lorenzo and, for the first time that day, actually saw his face. His brother had made sure to walk ahead of him as they descended the scaffolding and rushed to the Palazzo Medici.

Lorenzo's white teeth were biting into his lower lip, and Cosimo suddenly realized how distressed he was. Lorenzo's handsome countenance, which usually seemed impervious to tiredness, was sallow, and there were dark rings under his green eyes. He needed to rest, thought Cosimo. Over the past few days since their father had fallen ill, Lorenzo had been working tirelessly on the bank's financial affairs. An active, practical man – less gifted than Cosimo in arts and letters, but possessed of a quick and lively intellect – his brother had always been the one who stepped in to bear the brunt of whatever hard work needed doing and to shoulder the responsibilities of the family. Cosimo, on the other hand, had dedicated himself to following, together with several members of the Opera del Duomo committee, the progress of the dome. He was the member of the family entrusted with strategy and politicking, much of which was conducted through lavish displays of arts patronage. Though formally it was the committee which was responsible for the dome's construction, all Florence knew how much Cosimo had pushed for the candidacy and eventual selection of Filippo Brunelleschi. He had dipped into the family's resources to finance the wondrous edifice that was now approaching completion.

Cosimo embraced his brother and then entered his father's chamber.

The room was lined with thick brocades that allowed no more than a dim, almost unearthly light to permeate the darkness. Here and there were golden candelabras. The reek of wax made the air stifling.

When he saw his father, his eyes now dim and watery with approaching death, Cosimo knew there was nothing to be done. Giovanni de' Medici, the man who had raised the family to the city's highest rank, was dying. His face, once so confident and determined, was grey with illness and upon it was a shadow of resignation that rendered him a pale imitation of his previous self. Cosimo was deeply shocked. He could barely believe that Giovanni, once so strong and purposeful, could have been brought so low in a matter of days by a fever. Cosimo's mother was at the bedside, holding one of his father's hands in hers. Piccarda's face was still beautiful, even if her usual composure was now absent: her long black lashes were silver with tears and her pursed lips as red as the bloodied blade of a dagger.

She murmured his name and then fell silent – all other words seemed meaningless.

Cosimo looked back at his father and thought again how suddenly his illness had struck, and without any apparent cause. Their eyes finally met and Giovanni felt a surge of energy when he recognized his son. He might be weakened, but he had no intention of giving in. In that moment, his usual character was roused, urging him to fight on even if it were for the last time. Heaving himself up with a wheeze, he sat up in the middle of the bed among the down pillows that Piccarda had positioned for his comfort. He pushed them aside with a gesture of irritation and beckoned to Cosimo to come over.

Though he had promised himself he would be strong, Cosimo could no longer hold back his tears. Ashamed of his weakness, he quickly wiped his eyes with the back of his hand and went over to his father.

Giovanni had last words to impart before he left this world.

His dark eyes glittering like buttons of polished onyx in the flickering candlelight of the room, he strained forward towards his son, and Cosimo grasped him by the shoulders.

'My son,' he croaked, 'swear to me that you will be sober in your politicking. That you will live with moderation. Like a simple Florentine. But that you will not hesitate to act with force when necessary.'

The words came out quickly but were enunciated carefully, with the last reserves of his father's energy.

Cosimo looked at him, lost in the dark, shining pupils of his father's eyes.

'Promise me,' insisted Giovanni, with a last burst of strength. His penetrating eyes stared into Cosimo's and his expression was both determined and severe.

'I promise,' replied Cosimo, his voice breaking with emotion.

'Then I can die happy.'

Giovanni closed his eyes and the muscles of his face relaxed. He had battled against death just to be able to exchange those final words with his beloved son. They expressed all that he was and had been: his dedication to his city and its people, his restraint and humility, his moderation and discretion, never flaunting wealth or abundance, and – of course – his ruthless, hard-headed talent for making decisions.

His hand grew cold and Piccarda began to sob softly.

Giovanni de' Medici was dead.

Cosimo embraced his mother. 'Be strong,' he whispered. She felt frail and helpless in his arms and her cheeks were wet with tears. He broke away and lowered his father's eyelids, closing forever those eyes that had once burned with such vitality.

Lorenzo sent for the priest to administer the last rites.

As Cosimo went to leave the room, Lorenzo stepped into his path. He hesitated a moment before speaking, fearing that he might be disturbing his brother, but Cosimo nodded for him to proceed.

'Speak,' he murmured. 'What is it that cannot wait?'

'It regards our father,' said Lorenzo.

Cosimo raised an eyebrow.

'I suspect that he was poisoned,' said Lorenzo through clenched teeth. His words hit Cosimo like a blow from a hammer.

'What? How can you say such a thing?' As he spoke, he reached out to grab Lorenzo by the collar, but his brother, anticipating his reaction, caught hold of his arms.

'Not here,' he said in a choked voice.

Cosimo understood – he was behaving like a fool. He let his hands fall to his sides.

'Let us go outside,' he said.

3

In Cauda Venenum

The air in the garden was still cold.

It was 20 February and although spring was on its way, the sky seemed unwilling to relinquish its leaden colour. A bitter wind blew over the Palazzo Medici, and sheets of ice were forming where freezing water splashed into the basin of the fountain at the centre of the *hortus conclusus*.

'Do you realize what you're saying?'

Cosimo was distraught – and furious. He had just lost his father; now he also had to deal with a conspiracy. What did he expect, though? His father had been a powerful man, and over the years had made many enemies. And Florence was what it was: on the one hand the essence of magnificence and power, and on the other a den of vipers, whose most powerful families had always frowned upon Giovanni's rise. Cosimo's father had built up a financial empire over the last twenty years, daring to open banks not only in Florence but also in Rome and Venice. Worse still, his father had always refused to disown his humble origins and instead of allying his house with the noble families, he had chosen to remain among the ordinary people, carefully avoiding any political office. You could count the number of times he had entered the Palazzo della Signoria on the fingers of one hand.

Cosimo shook his head. In his heart he knew that Lorenzo spoke in good faith, but if what he said were true, who could have committed such a crime? And, most importantly, how had the poison reached his father's table in the first place? Cosimo's deep, dark eyes, full of questions, sought those of his brother and urged him to speak.

'I wondered whether it was right to tell you,' resumed Lorenzo, 'since I have only one piece of evidence for my claim. But our father's decline was so sudden that it made me wonder.'

'You're right – it was suspicious. But how could he have been poisoned?' asked Cosimo in exasperation. 'If what you say is true, the poison must have been administered by someone inside the house! Our father hadn't been out at all over the last few days, and even if he had, he certainly didn't eat or drink anything.'

'I realize that, and that is why it's only a suspicion. But Father had no shortage of enemies. And just when I was starting to think that it must be my own mad imaginings, I found these.'

Lorenzo held out a bunch of dark berries, as enticing as black pearls.

Cosimo stared at his brother uncomprehendingly.

'Belladonna,' said Lorenzo. 'It produces dark flowers and poisonous fruit. You find it in fields, often near ancient ruins. And I found this little bunch here in our house.'

The revelation filled Cosimo with dismay. 'Do you know what you're saying? If it's true, it means that someone in this house is plotting against our family.'

'Another reason not to let anyone know of our suspicions.'

'True,' nodded Cosimo. 'But that mustn't stop us getting to the bottom of this matter. And should your suspicions prove true, that will make this death even more tragic. I hope that these are just fancies, Lorenzo – because if they aren't, I swear, I'll kill the person responsible with my own hands.'

He sighed. He could hear how empty, how stupid his threats sounded, and was overcome with a feeling of impotence and frustration. How would he be able to bear this?

'It can't be difficult to get hold of poison like that in a place like Florence, can it?' he asked. It was unnerving to think how easy it was to end a person's life in this city. With what he stood to inherit, he would have to be doubly careful from now on.

'Any good apothecary can get his hands on such substances and prepare a concoction with them.'

Cosimo let his gaze linger upon the garden. It was bare and grey, just like that winter morning, and the climbing plants formed dark, restless webs on the walls.

'Very well,' he said, 'this is what we will do. You will investigate. We won't say anything to the rest of them at home. Follow your suspicions. If somebody really did murder our father then I want to confront him.'

'I will. I'll have no peace until I've uncovered the name of that serpent.'

'So be it. But for now, let's get back inside.'

Lorenzo nodded.

And so saying, they returned indoors, the grim revelation tearing at their hearts.

4

Last Wishes

A funeral vigil had been organized in the days following the death.

Representatives of all of the city's most important families, even those who had considered him a bitter enemy while he was alive, had come to pay tribute to Giovanni. Among them were the Albizzi, who had always lorded it over the city; even Rinaldo degli Albizzi, his eyes full of disdain and arrogance, had not been able to avoid coming. For two full days, a parade of notables had trooped through the Palazzo Medici.

Now that it was all over and the funeral had been celebrated – a refined, splendid affair – Cosimo, Lorenzo and their wives were in one of the palazzo's great halls waiting to hear Giovanni's will.

Ilarione de' Bardi, their father's trusted right-hand man, had just torn off the seals and was about to read out Giovanni's last wishes. Lorenzo's brow was furrowed and he seemed lost in gloomy reflection. His investigations must be proceeding, thought Cosimo. Soon they would discuss what progress he had made.

Ilarione began to read.

'"My children and sole heirs: I did not think it necessary to write a will because many years ago I appointed you to direct our bank, keeping you by my side in all matters of administration and business. I know that I have lived out the time that God in his goodness saw fit to grant me on the day of my birth, and I think I can safely say that I die happy, because I know I leave you wealthy, healthy and able to live in Florence with the honour and dignity befitting you, and comforted by the friendship of many. Death does not trouble me because I know that I have never given offence to anyone and indeed have, as far as I was able, done good to those who needed it. For this reason, I urge you to do likewise. If you wish to live safely and with respect, I urge you to observe the law and not to take anything that belongs to another, so you may remain far from envy and danger. Your freedom ends where that of others begins, and what makes men hate is not how much you give to a man but how much you take away from him. Look to your own affairs, then, since in this way you will have much more than all those who covet the assets of others. They only end up losing their own and at the last find themselves living a life of squalor and grief. That is why, in pursuing these few rules, I am certain – despite the enemies, defeats and disappointments which from time to time afflict the lives of each of us – that I have maintained my reputation in this city, and perhaps even enhanced it. I have no doubt that if you follow my advice you will maintain and enhance yours too. But if you wish to behave otherwise, I can predict with equal certainty that a single destiny awaits you – the destiny of all those who have ruined themselves, inflicting upon their families the most unspeakable woes. My children, I bless you."'

Ilarione's voice stopped. Piccarda had begun weeping silently and her cheeks were streaked with tears. She raised a linen handkerchief to her face and wiped her eyes, but she said nothing: she more than any of them wanted the words to hang in the air and mark out a code of conduct for her children.

'And now that I have read what I was told to,' said Ilarione, moving on to the most obvious but also the most urgent question, 'I must ask you: what do we do about the bank?'

It was Cosimo who answered.

'We will summon to Florence the men of all our branches around Italy so they can report on the situation of each. I would ask you to handle this matter, Ilarione.'

The trusted servant nodded gravely and took his leave.

Piccarda looked at Cosimo firmly, as she always did when she had something important to tell him; then she went to await him in the palazzo's library, settling herself in an elegant chair upholstered in velvet. The embers in the hearth sizzled and the occasional spark rose like a firefly towards the coffered ceiling.

Piccarda kept her long chestnut-brown hair gathered under a cap dotted with pearls and a hood embroidered in gold thread and decorated with precious stones. The contrast with the intense indigo blue of her fur-lined robe highlighted her soft, dark eyes; the robe was held tight above her waist by a magnificent silver belt, and the folds discreetly hinted at the substantial amount of precious fabric which had been used in its making. Its wide sleeves ended with more silver embroidery and were split in order to display the brocaded grey velvet of her equally beautiful *gamurra*.

Despite the difficulties of the past few days, Piccarda looked splendid, and was determined to speak to her son to make sure he understood what he must do now. Cosimo was no fool, but to her mind, his love for art did not sit well with the inheritance he was about to receive. And Piccarda could allow for no errors or misunderstandings. She had to be certain that Cosimo knew what was expected of him.

'My son,' she said, 'your father could not have been clearer or more affectionate in his words. And yet I know for a fact that on his deathbed he had other advice for you. Florence is like a wild stallion: magnificent, but in need of taming. Every day. In its streets you will encounter people willing to help and support your work but also villains and idlers ready to slit your throat, as well as subtler foes who will try to take advantage of your good heart and your honesty.'

'I'm not completely ingenuous, Mother,' protested Cosimo.

'Let me finish. I know that you are not, and you have played an important role in the success of this family. But life has grown more complicated, my son. I am sure that you will find your own path, which will develop according to your own beliefs – but I trust you will remain respectful of the wishes of your father? What I want to advise is this: follow the path traced out for you and thus model your behaviour on that of the Stoics. That is: let it be guided by the search for the common good, moderation in all its forms and a rejection of personal ostentation. I also want you to know that from now on I intend to be with you always, and that my first concern will be to ensure that the whole family follows you, whatever your decisions. But remember that even though our financial situation is strong and our prestige clear, our opponents are many and insidious.

In particular I'm talking about Rinaldo degli Albizzi. Be wary of him and his political manoeuvring. He is a ruthless man and there is no limit to his ambition. I'm certain he would do anything in his power to harm you.'

'I will be careful, Mother, and I'll prove my worth.'

'You can rely upon your brother, of course. Your personalities and thought processes complement one another well. He is more impetuous; you are more reflective and analytical: where he acts, you consider and then react, taking into account your broader vision of the world and of what is beautiful and useful in life. You should always remain close to one another and respectful of each other's ways. But to return to what awaits you: look after your own business and remember to anticipate your opponent's moves. Giovanni was always reluctant to take part in the political life of the city, and I was never fully in agreement with him on this. I think – while remaining close to the people, who have always been our allies – one should cultivate a political career and take on public roles and duties, making sure to address both the demands of the commoners and the concerns of the aristocracy. That way you can work to ensure support from both sides.'

Cosimo knew how true and wise Piccarda's advice was, and he nodded. But his mother had not finished.

'I do not need to tell you that Giovanni di Contugi has been provoking Giusto Landini in Volterra, and the reason lies in the land registry law which your father endorsed. I say this because we have no option but to take a stand, and that means we have to make a choice. I do not wish to criticize you for the attention you are paying to the work on the dome of the cathedral, but not being sufficiently involved in the world of politics could cost us dearly. Bear this in mind, therefore. I am not asking that you attract more attention to yourself than necessary – seeing you take a sudden interest in public affairs might make Rinaldo degli Albizzi suspicious, but we cannot leave the initiative to him and his family. Florence will be going to war with Volterra and our position must be clear.'

'But on the other hand, we cannot betray the people and the peasants,' said Cosimo. 'Father advocated the law on the land registry, which has helped the people of Florence see the aristocracy taxed higher.'

'And Rinaldo degli Albizzi never forgave him for it. What I am trying to tell you is that at this particular moment we cannot take them on.'

'No. Rinaldo has mobilized his army along with that of Palla Strozzi against Giusto Landini for that precise reason.'

'Naturally. Your father would have sided with the nobles but would have managed it without taking a clear position. And he would have been right – then. What matters now is to show where we stand. You can no longer refuse to take a clear political position or continue to be ambiguous about your intentions. And therefore, without disavowing your father's work, you must support Florence. Giovanni's intention was to allocate resources and sacrifices proportionally. There was nothing wrong with that idea, and there is no contradiction in supporting it to oppose a city that turns against Florence.'

'I know,' sighed Cosimo. 'I think I will join the other families so as not to give the impression that I wish to remain aloof, while maintaining our position as protectors of the people. If we lose their support, all that my father worked for will be lost.'

Piccarda nodded with satisfaction. Cosimo had chosen well and judiciously and despite her sorrows, a smile lit her face. But she had no time to speak further because at that moment, Contessina burst into the library as if the Devil were at her heels.

'Giusto Landini!' she cried. 'Giusto Landini is dead! Murdered by Arcolano and his henchmen!'

5

Rinaldo degli Albizzi

'Well, the old man is finally dead,' gloated Rinaldo degli Albizzi. 'That will be a blow for the Medici.' Clad in a green brocade doublet and pantaloons, he was perched on a bench in the inn.

Palla Strozzi gave him a look.

'What do you mean? That this would be a good time to strike at those damned usurers?'

Rinaldo threw his leather gloves on to the wooden table, smoothed down his brown curls, and said nothing as he waited for the serving wench to come over to them. He loved making Palla Strozzi wait – it emphasized the differences between them. The Strozzi family was powerful, but not as powerful as his, and Palla was a humanist: a slim, elegant scribbler who never accomplished anything of value. To change things, one needed steady nerves and a taste for blood, and Rinaldo had both.

'Bring us a quarter of mutton,' he ordered the innkeeper when she arrived, 'and bread and red wine. And hurry, because we have fought much today and we are hungry.'

While the woman returned to the kitchen with a great rustling of skirts, Rinaldo shot her a sideways glance. She was certainly pretty, with an honest face, long dark curls and brown eyes flecked with gold, and her figure warmed his blood.

'So you're boasting of our soldiering skills when we haven't so much as lifted a finger... I suppose that's just your way of trying to impress the common girls,' said Palla Strozzi, not without a hint of resentment. He hated it when Albizzi didn't answer him, which he frequently didn't.

Rinaldo smiled and turned to look at Palla sitting across from him.

'My good Palla,' he began, 'Let's look at the question another way. Is it not true that the Council of the Ten of Balia instructed us to lead our men against Volterra to punish the city for rising up against us, and that the situation then settled itself without our intervention? You saw it for yourself, no? Giusto Landini's head set on a pike? And you do remember *why* Giusto wanted to rise up against Florence, don't you?'

'Of course!' replied Strozzi. 'Because of the new taxes imposed by the law on the land registry.'

'Which was advocated by...?' prompted Rinaldo degli Albizzi.

'Giovanni de' Medici.'

'Precisely.'

'But Giusto's arrogance was punished by his own people. Arcolano gathered his men, and they chopped off his head.'

'And as you yourself observed, by so doing, they saved us the dirty work and we come out of it as clean as a May sky and victorious at having brought Volterra back under Florence's jurisdiction.'

'All without lifting a finger,' concluded Palla Strozzi.

'Exactly. Now,' continued Rinaldo 'it's no mystery why Niccolò Fortebraccio is wasting away in Fucecchio. Giovanni de' Medici was the leading advocate of peace in Florence and also the man who had him dismissed by the Florentines. Can you deny that?'

'I wouldn't dream of it,' said Strozzi impatiently, 'but stop playing games with me, Albizzi.'

'I'm playing no game, as you will soon see. It is a fact that the city of Volterra, which seemed about to rebel, has been returned, *obtorto collo*, by Arcolano thanks to his dextrous handling of the affair.'

'If you define lopping off someone's head with a sword as "handling", yes.'

Rinaldo waved away Palla's words with annoyance. The way the man continually dwelt on silly details was intolerable.

'Nonsense,' he said. 'Unless we're willing to spill blood, we can forget making Florence ours.'

'I have no problem spilling blood, Albizzi, I just like things to be called by their proper names.'

Palla knew what he said would irritate his companion. He had no wish to make things easy for him. He was not, after all, Rinaldo's inferior.

'Come, my friend, let's not get bogged down in the nuances. Leave that for others. Niccolò Fortebraccio ardently desires to get back to burning cities and raping women—'

'How can you blame him?' interrupted Palla. As he spoke, his eyes fell on the beautiful innkeeper as she placed a loaf of fragrant bread and a jug of wine on the table along with two wooden cups. The low neckline of her dress revealed full white breasts that made Palla lick his lips as though anticipating some irresistible delicacy.

She didn't seem to notice, and he kept his eyes upon her while she returned to the kitchen.

'Listen to me and leave her alone, you old satyr,' reprimanded Albizzi. 'I realize you share Fortebraccio's appetites but that's not the point at issue here.'

'So what *is* the point, then?' enquired Strozzi, filling the cups with wine, raising one to his lips and downing it in a few gulps.

'What I want you to understand is that we have to provoke a battle. Only by starting another war can we throw the city into confusion and take the opportunity to seize it.'

'Really?' responded Palla incredulously. 'You really think *that* would be the best strategy? Let's see if I've got this right: you want to use Fortebraccio's resentment against the Florentines by secretly bribing him and getting him to wage war against Florence. And while he does so you'll take advantage of the blood and terror to appropriate the city?'

'That's the idea. It would be a sham war. We let them kill a few peasants, and maybe Cosimo and his family will end up getting dragged into it too, and then we step in to stop the massacre and we take power. Easy and clean, don't you think?'

Palla shook his head.

'Not at all,' he said. 'Shouldn't we wait for a better moment? You know that Niccolò da Uzzano is a friend of the Medici, and with him at their side it will be no easy thing to get at Cosimo, or to take possession of the city.'

'So what do you suggest?' snapped Albizzi impatiently. 'Giovanni de' Medici is dead and the family and its assets will now be controlled by his children. Lorenzo is a fool, but Cosimo could be dangerous. He has shown more than once that he knows how to handle himself. He is behind the dome of the cathedral and we all know what his relations with the papacy are. He might make a great show of being a benefactor and pretend to keep to the sidelines, but he is as cunning and ruthless as his father – perhaps even more so. The truth is that he's a briber and a moneylender, and if we let him be, it will be the ruin not only of our families, but of the whole Republic.'

Palla snorted.

'The dome of Santa Maria del Fiore isn't exclusively a Medici initiative. It was the Opera del Duomo committee who sanctioned its implementation. And from what I hear, Filippo Brunelleschi's work is coming along quickly—'

'Too quickly,' interrupted Rinaldo.

'Yes, too quickly,' agreed Palla, 'and what's worse, to the detriment of Lorenzo Ghiberti, who was in charge of supervising the work with Filippo!'

'Yes, yes, I know that is your greatest worry, but you must put it to one side – we're not going to solve our problems through culture!' snapped Rinaldo. His friend's constant digressions on to topics like art were completely baffling to him – and infuriating.

'In any case,' continued Strozzi, 'I don't see what objective advantage we would gain from destroying our own city for the sole purpose of killing the Medici. At that point, you might as well just hire some assassins. Wouldn't it make more sense to set Fortebraccio not against Florence but against a different target? Perhaps one legitimized by the Council of the Ten of Balia?'

While Palla Strozzi's words floated seductively through the air, the innkeeper appeared again with a wooden tray bearing a huge leg of lamb. Two smaller bowls gave off an intense aroma of stewed lentils.

'Magnificent,' said Rinaldo when the food was laid out before him. 'You were saying?'

'I was saying that we might have better luck convincing Fortebraccio to devote his murderous attentions towards Lucca.'

'To what end?'

'To expand our territories, thus legitimizing a new war but without risking an assault on our own city. That would be complete madness. I repeat: the idea of filling Fortebraccio's pockets to convince him to attack is a good one, only I would make him attack Lucca. He's sick of rotting away in Fucecchio. As you said, he's dangerous – out of control even – and that means we'd be justified in engaging him against Paolo Guinigi's city. At this moment I am one of the Ten, and I have my own allies, as do you: it wouldn't be difficult to convince the Chief Justice to vote in favour of an attack on Lucca to impose our hegemony once and for all, just as we did with Volterra. Fortebraccio will attack and besiege Lucca, and once he has taken the city, we, the emissaries of the city of Florence, can come in to calm tempers and make peace. That way we gain the support of the common people and of the people of Florence in general. And as saviours of the Republic we will have strengthened our positions in the city against the Medici.'

Rinaldo thought about it. The idea was not a bad one, but Palla's scheming *was* somewhat elaborate. Saying nothing, he bit into the meat, tearing it from the white bone.

They had just won the battle against Volterra but the war must continue, on that he and Palla agreed. Further strengthening their prestige and political power through military superiority and the enlargement of the Florentine hegemony was an intelligent way of increasingly marginalizing the role of Cosimo de' Medici. And in war, a sword through the back or a fatal blow could happen at any moment. There was death everywhere, and he had every intention of being the one who decided how and when it would happen. He had no intention of standing watching from the sidelines.

'We will fight then,' he said, and raised his cup. Palla Strozzi did the same, sealing the toast.

'And we will silence that descendant of the damned Medici family once and for all.'

Rinaldo drained his cup and grinned, the wine on his lips looking like blood in the candlelight.

'Cosimo's days are numbered,' he whispered hoarsely.

6

The Perfumer

Lorenzo wasn't new to poisons. He was no expert, but among the many interests he had inherited from his mother was an interest in herbs and powders, even if only enough to know which of Florence's apothecaries could obtain poisonous powders or herbs with relative ease.

It wasn't much, but it was a start, and if he was certain now of one thing it was that his father could not have died a natural death. Something told him that the sudden, incurable illness had been induced.

But by whom and to what end, he still did not know.

The possible answers to the questions crowding his mind multiplied dizzyingly, so he had decided to take a rational approach and address the problem by adopting the simplest, most reliable method: start with the end result of the plot and trace it back to its beginning. Therefore, in the days following Giovanni's death he had questioned a few of the local apothecaries. He had pressed them hard, and in a couple of cases might even have gone too far, but everyone knew who he was so even those he had intimidated or physically hurt had said nothing for fear of upsetting the Medici. Unfortunately, though, he had achieved nothing.

Meanwhile, he and Cosimo had been observing all the servants who worked at the Palazzo Medici. It was a complex business, but his suspicions had focused on a beautiful raven-haired maid they had taken on a while ago, who came in a couple of days a week to do some minor tasks around the house. After some investigation, Lorenzo had discovered that the woman had for some time owned a perfume workshop in Florence and that her name was Laura Ricci. If anybody knew something about concoctions and potions it would be her.

Naturally, he had made sure not to display his suspicions. Lorenzo decided to follow her to find out where she lived and to ask her some questions. He had to move with caution, though – after all, there was no evidence that she was guilty, even though she was certainly the most likely suspect.

For this reason, Lorenzo was at that moment following the perfume girl. He had been on her heels for a while now, trailing her through the city's alleys: dark, muddy, encrusted with blood and offal.

The butchers were a *vexata quaestio* in the city. The comings and goings of their carts and wagons left trails of blood and scraps of meat along the streets of the town, which filled the air with a stomach-turning stench. The Council of the Two Hundred had been debating the issue for some time, but none of the competent institutions had yet decided what to do. Some had suggested transferring all the Florentine butcher's shops on to the Ponte Vecchio, but nothing had come of it.

After passing the Mercato della Paglia, Lorenzo had then followed the woman to the Ponte Vecchio, reaching the Oltrarno where, after passing the Ospizio per Viandanti, the perfumer had continued on towards the bridge of Santa Trinità before turning into an alley on the left and finally stopping in front of what must be her workshop.

She pulled out a key and slipped it into the lock.

Unable to hide a shadow of concern, she peered around herself and then went inside. She seemed to sense that she was being followed.

The room was dimly lit by four candles in an iron chandelier hanging from the ceiling. In an attempt to make the place look less gloomy, she opened a drawer and pulled out a few more, putting them in a three-armed silver candelabrum which she placed on the counter amidst a profusion of glass pots containing herbs and coloured powders.

Taking care to keep the shutters well closed, she had just finished illuminating the room when a voice made her jump.

Sitting in a velvet armchair in a corner was a striking-looking man. He had long reddish-blond hair and deep-blue eyes and was dressed all in black, including the cloak which hung from one shoulder. His doublet, reinforced with iron plates, showed him to be a man-at-arms, and for further proof he held in his hands a short dagger with which he had sliced and cut into quarters the apple he was now eating with great relish.

'So you've arrived, *mein Kätzchen*.'

His voice was cruel and unpleasant, somehow contriving to waver in pitch from high to low as though he were unable to modulate it.

'My God, Schwartz,' said Laura, 'you frightened me.'

The Swiss mercenary looked at her for a long time without speaking, watching her tremble under his icy stare.

'You are afraid of me?' he asked.

'Yes.'

'Good. Do they suspect anything?'

'Yes.'

'I imagined that they would. In any case, you did what you had to do. By the time they have realized, it will be too late.'

'What do you mean?'

'Come here.'

She remained where she was.

He would never have admitted it, but this pleased him even more. He loved women with character, and Laura had it in abundance.

He stared at her a moment – she was a true beauty. Even in the flickering light of the candles he was dazzled by that olive skin and he gladly allowed himself to become lost for a moment in those eyes, as green as a summer forest. A cascade of black curls framed her perfect oval face, but perhaps it was her scent which captured his soul; intriguing and seductive, that splendid aroma of mint and nettle now seemed to fill the entire room.

'Why did you close the shop?' he asked, changing the subject.

'Business wasn't going well. And anyway, it's none of your business.'

'Very well, very well,' he replied, raising his hands. The blade of the dagger shone in the candlelight.

'Will you tell me why you've come?'

'To save you.'

'Ah, really?'

'The Medici will have worked out what happened by now, as the fact that Lorenzo has followed you shows. And that's not all – he's out there waiting for you. I saw him.'

'My God!' Laura flinched. 'I hadn't realized! Are you afraid of him?'

'Not at all.'

'You should be.'

'And why?'

'Have you any idea who the Medici are? Obviously not.'

'Come here,' he told her again.

'And what if I don't want to?'

'Don't make me repeat myself. I'm not in the mood to be refused a small favour by a woman who needs my help.'

For a moment Laura seemed to consider Schwartz's request.

'A *beautiful* woman,' she said with a smirk. 'Too beautiful for someone like you, Schwartz.'

'Ah, of course,' he jested. 'But don't give yourself airs and graces, or by God Almighty I'll make a few adjustments to your face with this dagger of mine and you'll lose all your charm in a flash.'

Laura felt something indescribable: something inextricably linked to a distant past that she had hoped had been washed from her memory forever. An intense anger whose source only she knew welled up inside her. But only for an instant, and she made sure not to let it show. She hoped she had been quick enough to hide it from Schwartz. Especially since, in some inexplicable way, she was attracted to him.

Schwartz took her by the hair and pulled her down to her knees.

'This time, I want you to show me how grateful you are.'

'What will *he* say...?'

'Our lord and master? Don't worry about him – concentrate on the matter at hand,' and so saying he put his knife to her throat.

Laura understood and, without another word, knelt down and opened his breeches. She did it slowly so as to prolong the wait and Schwartz's pleasure. And hers. She knew very well how to please a man. She took his penis between her hands. It was already swollen and large, the first dot of moisture beading his glans.

'Suck it, now,' he ordered, 'or I'll slit your throat.'

Laura took it in her mouth, giving Schwartz such pleasure as he had never before experienced.

7

Faith and Iron

Cosimo needed to be alone, and it was so peaceful here in the cathedral. Many things troubled him in those painful days. The death of Giovanni had left a huge empty space, and the thought that he might have been poisoned had opened a still deeper wound and made Cosimo aware of his own vulnerability. Someone in their own house had conspired against them. It might just be Lorenzo's imagination – but Cosimo doubted it. Giovanni had fallen ill and died so suddenly, when until a few days previously he had seemed so healthy.

That wasn't enough to be certain, of course. They had practically no evidence, apart from the belladonna berries and the suspicions regarding the servant, and yet...

And yet even his mother had said it: they had many enemies, so why continue being ingenuous?

Lorenzo had been keeping a close eye on all the servants and new food tasters had been selected. Moreover, a whole new group of *offiziali della bocca* – table servants – had been taken on. When Piccarda had asked for an explanation, Cosimo had tried not to alarm her, simply saying that there'd been some minor issues so he'd decided to change most of the staff.

Piccarda had given him an incredulous look but had pressed him no further. She would trust him as she had promised.

He looked up at the beautiful dome above him. The rays of winter light filtered through the roof lantern and the windows at the base of the ribs, falling upon the interior like gentle rain.

The sight of it revived him and his thoughts turned to Filippo Brunelleschi. What a combination of genius and determination the man was: obsessed by buildings, architectural flourishes, calculations and solutions into which he plunged himself day after day with seemingly inexhaustible energy, transforming his vision into wonderful shapes like the arches in the Chapel of San Lorenzo, which alternated with the form of the building to create perfect lines and circles.

That was the pattern he should follow, Cosimo thought: the simplicity of the straight line and the circle's ability to take a risk. Which, in so many words, was what his father had told him.

He wasn't worried about managing the bank – he knew how to do business and Lorenzo was there to help him – but the difficult art of politics and compromises frightened him, and he was afraid of disappointing his father. He had every intention of doing his best for his family and helping those who needed it, but he also felt upon his neck the breath of the Ten of Balia, who seemed to devote all their energies to annoying him. And, perhaps, even to pushing him out of the way altogether.

And then there were Giovanni and Piero, his own children.

Piero in particular worried him. At almost fourteen, he was becoming a man and had even expressed a desire to learn swordsmanship and to have a master of weapons. Not that there was anything wrong with that – Cosimo himself had learned the rudiments of fighting and was well able to defend himself if attacked, even though he was certainly no professional soldier. But since the trouble Albizzi had fomented in Volterra and the resulting conspiracy which had put an end to its principal conspirator, Piero had started carrying on about wanting to be a man-at-arms.

Cosimo sighed, put his hands together in prayer, closed his eyes and listened to the silence.

There was something mystical about the absolute stillness. He didn't need to speak nor take a position against anyone. It had been a while since he'd been there to meditate.

It occurred to him that Lorenzo hadn't returned yet. He hoped the beautiful perfumer hadn't been more problematic than they'd anticipated.

His brother knew how to look after himself. And yet, his lateness unnerved him.

Lorenzo had been waiting for a long time. He had lost track of just how long, but he knew deep down that he couldn't leave. Only by waiting for the woman to come out could he get to the bottom of the mystery. It might take the whole day, but if it did, then so be it. He had no intention of giving up and going back to his brother empty-handed. That wasn't his way. As his father always used to say of him, when he put his mind to something, he had to finish it.

The sun had set when the door finally opened. That was certainly Laura he saw emerging – he recognized her figure and the long black curls under the hood which served to hide her from prying eyes.

Frustrated by the endless waiting, he had no intention of letting her go a second time. He went over to her and impulsively grabbed her by the wrist. If solving the mystery meant making threats and twisting arms, he had no qualms about doing it.

'Laura,' he said, 'you and I need to talk, don't you think?'

He saw her turn towards him but as soon as he looked into her deep-green, feline eyes he felt a vice-like grip on his shoulder and then was thrown against a wall; his shoulder smashed against the stone and pain shot through his entire body.

A tall, impressive-looking man stood before him. Judging from the dagger at his belt, he could only be a soldier. He was dressed completely in black, and a cloak of the same colour hung limply from his shoulder. He had a self-confident, cocky air, as though he were eager to get about his business.

Lorenzo steeled his nerve.

'Who are you?' he asked angrily, his hand going to the dagger he kept hidden in the lining of his robe.

'*Du, Schwein!*' the other snapped. 'If you imagine you can get that dagger out before I alter your features, you are as much of a fool as I imagined you would be.' The man smiled, his teeth shining white in the dim torchlight that was the only illumination in the gloomy alley.

Lorenzo ignored him and drew his knife, throwing himself at the man and swinging for his abdomen. But the soldier feinted, easily avoiding the blow and tripping Lorenzo, sending him sprawling once again to the ground.

'You have understood nothing, then.'

'No,' said Lorenzo, wiping away the blood that trickled from the side of his mouth.

The man allowed himself a laugh, a harsh bark that chilled the blood.

'You Medici,' he said. 'What fools you are! Do you believe this woman poisoned your father?'

As response, Lorenzo spat at him, shocked at how many moves ahead of him his opponents were. It was a particularly bitter pill to swallow.

'Ah, you'll have to do better than that if you want to frighten me,' resumed the soldier. 'And in any case, you are far from the truth... You miserable pigs!' He filled the word with all the hatred he could muster. 'Didn't you wonder why you managed to work out so easily that it was her?'

'Kill him,' said the girl, pointing to Lorenzo. Her eyes blazed with cold fire, as though a possible murder was now the safest way for her to get rid of a troublesome witness.

'Why, no,' said the man. He turned back to Lorenzo. 'You managed it because we allowed you to. There *was* no poisoning, my lord. We only left the belladonna berries in the bedroom to make you *believe* there was! Your father died from his illness, and the sole purpose of this charade was to give you a warning: we can get to the Medici whenever we want to, do you understand me? Be very careful, or next time we might *really* decide to kill you.'

At these words, Lorenzo leapt to his feet, feinted a lunge and then brought his dagger down in one last attempt to wound the man, but the soldier parried the blow with his own knife. The blades ground together, iron against iron; then the soldier freed himself and pointed his dagger, which was much longer than Lorenzo's, at the young Medici's throat.

'This is a duel you have no chance of winning,' said Schwartz. 'We will be on our way now, but fear not, Lorenzo de' Medici, we will meet again. Just pray it isn't too soon, because the next time I will have to kill you. And believe me, I will.'

And so saying, his dagger still pointed at Lorenzo, the man backed away, clutching Laura's hand tightly. She did not seem to mind the closeness, though, and as they walked down the alley, Lorenzo was certain he saw her smile.

August 1430

8

An Important Interview

The horses sped along the dirt road. To the right, fields of pale wheat filled the vista as far as the eye could see, while to the left the green foliage of cypresses strained upwards like dark flames.

Cosimo felt the sweat drenching his collar, plastering it to his soaking skin. He spurred on his horse. Lorenzo, on his chestnut mare, could barely keep up with him.

There was no time to lose. He knew that Niccolò da Uzzano had spoken out against the war on Lucca and now that Francesco Sforza was descending the Val di Nievole and crushing Fortebraccio's men he could no longer put off the decision. But he didn't want to upset his most committed ally. Niccolò was old and unwell, and tired of these pointless battles. Ignored and dispirited, and with the Albizzis and their followers against him, he had decided to spend the torrid summer days at his villa in the countryside outside Montespertoli, as though to follow in the footsteps of Cincinnatus.

Cosimo used his spurs even more violently and smiled at the splendour of the Florentine countryside while the wind blew gently on his face. His long black hair streamed out behind him like a cloud of ink.

The fields were dotted with the occasional farm, and after taking a narrow lane he found himself before a dark gate facing two guards in leather armour and boots. Each held a long spear and they looked as though they were melting in the searing heat.

Cosimo brought his horse to sudden stop and the animal reared up, raising a cloud of dust when its front hooves fell back to earth.

'Who goes there?' asked the guard, half-heartedly holding out his pike.

As the horse snorted, foaming at the mouth from the long ride, Cosimo glared at the soldier.

'Who?' he said angrily. 'Do you not recognize the colours of the Medici?' And so saying he pointed to the trappings of his steed, which bore the family coat of arms: the six red spheres on a golden background.

The other guard shook his head as though to apologize, and ran a gloved hand over his thick brown moustaches.

'Forgive him, *messer*. Our lord Niccolò da Uzzano was hoping to see you. Your visit will be most welcome. Go through the gates and follow the paved road.'

Without further ado, Cosimo set off at a gallop, Lorenzo at his heels. The hooves of their mounts rang on the flagstones while they galloped between myrtle and laurel hedges and bushes full of blackberries.

When they reached the villa, Cosimo leapt down from the saddle and handed his horse's reins to a groom.

'Give our horses oats and water. They have earned them.'

A servant welcomed them, and led them inside.

'Please try to understand, Cosimo. The war with Lucca will bring no benefit to our beloved Florence. Rinaldo degli Albizzi is throwing himself into it because he can see no other way than to put weapons in the hands of Niccolò Fortebraccio, who is greedy for booty. He and Palla Strozzi have long been plotting to take Lucca, but this is not the way to achieve prosperity and peace, believe me. We learned how hateful it can be to suffer the impositions of others when we fought against Milan – a war that cost countless florins and led to nothing except the death of our most courageous young people. What, then, would be the benefit of a war against Lucca? Not to mention that Francesco Sforza is currently moving against Fortebraccio – and you know how ruthless and formidable *he* is.'

Niccolò da Uzzano let his arms drop to his sides. The silver tufts of hair poking out from under his chaperon spoke volumes of his wisdom and fatigue. His purple cloak swung from his shoulders as he restlessly paced the hall with great strides. Cosimo knew perfectly well how much Uzzano wished to keep peace in Florence and how Albizzi, instead, was doing everything in his power to destroy it. First Volterra, then Lucca – Rinaldo seemed to live for war. Fought at the cost of others' lives, of course.

Cosimo exchanged a glance with Lorenzo.

They had met Uzzano in secret because it was unwise to be seen in the company of one side rather than another, and all Florence knew that Albizzi wanted war and Uzzano wanted peace. On the other hand, Cosimo could only pass on the decision expressed by the Ten of Balia. A decision that he himself had taken care to ensure that they took.

'We did everything we could, Niccolò. And in any case, the Ten of Balia have decided. On the advice of my people, of course. And you will see that the solution we have reached, and for which I can vouch, is not to be despised. These are grim times and Paolo Guinigi has been overreaching himself lately. You're right when you say that it would be a mistake to attack Lucca, especially now that Sforza is defending it, but should we just let it go and give up hopes of extending our hegemony? You know how much I detest Rinaldo degli Albizzi but it is also true that if we accept the Milanese intrusion we will soon find ourselves reduced to begging just to stay alive in our own city.'

Niccolò's eyes flickered. He hadn't missed the implications of Cosimo's words: the young man might look like his father, but he seemed also to possess a certain duplicity – on the one hand he didn't want to get involved while on the other he was suggesting going to war.

'Careful, Cosimo. I know that what you say isn't far from the truth, but remember that you cannot side with me and with Rinaldo degli Albizzi at the same time, so choose your allies wisely.'

Cosimo sensed the irritation beneath Uzzano's words. He knew he had to flatter him and allow him to intuit for himself how he intended to proceed and why, but he couldn't keep him in the dark about his strategy either.

'Niccolò, I understand you, and believe me: the Medici are your allies and defenders of the peace. And we all know how dangerous Francesco Sforza can be. Milan has already harmed us in the past, and it would be a mistake to let them have Lucca as well. There is no doubt that Sforza will free the city from Fortebraccio's siege. He has more men and is better armed, and it's quite likely he's marching triumphantly towards Lucca right at this moment.'

'I don't doubt it – they're unevenly matched, and if I heard right, Fortebraccio is going to be dismissed from the command.'

This was news to Cosimo, but it was also irrelevant.

'What I think, Niccolò – and the Ten agree on this – is that we can get rid of Francesco Sforza without a single sword being swung.'

'It would be an enormous advantage, don't you agree?' chimed in Lorenzo, unable to help himself from pointing out the brilliance of the solution they were about to propose.

Uzzano raised an incredulous eyebrow, but Cosimo continued.

'I don't think there is any doubt about what the war dogs who lead the mercenaries are after. The problem is that none of us have had any military training, and we have let fighting become a trade. One which is often well paid. Well, that is what I intend to do.'

'Pay him?' asked Niccolò.

'How I get rid of Sforza is my concern. What I want you to understand is that I desire peace and wish to avoid any unnecessary bloodshed. Even more so if those who fight are ultimately doing it for money. And there is no doubt that it is money which drives them.'

The old man sighed.

'So be it, then. You have my blessing.'

Lorenzo smiled.

'But remember,' Niccolò da Uzzano continued, 'I don't want to see a single sword swung.'

'You have my word, do you not? In the name of the friendship that has always united our families.'

Niccolò nodded.

'Very well then,' he said, sounding satisfied. 'You should stay for dinner and rest before returning to Florence. I've already had the rooms prepared and I have one of the best partridge pies you've ever eaten to offer you.'

Lorenzo didn't need to be asked twice.

'I would be delighted,' he said. 'The ride here gave me an appetite.'

'But before you go, my friends, remember. Bargaining with Francesco Sforza will take time. The man is possessed of powerful appetites and ambition. He won't grant you any favours – you must know this.'

'I don't intent to underestimate him, if that is what you're afraid of, my friend,' replied Cosimo.

'You do well to bear that in mind. Otherwise, God have mercy on us all.'

Gloomy and ominous, Niccolò da Uzzano's words hung in the air.

9

The Battlefield

The blue smoke from the hand cannons rose to the sky, and Neri watched as Francesco Sforza's cavalry charged headlong towards him. Despite the pounding of the mortars, they were approaching rapidly, and when they arrived it would be the end. He braced himself for the impact. Suddenly, the frothing mouth of a horse appeared in front of him and the blade of a sword was swinging down over his head. Neri raised his *Zweihänder* sword, and blue sparks flew from the clanging metal. Somehow, he managed to remain standing, but he saw many of his comrades falling around him.

The horseman who had attacked him rode on, but then pulled his glistening cinnamon-coloured mount to a halt. The animal was restive, pawing the air with its front legs before turning back to gallop at him.

Neri didn't know what to do. He was scared to death and he could feel urine gushing down his legs, soaking his breeches. When the man was a few feet away from him, he suddenly stopped his horse and, in a single agile movement, swung himself down from the saddle, leaving the animal to run on.

The man's feet hit the ground, raising a cloud of brown dust, and he swung his blade in a single, fluid motion that for a moment left Neri completely paralysed. Eyes transfixed, the boy raised his two-handed sword and put himself on guard, somehow parrying the thrust, but the violence of the assault and the weight of his own weapon were such that he fell sprawling to the ground.

His mouth was full of dust, but there was no time to waste. In an instant he was back on his feet just in time to fend off a hail of blows. Neri had the distinct feeling that this accursed horseman was playing with him – amusing himself by waiting for him to make his first mistake so that he could skewer him like a thrush.

The battlefield had become a chaotic mayhem of shields, iron and leather, and he struggled to imagine how he would be able to get himself out of this situation. Someone banged into his shoulder, and then suddenly his opponent was back again. Neri parried, but when he tried to attack in his turn, the man dodged, avoiding his lunge and swinging at him again.

There was a sharp, poisonous pain and, suddenly, Neri could no longer feel his left leg. He felt something flooding his thigh and barely had time to look down to see his grey breeches growing dark. The liquid soaking the pearl-coloured cloth of his garment was the colour of wine.

He collapsed to his knees. The slash in his thigh was so deep that he couldn't understand how his leg had not yet detached itself from the rest of his body. Blood continued to pump from the wound, and he cried out in pain. And as he knelt there, helpless and drenched in gore and sweat in the middle of that battleground, he saw the horseman's sword coming down upon him like the Day of Judgement.

Francesco Sforza swung his sword down diagonally and the blade bit into flesh, sending the soldier's severed head flying from his neck and rolling away. A geyser of blood sprayed from the decapitated body and what was left of the Florentine warrior struck the ground of Lunigiana with a thud.

Francesco Sforza raised the visor of his helmet. Around him, the soldiers of Niccolò Fortebraccio were taking to their heels, the horses and foot soldiers retreating as they tried to avoid the devastating impact of his men.

He spat on the ground. It was a dirty war, as he knew better than anyone else. There was no honour to be gained from it, just money, and the small change he had been offered by the Duke of Milan and Guinigi of Lucca certainly wasn't worth the endless struggle to take the city in which he and his men were engaged.

But orders were orders, and Francesco had to carry out the contract he had agreed to, otherwise he might as well look for a new occupation.

He threw his helmet to the ground, freeing his brown hair, which was wet with perspiration.

Florence must be weary if she sends young boys against us, he thought bitterly. The one he had just killed couldn't have been older than sixteen, and it was obvious that he'd had no training in the profession of arms. His fate had been sealed from the moment he had tried to fight back under the blazing sun, clumsily swinging away with a sword that was larger than he was.

This damn armour was suffocating him. The heat showed no sign of abating and sweat was streaming down his tension-lined face.

There was no honour here, he thought. And he was damnably tired. He hadn't washed for days and he needed a bath. He tried to force himself to look on the bright side: now, at least, he would enter Lucca as a hero and Guinigi would treat him with respect. He would eat until he was fit to burst and then mount a couple of shapely peasant girls.

He smiled at that thought and looked up to see his man Bartolomeo D'Alviano trudging towards him between the dead bodies whose blood drenched the battlefield.

'Captain,' muttered Bartolomeo, breathless from the exertion of the battle, 'they're retreating.'

'I can see that for myself, my good D'Alviano,' replied Sforza, unable to hide his satisfied grin. 'We have done a marvellous job today. I doubt that dog Niccolò Fortebraccio will show his face around here anytime soon.'

'I'm sure he will not, my captain.'

D'Alviano also smiled, exposing a mouthful of black, rotten teeth, consumed by wine and neglect.

'Are you all in one piece, at least?'

'A couple of scratches, but nothing to worry about. I certainly wouldn't accuse Fortebraccio of having fielded an impregnable defence.'

'Not really, old man. Had I known, I wouldn't have bothered wearing my mail,' joked Sforza.

'Yes,' sighed D'Alviano, 'it's so hot.'

'Anyhow, we've done it. Any idea of the losses?'

'Too early to say, my lord, but I think I can say that this little skirmish has turned out to be a total success.'

'I think so too. That being the case, let's bury our dead and loot theirs – what's left of them. In the meantime,

I'll lead the vanguard to the outskirts of Lucca and await your arrival there, and then we'll enter the city.'

Bartolomeo D'Alviano nodded and saluted him, then returned to his men to carry out his orders.

Francesco Sforza called for his horse and climbed back into the saddle.

Life wasn't so bad after all, he thought. With a little luck, in two days' time he might even be sleeping in a bed with clean sheets.

10

The Honour of Blood

'But don't you understand, I want to fight!'

'Don't you care about me at all? Sforza has gone to war against Fortebraccio and soon he will liberate Lucca. They say that whoever stands in his way is swept away like an autumn leaf.'

Piero looked at his mother, Contessina. Her face was flushed and tears glistened on her cheeks. Her beautiful red lips trembled with fear and anger. How was it possible that she didn't understand? He had to *fight*! He wanted to prove to his father and to all of Florence what he was made of!

'I'm a Medici like my father, and his father before him, don't you see? I'm not a politician, nor a merchant – I'm not *like* them, Mother! I have no talent for numbers, nor for art or political games. I only have these arms and this heart, which beats for our people.'

Contessina was sitting on the edge of the canopy bed with her face in her hands. She was sobbing now.

Piero turned away. Seeing her in that state was upsetting but he had made his decision. He stared at the orange flames of the candles, their reflections flashing in his pupils like burning tongues. He knew he wasn't like his father, or even like his uncle Lorenzo, and it distressed him. He wanted to prove to everyone that he was a true Medici, and this war was an incredible opportunity. He didn't want to miss it.

After all, no one else in the family had undertaken a military career, so why shouldn't he be the one to do so? His constitution was somewhat frail and he wasn't a professional soldier, but he knew how to use a sword.

It was then that his grandmother, Piccarda, entered.

At the sight of her, Contessina seemed to perk up, as though her courage had suddenly returned.

A breeze blew through the windows of the room, bringing with it the moist scents of the warm August evening. Piccarda looked at her grandson and her beautiful daughter-in-law, still red-eyed and teary.

'What is the matter?' she asked, her voice incredulous with surprise.

'Oh, Milady Piccarda,' said Contessina, who had no intention of missing the opportunity to turn the sudden appearance of Piero's grandmother to her advantage, 'Piero won't listen to me. He wants to go and fight against Sforza. But what would be the point, I asked him, if Fortebraccio's fate is already sealed?'

'Should we just stand by and watch Milan take Lucca, and then perhaps come here too?' asked Piero in exasperation.

Piccarda glared at him.

'Is this true, Piero?'

'What?'

'That you wish to enlist in Fortebraccio's army?'

'I want to fight for my city,' he said, this time angrily.

Piccarda didn't flinch.

'Have you any idea what is happening?'

Piero shook his head.

'Francesco Sforza has come down through Val di Nievole and is advancing. He is encountering practically no resistance. He set up camp a few days ago in Lunigiana. Fortebraccio's days are numbered, and that is why your father and your uncle have gone into action.'

Piero's eyes widened.

'Are you surprised?'

'But... where have they gone?' was all the boy managed to say.

Piccarda narrowed her eyes until they became two slits. Piero still had much to learn. His mother ought to be harder on him – but what Contessina couldn't manage for herself, Piccarda was more than capable of.

'Cosimo and Lorenzo left for Montespertoli to speak to Niccolò da Uzzano, our main political ally. They will convince him that we Medici do not wish to encourage war but at the same time cannot tolerate Sforza taking Lucca in this way.'

'And how will they do that?' asked Contessina, who was listening to her mother-in-law as though to the wisest of women.

Piccarda stared into her eyes and sighed.

'My girl, they will do it with the only thing that really matters to Sforza – money. But we don't know if that will be enough. That's why, in the event that they are unlucky in Lunigiana, Lorenzo is ready to go to Rome, not only to inspect our bank there but, if necessary, to be received by the Pope. Fortunately, our family has always enjoyed papal favour – at least since Giovanni, with great foresight, decided to help Baldassarre Cossa – sorry, His Holiness Pope John XXIII. And of course we continue to do so with Pope Martin V. Will that suffice? That is a question I ask myself constantly. In my heart I truly hope it will, but if Cosimo's plan doesn't work, the pontiff will certainly be able to influence the fate of the conflict.'

'And so...?' asked Pietro hesitantly. He knew that there was little point discussing it with his grandmother. She always had the last word and before her, his boldness seemed to have melted like snow in the sun

'And so, my beloved grandson, all your enthusiasm would be wasted in pointless sacrifice! Battles are won long before they are fought: always remember that! You belong not to a family of soldiers but to a family of bankers, politicians and artists. Put to good use the education that your father has provided you; not everyone who has Carlo Marsuppini and Antonio Pacini as preceptors. You should be grateful for that education and devote every moment of your time to learning. One day, the responsibility for this family will be yours – and having received so much, you will need to give something back!'

As she spoke, Piccarda admonished her grandson with a finger. Her firmness and severity were such that the young man was immediately silenced.

Contessina said nothing, just looked at her admiringly.

It had only been a few months since Piccarda had lost her beloved husband, but that terrible event seemed to make her stronger with each day that passed.

'Now prepare yourself for the night and go to bed,' she concluded. 'Your mother and I are going to pray for the happy outcome of your father's negotiations.'

11

Triumph

As he made his entry into Lucca, Francesco Sforza tried to look radiant with joy. Despite the toll taken by the battles he had fought over the last few days, he sat stiffly upright on his black horse. His long hair was soaked with sweat and his armour, finely tooled and decorated, gleamed under the relentless sun. He wished he could have taken it all off and worn a simple tunic. He hated the heat, but at least he would be paid well for enduring it. The profession of arms demanded a show and victory demanded pomp. And pomp required some small sacrifices.

That triumphant entry into Lucca was one of them. According to Paolo Guinigi, the tyrant of Lucca, it was what the people desperately wished to see. And so he had to grit his teeth... and sweat.

And the people were there waiting for him. In long lines, they filled the narrow streets of Lucca, thronging its squares and crowding its streets, waving rags of white and red – the city's colours. There were so many of them that it almost made him dizzy.

Bartolomeo D'Alviano, who rode alongside Francesco Sforza at the head of the parade, kept peering around him, not knowing where to look.

Damsels threw down flowers from the windows of the houses and murmured promises of love. The common girls shouted up to them and bared their white breasts, while the men cried out the name of Sforza, who had freed them from the Florentine yoke, and the children on their fathers' shoulders stared wide-eyed at the splendour of the soldier of fortune.

If only they knew what his job was really like, thought Francesco. Stabbing people in the back, *that* was his job. Always playing dirty. In war, there was no such thing as honourable conduct, just tricks to make sure you got home with your hide intact. He had won many more battles through ambush and subterfuge than on the battlefield. But in that moment, he didn't give a damn. And anyway, when it was time to fight, he had never been one to hold back.

Florence, Lucca, Siena and Pisa were nothing but rabid dogs whose only thought was to snap at one another in the name of a hegemony none of them could actually impose.

The shouts rose up into the sky and the white and red flags of Lucca hung immobile and limp in the infernal heat of that August day.

Under the blazing sun, they made their way through the city until they reached the Cittadella: a compact fortress with twenty-nine towers which stood before them in all its grandeur, its gates guarded by soldiers clad in the colours of the city.

'He might be the lord of the place,' murmured D'Alviano, 'but it looks as though he lives barricaded up in his own house.'

'His days are numbered,' Francesco Sforza murmured back. 'Don't you know what they call him?'

'No, I don't,' replied Bartolomeo.

'The wife-killer,' said Sforza.

'Curious nickname... Why?'

'Because he's gone through four in the space of twenty years. Maria Caterina degli Antelminelli, married at eleven years old – she died soon after giving birth. Ilaria del Carretto, who didn't survive the second son, and then Piacentina da Varano and Jacopa Trinci.'

'Good God, it's a massacre.'

'That's right. Now do you understand who we're dealing with? The man is a snake, so let me do the talking, my friend, because I fear that we will have to fight for every single ducat. For this same reason, let me tell you that tonight I am expecting the Florentines at our camp, on the far bank of the Serchio River. They have an offer for me. So remember: don't say a word.'

'The *Florentines*?' asked D'Alviano incredulously.

'Cosimo de' Medici.'

'Really?'

'Really.'

And so saying, Francesco Sforza set off towards the entrance of the Citadel. D'Alviano and his men followed him and were soon swallowed up by the large gate of the fortress, which closed behind them, blocking out the cheers of the people who continued to fill the city of Lucca with cries of joy.

'My friends,' Paolo Guinigi greeted them when Francesco Sforza and Bartolomeo D'Alviano made their entrance in the hall of the Signoria. His voice, which could not have been more cheery, was in complete contrast to the grim expression upon his face, which was adorned by a curly, pointed beard that made him look like a vulture.

He had been waiting for them for a long time. He was wearing a beautiful dark-blue jacket, richly embroidered with silver thread and loosely closed at the waist with a fine silk sash.

'My beloved lord, how are you?' asked Francesco Sforza.

'Very well, now that I have you in my house. I trust that Florence will stay away from the battlefield now.'

'I am sure of it,' said Sforza. 'Niccolò Fortebraccio took such a beating in Lunigiana that he won't be back. Not as long as I'm here to protect you, at least.'

'And that,' exclaimed Guinigi, pointing to the sky as if he had just been struck by divine inspiration, 'is what matters! As long as you watch over Lucca, my friends, I can sleep soundly. Despite the enthusiasm you have seen for yourselves today, the people are not exactly enamoured of me.'

'Really?' asked Sforza, feigning surprise.

Paolo Guinigi seemed not to notice the amused grin that had flickered across the mercenary captain's face.

'Ungrateful wretches!' he said. 'I've broken my back for them. I have commissioned works of art for them, had this impregnable fortress built to defend them... And this is how they repay me.'

'Built for them or for yourself, my lord?'

Sforza had no intention of passing up the most amusing part of the absurd situation.

Guinigi noticed his sarcasm but he was a man of spirit and quite capable of coming up with a witticism in response.

'Now, Captain, a lord and his people are the same thing, are they not?'

'Of course, my lord, of course,' granted Sforza. 'Would you, therefore, in the name of our covenant and agreement, now give me ten thousand ducats to settle our bill and add as many again as advance payment for future protection? I have lost at least a hundred men over the last few days, and defence, as you know, costs dearly.'

'A debt is a debt,' replied Guinigi promptly. He snapped his fingers and, a moment later, two men came into the room carrying a chest which they deposited at Sforza's feet.

'There,' said the lord of Lucca. 'Feast your eyes, sirs: ten thousand gold ducats. You have earned them.'

Bartolomeo D'Alviano was almost blinded by the sight of all those shiny coins, but Francesco Sforza was made of sterner stuff.

'Very well. The debt has been settled. But what about the future?'

'What do you mean?'

'You heard me.'

Guinigi's face twisted into what was supposed to be a smile. The result would have sat very comfortably upon the muzzle of a weasel.

'Ten thousand ducats to secure the future of this city, and before even having even lifted a finger against the enemy? Come, Captain, you didn't ask for so much last time. Don't you think you're being a little greedy?'

'Do you wish to put your safety and that of your people at risk by bartering with me? Because, as you know, the Florentines will soon regroup and come back to lay siege to the city. Perhaps they won't send Fortebraccio, but they will certainly find someone capable of commanding a gang of villains in exchange for a handful of gold. Do you really want to take such a risk?'

Paolo Guinigi sighed.

'Five thousand now,' he said between gritted teeth, 'and another fifteen at the conclusion of the job. But I don't want to see a single Florentine anywhere near my city.'

Sforza cocked his head to one side.

'Five thousand is better than nothing, but it's not enough. I will attempt to make it do for the moment, however.'

'Do so, and I will go up to twenty thousand ducats at the end of the job. You know how deep my devotion to the Duke of Milan is.'

'As deep as your purse, my lord.' As he spoke, Francesco Sforza looked around him at the frescoes on the walls depicting the seasons in vivid hues, the armour, the racks of swords – for parades only, of course – the dressers and closets of Franco-Flemish manufacture with carvings of grapevines, and beautiful accessories in wrought iron. There was a pair of triptychs on wooden panels, and the imposing table in the centre of the room was impeccably laid with porcelain, solid gold cutlery and magnificent goblets, with twelve wooden chairs, elaborately carved and decorated, around it. From the exposed beams on the ceiling hung impressive wrought-iron chandeliers, each with twelve candles.

For a tyrant who was hated by his people, Paolo Guinigi seemed to be doing rather well for himself. And it was all thanks to people like Sforza – the soldiers of fortune who risked being skewered while they did his dirty work for him.

'Those frescoes of the four seasons are beautiful, aren't they? They're by Priamo della Quercia.' Guinigi's voice was mellifluous. 'While my men count out the five thousand ducats, I hope you will join me for lunch?'

Without waiting for confirmation, Paolo Guinigi picked up a small golden bell from the table and rang it so hard he seemed to wish to break it.

Within a few moments, a head servant appeared along with an entire squadron of table staff: a carver, a butler, a bottler and a napkin bearer, each in turn describing the characteristics of the food and the wine that would be served.

After the endless descriptions of hams, sausages, filled pastas, pies, roasts and stews, cheeses, fruits and pastries, D'Alviano looked ready to draw his sword and send the sextet of servants on their way to a better place. Sforza gave him an affectionate glance and motioned for him to resist.

When the six had finished informing Paolo Guinigi and his two guests of the wonders that awaited them for lunch, the lord of Lucca finally invited the two soldiers to sit down.

Francesco Sforza didn't need to be told twice, and as he went towards his chair – which bore more than a passing resemblance to a throne – he reflected how art, clothing, textiles, furniture, chandeliers, frescoes, fine food and wines might be wonderful but were also poisons which could weaken a man to the point of making him unable to take care of himself and his people. It was a destiny he hoped to avoid.

It was with double satisfaction therefore that he took his place at the table while the servants busied themselves bringing before them all that fabulous food.

He knew that the meal would be a pleasant interlude in a day that would end with an important negotiation. He hoped that it would all go well. If Guinigi had even a suspicion of his double-dealing, he would have far worse problems to deal with, and he did not want to have to slit his Amphitryon's throat.

But if Guinigi didn't behave, he wouldn't hesitate to do so.

12

The Camp

After all the blood and the booty, and after entering Lucca as a hero and dining with the debauched Paolo Guinigi, Francesco Sforza was happy to get back outside the city and make camp across the Serchio River at Colle del Lupo, outside Pescia.

It had been a long day, and all that frivolousness had been so wearing that he'd almost rather have been back on the battlefield. It was always the same: when he was fighting he wanted to be somewhere quiet, but when he *was*, he wished he was back fighting again. The part of the job that he hated most was the endless meetings with the lords and dukes who gave him his assignments. He was happy to get paid but would have preferred to spend his time doing very different things with very different people. As far as Sforza was concerned, Guinigi was an imbecile, just like his ducal master, Filippo Maria Visconti. And what good was accumulating money in military campaigns if you didn't have time to retreat to a castle and spend your days hunting and making love to young maidens? One of whom you could take as your favourite, or even better, as your beloved wife? Why should such a possibility be denied him? Why couldn't *he* have been in Guinigi or Visconti's place? What did *he* lack? Nothing, as far as he could see – and he was able to fight too. Perhaps it was their political acumen and their love of plots and intrigues that he was missing.

Allies! he thought. *That* was what he needed! Men of ambition to help him in his ascent and benefit from what he could give them in return.

Absorbed in these thoughts, he lay on the bed he'd had made up in his large tent and waited for his reward to be brought to him. In a corner, some kind soul had placed a table with a couple of flasks of Chianti.

Eventually, the reward arrived.

They were just as he had requested: a tall peasant girl with raven black hair, full lips and generous curves and a blonde northern beauty who was just as voluptuous.

Francesco wasted no time – all that thinking had made him impatient. He pounced on the dark-haired girl immediately, grabbing her big brown breasts from behind and pinching her nipples with his stubby fingers until she gave a squeal of pleasure, and then sucking at them like a hungry baby. The girl gave a silvery laugh, her complicity increasing his pleasure enormously.

While the great leader hung from the peasant girl's breasts, the other girl pulled down his breeches and grabbed his penis, tickling his scrotum with her nails and making him moan with desire before wrapping her full, moist lips around his member.

Sforza felt as though he had gone to heaven. Women and weapons, *those* were his passions. And they were passions he should encourage, because the years were passing and he really ought to think about constructing a respectable old age for himself.

Cosimo's horse was circling nervously. He was with Lorenzo on the road to Pescia, accompanied by a dozen Florentine horsemen, their armour dark and shiny, their sallets tight upon their heads. Francesco Sforza's camp wasn't far.

Cosimo and his men bore a white flag so Sforza would know that their purpose was to come to an agreement, and two black horses carried sacks half full of seeds, beneath which were concealed gold florins. The reason for their journey was clear: to meet Sforza and bribe him to leave Lucca under the blade of Florence. Thus had the Ten – under pressure from Cosimo – decided, and now that Niccolò da Uzzano had been informed accordingly, the new lord of the Medici family would do all that was necessary to rid Tuscany of the oppressive influence of the Milanese.

Of course, he had no intention of antagonizing Filippo Maria Visconti, since it was he who had sent Francesco Sforza in the first place. Cosimo wanted to proceed in the way most profitable for both parties so as not to jeopardize an equilibrium which might turn out to be useful in the future. Peace was necessary for business, but since his father had passed away it seemed that all and sundry were hell-bent on compromising it. Unable to develop their own lines of credit the way the Medici had done with their bank, Albizzi and Strozzi were seeking profits through political influence dictated by fear and war. This was on Cosimo's mind while he motioned to his men to follow him.

The sun was setting behind the black hills, a copper disc that flooded the sky with shades of red.

They had to hurry.

Cosimo spurred his horse forward at a gallop, followed by Lorenzo and the twelve men who rode with them. They raced down the track through a forest of pines until the vegetation began to thin and they came in sight of the plain hosting Francesco Sforza's camp. It was dotted with tents and weary soldiers crawling around a campfire over which a spitted kid was roasting. The torches and braziers glowed red.

As they approached, a pair of guards ordered them to stop, but Cosimo immediately indicated the white bands he and his companions wore on their arms.

'Who are you?' asked the sentry, his voice hoarse with wine and fatigue. His eyes were rheumy from drinking and the filthy locks which emerged from beneath his helmet were plastered to his temples by sweat.

'We come in peace from Florence. Francesco Sforza is expecting us. If you could lead us to the captain's lodgings we would be much obliged.'

The soldier conferred with his partner for what to Cosimo and his companions seemed an age. A third man arrived; then he broke away from the other two and headed off towards the tents. Eventually, he came back and spoke briefly to the first guard. When the man was sure he had understood, he returned his gaze to Cosimo.

Why must I always deal with idiots? Cosimo asked himself.

'You're Florentines, you said.'

'Precisely.'

'You came to talk with Captain Sforza.'

'Yes,' confirmed Cosimo with a hint of annoyance. 'And let's get a move on, otherwise we'll go back to where we came from just as quickly as we came here and your lord will be poorer by a substantial sum – at which point he will flay your hides. Is that what you want?'

'It certainly isn't. My comrade-in-arms will guide you to Sforza's tent. Only you and your load though!' he ordered, pointing first at Cosimo and then at the two horses with sacks.

'How dare you?' snapped Lorenzo, his hand moving to his dagger, but Cosimo gestured to him to stop.

'So be it,' he said. 'Let's see what this Francesco Sforza is made of.'

And finally the sentry stepped aside.

13

Cosimo and Francesco

Francesco Sforza was a very large man, and his frank, pugnacious face bore witness to a lifetime dedicated to the art of warfare. His frank eyes commanded respect and, Cosimo was certain, fear if necessary, because there was a harshness in them despite the smile on his face. The broad, strong shoulders were like those of a bull and his considerable height completed the fearsome image.

His face, though, betrayed his fatigue and his modest sage-green garment, filthy and creased, was soaked with sweat. He looked worn out by the fighting.

The tent was furnished sparsely: there was a simple bed, a brazier of glowing coals and a small table with two cups and a bottle of wine. Scratched, dirty and covered in dust from the battlefield, his armour was propped up in a corner.

'My lord,' said Sforza, 'how marvellous that you come to visit me on this hellishly hot night.'

'Thank you for seeing me, Captain,' replied Cosimo. 'Because, you see, your conduct – which is impeccable from the point of view of your profession – has caused great embarrassment to my beloved Florence.'

'It pains me to hear that, Messer Cosimo. But Paolo Guinigi of Lucca has paid me for my services, and it was Filippo Maria Visconti in person who ordered me to intervene and force Fortebraccio to take to his heels.'

'I am aware of that. Tell me honestly, Captain: what has Guinigi paid you to defeat Niccolò and his men and resist the Florentine militia?'

Sforza seemed to hesitate for a moment.

'Twenty-five thousand ducats: five thousand in advance and twenty thousand upon completion of the job.'

Cosimo nodded.

'A reasonable fee, but not shockingly high,' he said with a smirk. 'I would have thought the tyrant of Lucca more generous.'

'Frankly, *messer,* he seemed to me to be in a bad way.'

Cosimo raised an eyebrow. 'How so?'

'He's locked up in his citadel, surrounded by the ghosts of four wives, and to judge from the way D'Alviano and myself were greeted in the city as heroes, it is my opinion that Lucca is ready to rise again.'

'What makes you believe that?'

'The fact that a true lord would not be afraid of his people. Look at yourself, Messer Cosimo: you've come here, and we both know very well why, and I know for certain that through the art of compromise and politics, you will obtain what you want. Because you *are* Florence.'

Cosimo was unmoved. It was hard to tell whether that statement had pleased him or not. He nodded.

'I am surprised how well appraised you are of our situation.'

'I'm a man-at-arms, my lord, and a mercenary: in my profession, being informed is part of the job,' said Sforza, striking his chest above his heart with his hand. 'Would you like a cup of wine?'

'I thank you greatly, but I would prefer to get down to business.'

The captain walked over to the table, poured himself a cup and threw it back in a few long gulps. He smacked his lips in appreciation and wiped his lips with the back of his hand.

'I'm listening.'

'I have come to offer you the sum of fifty thousand florins in exchange for a promise to deliver Lucca to Florence. The sum is not negotiable. What do you answer?'

Cosimo's dark eyes stared into those of Francesco Sforza and for a moment it seemed that neither of them would look away. Sforza sensed a will of iron in the man before him and a determination that could not easily be halted. Cosimo de' Medici appeared to have inherited the noble temperament of his father after all.

The sum Cosimo was offering him was far greater than what Paolo Guinigi had promised as an advance, so there was no reason to refuse. The men would be happy and he would be able to buy a new horse and that castle in which he hoped to grow old. Perhaps together with a beautiful woman. Or more than one...

He knew that he would accept, but there was one thing that vexed him.

And unless that was cleared up, their meeting would have been for naught.

14

The Agreement

'I would gladly accept,' said the captain, 'but there is just one problem.'

Cosmo waited to hear what it was.

'My honour.'

'Be more explicit.'

'You see, Messer Cosimo, though it may seem strange, we soldiers of fortune have our obligations – obligations towards our clients, which cannot be simply disregarded.'

'Obligations that prevent you from accepting the sum I offer you?'

'Not at all.'

'As I thought,' retorted Cosimo with a hint of sarcasm.

'I can imagine what you're going to say—'

'Can you?' interrupted the Florentine lord. 'Because you may be mistaken. I realize that having accepted a commission prevents you from doing what I ask without due consideration. I realize that a soldier of fortune has principles which, although they may differ from my own, dictate his conduct, and that he is therefore required to act accordingly. On the other hand, I see just as clearly that you would be happy to make these fifty thousand florins your own. So here is what I think: instead of handing over Lucca to me, why don't you simply abandon Paolo Guinigi and his city to Florentine swords? Would that not be a solution that works in both our interests and allows each of us to derive a legitimate profit from this nocturnal conversation of ours?'

So saying, Cosimo went out to the horses, which were tied to a wooden pole outside the tent, and returned with one of the bags tied to their saddles.

While Francesco Sforza was still trying to understand what he was about, Cosimo poured the contents of the bag on the table. Seeds flooded out, followed by a cascade of tinkling florins.

At the sight of the gold, Sforza grinned and his eyes flashed greedily.

'And now what have you to say? I have another forty-nine bags like this one on the backs of the two horses outside.'

Sforza swallowed. It was clear how tempted he was by the offer. Cosimo had known that he had him as soon as he had seen the gleam in his eyes. He must only remember to conduct the negotiations carefully, because the captain was no fool. Indeed, an idea had occurred to him: why not maintain a friendship with this man? He might prove useful to him in the future.

'So? Are you lost for words, Captain?'

Francesco Sforza took a sharp breath.

'Well, my lord, you speak wisely, and to be frank, the solution you propose is not only intelligent but also fits with what I've heard of you.'

'So you agree, then?'

'I agree...'

'To my conditions?'

Cosimo sensed that Sforza was about to give in, and had no intention of passing up the opportunity. He was offering him a lot of money and therefore demanded all necessary guarantees, and more besides.

'What would they be?'

'Essentially the following: tomorrow you will pack up camp and leave the Colle del Lupo without further delay. You will not bother to inform Guinigi, of course, and you will go wherever you feel is appropriate, provided it is far from here. As for Florence, you will not interfere in any way with what we see fit to do. In full and final settlement of all claims, I deliver to you, on behalf of the Republic, the fifty thousand florins which are tied to the back of the two black horses out there. Does that seem to you to be sufficient and do you feel able to honour these conditions?'

Francesco Sforza pondered the question a moment, but it was clear he had already decided.

'My lord,' he said, 'not only do I welcome your request but I am also convinced we are creating the foundation for a long and profitable alliance.'

'I am convinced of it, too,' said Cosimo. 'Are you sure that what I have said will apply to you and all your men?'

'I guarantee it, as sure as my name is Francesco Sforza.'

'Very well, then.'

'I believe that this agreement is worth a handshake,' said the captain, proffering his right hand to Cosimo de' Medici.

Cosimo grasped it, feeling in his heart that he had not only avoided Florence being usurped by Milan that day, but had also created a precious alliance.

Sforza was not the Duke of Milan – the Visconti were powerful and had deep roots in their territory, and Filippo Maria was no fool. But on the other hand, this man-at-arms had not only courage and valour but political insight and business acumen, which properly utilized, could take him far. Far enough, Cosimo hoped, to become an important ally in his future plans.

September 1430

15

The Plague

They said that you woke up shivering and felt as though death had just passed beside you. Schwartz had awoken that morning with a start and had felt the icy sweat covering his pale skin like a shroud. It must be early, because no light filtered through the cracks in the shutters. As soon as he opened his eyes he smelt the sour sweat of the other men sleeping nearby. The air in the barn was hot and oppressive because of all the beer the soldiers had drunk, so his cold sweat and shivers made even less sense.

It had been a while since he'd slept with his fellow fighting men, but Rinaldo degli Albizzi had ordered him to put his sword at the service of Guidantonio da Montefeltro at the siege of Lucca, which was being defended by Niccolò Piccinino's troops. Schwartz had obeyed, and that was why he had ended up in that barn with several other men-at-arms after carousing until late the previous night.

The Swiss mercenary was not particularly enthusiastic about the assignment – indeed, he thoroughly missed the well-paid intrigues that had previously been his lot – but since Albizzi had spared no expense and the job was a short one, he had joined the ranks of the Florentines in order to keep his master informed about the progress of the siege after Francesco Sforza had left the Val di Nievole along with the fifty thousand florins he had received from Cosimo de' Medici.

He suspected that the stupid job had not come his way by accident, but rather because Albizzi had discovered his liaison with Laura Ricci and had sent him there to punish him. Laura Ricci belonged to Rinaldo degli Albizzi and no one else, or so the arrogant fool believed. The fact that Schwartz worked for him didn't mean that he was afraid of the man, though, or that he was obliged to comply with his rules.

He could have chosen to leave, but the iniquitous jobs Albizzi gave him were not only welcome – they were necessary. Finding a new master was no easy business these days. There were many men about who knew how to wield a sword, and however good his reputation, his services were far from unique.

He had thus decided that it was worth suffering a little indignity to complete the mission. In two weeks he would return to the Palazzo Albizzi with news from the battlefield and await new orders.

In any case, he had no intention of giving up Laura Ricci and her devastating beauty. She had bound him to her very closely, and he must be careful not to let her pull the leash too tight – otherwise he might end up strangling himself.

He decided to get out of that pigsty crammed with filthy bodies, and procure some fresh water from the well to drink.

The barn door creaked on its hinges as he closed it behind him.

The September air was even warmer and more humid than that inside the barn, and the sky was filling with the golds and reds that announced the arrival of dawn. Shivering, he pulled close his black cloak and walked over to the well, where he picked up the wooden bucket and dropped it in.

It seemed to take him forever to pull it back up, the thick rope crawling over the pulley as he hauled it aloft. Once it was in his hands, he looked up at the sky, now pale with dawn, which was reflected uncertainly in the circle of water, then immersed his face in it.

The water was warm, as if it were full of disease and fever, and the sensation was so disgusting that he thought he might faint. It took him completely by surprise – it was as if he had plunged his head into all the filth of the night before.

He wiped himself off as best he could with the cloth he carried with him; then he raised the ladle to his mouth and, despite everything, drank.

Others began to awaken, and the sound was a relief. It was incredible how the miseries of war made one appreciate even the smallest things.

He was considering how he might find some breakfast when he saw a man approaching. He looked like a soldier, but his clothes were ragged and he was worryingly pallid.

As the fellow drew closer, Schwartz saw tears of unspeakable torment in his watery blue eyes. He was extremely thin, and his gaunt face, devoured by hunger and jaundice, made his head look like a skull. The effect was intensified by the hooded cloak covering his head, from under which his eyes peered out.

Schwartz was about to ask him where he came from, but what he saw choked off the words in his throat. The man turned towards him, revealing something Schwartz had hoped never to see again: from the pale skin of his neck hung a sort of monstrous purplish swelling the size of an egg – swollen and throbbing, it looked as though death itself lurked within it.

Schwartz stepped back unsteadily, but the man came right up to him and fell to his knees. Without saying a word, the unfortunate pulled open his cloak, revealing his chest and allowing Schwartz to see other buboes which bloomed like monstrous fruits on his flesh.

For a moment, the Swiss mercenary was at a loss as to what to do.

'S-s-sir,' croaked the man in a trembling voice, pointing to Schwartz's sword, 'p-please, k-kill me.'

He pulled out from under his cape two hands reduced to stumps and covered with sores and brown clots of blood; waving them in front of Schwartz as though to make him understand that he had no way of putting an end to his tortures himself, he began to weep.

Moved to compassion, Schwartz took his gleaming sword from its sheath and slashed his chest open from the right shoulder to the left hip.

The man fell forward and died.

Schwartz backed away from the body. His vision was blurred and there was bile in his throat. He fell to his knees and vomited up the water he'd drunk and the food from the night before, heaving so hard his chest ached. As soon as he had recovered, he got to his feet, ran to the barn where he had left his horse and tried to climb into the saddle, but his legs were trembling too hard: the sight of the dead man had filled him with fear. Eventually, though, he managed to pull himself up and set the animal racing at full gallop towards Florence.

He put his hand to his forehead to wipe away the icy sweat. The man and the chills he felt had brought back memories of a time when he had been a different person, a time he wanted to forget forever, but which still occasionally surfaced to take possession of his thoughts. He had half believed that certain images had been erased from his mind, but the chills which shook his limbs took him back to when the disease had invaded his body, consuming him.

His mind went back to the man he had killed, and the vision haunted him for the duration of the journey.

The plague, thought Schwartz.

The plague was among them.

16

Carts Stacked High with Death

The plague had descended upon Florence like a pack of hellish hounds, mauling men, women and children, disfiguring bodies, mutilating limbs and spreading terror and depravity throughout the city. Almost all the noble families had taken refuge in their country residences in the hope of avoiding infection while the malady had spread with incredible speed, assisted by the deathly sultriness of the September heat.

The city had sunk into delirium – the population was quickly decimated, and work on the cathedral had slowed to an almost complete halt. The streets had become open sewers and, in spite of the ceaseless efforts of the citizens, a solution to the crisis seemed far off.

The square of San Pulinari felt as if it were smothered by a humid nocturnal blanket and despite the hell which had descended upon the earth, it was so crowded that Cosimo decided to remain at the edges. Large numbers were dying from the disease, but the townspeople still wandered the town like ghosts and the whores solicited with greater conviction than ever. Illuminated by the red glimmers of the flickering fires, gravediggers were loading the deceased on to carts, the corpses heaped up in stinking black mounds and the moist air increasing the stench of death. All about were heaps of stone and building materials for the construction of the dome, awaiting the resumption of work.

The city guards patrolled the area, their black uniforms only adding to the gloom of the haunted warren that Florence had become. Crippled by plague and internal strife, the city was a shadow of its former self.

Some days earlier, Cosimo had ordered his family to leave the city and take refuge in their villa in Trebbio. He and Lorenzo had stayed behind to attend to the most urgent business, but in these last few hours he had realized how foolish he had been, and was now resolved to get out of the city. First, though, he had wanted to speak to Filippo Brunelleschi in the hope of convincing him to leave too, but it had proved impossible. The lunatic intended to stay where he was – in the dome, to finish his job, even though the workers were dropping like flies.

Cosimo had tried everything. If he died, he'd said, who would finish the damned dome? He had begged him, pleaded, even threatened him, but Filippo had just looked at him with those bloodshot eyes full of crazed determination and refused point blank to go.

So Cosimo was still there.

Together with the peasants and the common people, who had no other place to go except their homes or the accursed streets of that city which had come to resemble one of the circles of hell.

He sensed that behind the unlit windows and bolted doors, entire families of the poor were sitting with their hands joined, uttering words of prayer. The guards had drawn crude white crosses on some doors to indicate they contained plague victims. Corpses lay along the street, stray dogs licking at the dark blood and plague fluids seeping from under their nightgowns.

Cosimo looked across the square of San Pulinari and, by the light of the torch he carried, saw the great mass of the Santa Maria del Fiore cathedral looming over the space. When he reached it, he found more corpses, and more carts.

Some villain was kicking an old man who must have been suspected of being a bearer of the disease, and Cosimo watched as the victim gasped under the blows which were surely cracking his ribs.

The world had gone mad.

The epidemic had brought with it anger and anarchy. With the imposition of new taxes, the war against Lucca had already broken the working people's backs, and now the plague was robbing the city once again, this time of its workforce.

There was no hope, that much was certain.

In that primordial chaos, even leaving the house had become dangerous. Emboldened by the confusion into which the city had fallen, the worst kinds of brigands and mercenaries felt free to roam the streets, attacking the inhabitants and plundering what they could, aware that it was impossible for the city guards to maintain control.

He had just passed the cathedral and was heading for the Via Larga when a couple of thugs appeared in front of him, blocking his way. It was as though they had read his thoughts.

He had no idea who they were but from the way they were dressed he deduced they were not of the most refined stock.

'Good sir,' whispered one of them in a low, unctuous voice as he pulled a sharp dagger from his belt, 'what fortune to encounter you on this beautiful evening.' He wore an eyepatch and a tattered leather doublet, beneath which Cosimo glimpsed a ragged shirt that must once have been white.

The other didn't utter a word, but Cosimo saw a dagger shining in his hand too. He was bald and clad in a threadbare tunic.

Being unarmed, Cosimo had no idea what to do. He backed away. He wasn't far from home, so if he could surprise them, there was a chance he could lose them in the back alleys. The one who had spoken was coming towards him while the other remained where he was.

As he was wondering what to do, something unexpected happened. A voice shouted his name and pounced upon the second man, sending him sprawling to the ground. The man's face smashed into the pavement, blood gushing from a deep cut on his forehead.

Caught by surprise, the first thug hesitated.

That moment of indecision was fatal.

Cosimo leapt forward and shoved the torch into his chest. The man raised the hand that held the dagger in an attempt to ward off the blow, but burned himself on the flame and howled with pain.

'Quick,' called his saviour, 'let's get out of here.'

Cosimo recognized his brother's voice and ran without looking back.

They slipped into an alley and from there into another. He could hear the noise of his shoes pounding on the pavement and his breath was short with the effort of running. His brother was at his side. Soon they neared the palazzo and realized that the two attackers had given up the chase.

Once they were finally home, Lorenzo looked him in the eyes.

'Good thing I came looking for you,' he said. 'I hope you'll come to the country now, at least until the epidemic is over. Staying in Florence with this heat and the plague is pure madness.'

'We've already discussed it,' said Cosimo.

'Yes, and it doesn't seem to have made any difference.'

'What matters is that we did.'

'Do you think those two were there by chance?' added Lorenzo in exasperation.

Cosimo looked at him incredulously. 'What do you mean?' he asked.

'That your meeting with them this evening was no accident. Believe it or not, my dear brother, someone wants you dead – and tonight, they tried to take your life.'

17

A Nocturnal Discussion

Rinaldo degli Albizzi could not believe what he was hearing.

'What? You failed to kill him again?'

The two killers stood in front of him, the one with the eyepatch sporting an enormous bandage around his hand and the other's face swollen from the injury sustained when he had struck the paving stones.

'My lord, it wasn't our fault, believe me. We had him, but then somebody came to his aid and caught us unawares.'

His companion nodded.

Rinaldo smiled but there was no sign of amusement on his pursed lips.

'And naturally, the mute is in agreement. Excellent, marvellous work! Obviously this is a job which can only be carried out by a woman,' and he turned his gaze to the beautiful girl to his right who was gazing out of the large windows of the hall. She was dressed in a long emerald-coloured gown embellished with pearls and silver embroidery, its plunging neckline emphasizing the ample curves of her cleavage.

She gave a silvery laugh.

'Perhaps it is for the best,' continued Rinaldo. 'You two have proved to be a disappointment.'

'But your excellency,' protested the hireling, 'we weren't expecting there to be two of them.'

'You should have thought of that, you fools. You know that he has a brother. Where there's one, the other is never far away. You should have taken a friend along; perhaps then you would have managed to finish this task – God knows it was simple enough! Who knows when we'll next have the good fortune to be visited by a plague!'

By now, Rinaldo was shouting. It was true: the circumstances had never been so favourable. When would they have such an opportunity again? And those two imbeciles had failed.

He was sick of incompetence. How could he expect to get the better of the Medici with men like these? He had given battle in Lucca and that damn Cosimo had managed to get around the councillors of the Ten of Balia and bribe Sforza in an attempt to restore peace. Luckily for him, the manoeuvre had simply allowed the Florentines to return and besiege Lucca after the death of Paolo Guinigi. The new Florentine captain, Guidantonio da Montefeltro, was, however, proving to be inept and his opponent from Lucca, Niccolò Piccinino, was once again beating him on every type of terrain. That, at least, was how Schwartz told it after having left the battlefield early in an attempt to save himself from the plague.

And now that he, Rinaldo, was presented with this golden opportunity, these imbeciles had wasted it.

Rinaldo was furious. While he brooded over everything that had failed to go to plan recently, there was a knock at the door.

'Come in,' he barked.

Although the plague had Florence on its knees, Schwartz, who had been wandering in the midst of it, was in annoyingly good shape. It must be his Germanic ancestry, thought Albizzi.

His black clothes, pallid face, long red hair and blue eyes made him look more like a pirate than a soldier of fortune – not that there was that much difference between the two. Whichever, he was a disturbing sight.

Albizzi greeted him with a nod: they had many pressing matters to attend to, and it suddenly occurred to him that Schwartz's arrival might be timely.

He watched him approach a table, sit down, take an apple from a silver tray and begin to peel it with the dagger he kept on his belt.

Rinaldo degli Albizzi took a deep breath. He needed to make it clear to his men that they could not err with impunity. If that idea spread then all the thugs on his payroll would feel entitled to make mistakes.

The man with the black eyepatch seemed to sense his intentions.

'We won't disappoint you again, my lord, I swear it.'

'It is *I* who swears that this is the last time you will.'

'W-what do you m-m-mean, my lord?'

But his voice suddenly stopped, and turned into a strangled gurgle.

The sharp tip of Schwartz's dagger emerged from the side of his neck and blood spattered on the floor. The mute started to make a run for it but Schwartz's dagger struck him in the leg, causing him to stumble, and then was plunged into his side, sending him to the floor. At that point, the Swiss mercenary was upon him, pulling his head back and exposing his throat. The dagger flashed again, slicing his artery.

Schwartz released him, leaving his head floating in a scarlet lake.

Rinaldo degli Albizzi rose to his feet.

'Well done,' he said to Schwartz. 'A dirty job, but it needed doing. Now, call the servants and have them clean this up. Later, we will think about how to eliminate these damned Medici. I'm tired of having to settle for their leftovers, and I can't find men capable enough to carry out the tasks I assign them. But you, thank goodness,' he concluded, pointing first at Schwartz, then at Laura, 'have never let me down.'

'As you know, I am always at your disposal, my lord, in every possible way,' said Laura. 'Your wish is my command.'

'Tonight, I will await you in the bedchamber,' said Albizzi. 'And bring a friend with you.'

April 1431

18

Nobles and Peasants

Niccolò da Uzzano shook his head and raised his eyes to the ceiling. What he was hearing pained his ears.

The Ten of Balia had gathered at the Palazzo della Signoria. Warm light poured in through the large windows, turning the dancing motes of dust into tiny specks of gold. The room was spartan, containing only a large, heavy table around which sat the members of the Supreme Magistrature of War: the men who held the destiny of the Republic in their hands. The heads of the carved cherubim who looked down from the coffered ceiling above them seemed to be awaiting their decisions with curiosity.

In an attempt to ensure they understood how serious things were, Niccolò Barbadori spoke.

'Friends,' he began, 'I wish to emphasize to you all how desperate the situation is for our Republic. It is plain for all to see that the soldiers of Lucca, far from having been routed and discouraged, have more life in them today than before – so much so that since Niccolò Piccinino took the field, he has overrun Nicola, Carrara, Moneta, Ortonovo and Fivizzano in the last month alone. A total of one hundred and eighteen castles, of which fifty-four belonged to the Florentines, the Fieschi and the local Guelphs, and the rest to the Malaspina. This war is being conducted in a wicked and foolish way, and the worst crime of all was Cosimo de' Medici's corruption of Francesco Sforza. That deed not only cost us the vast sum of fifty thousand florins but also got us absolutely nowhere. Since that day, our men have been waging war to no purpose. And if we take into consideration the plague, well... I doubt the picture could be much bleaker.'

When he heard those words, Niccolò da Uzzano could no longer remain silent. He wanted to avert any imprudent reactions. Lorenzo de' Medici sat at his side waiting silently to hear what he had to say.

'I have listened to the words of my good friend Niccolò Barbadori,' he said, 'but I must disagree with him. It is obvious that the current state of affairs is not to be laid at the door of Cosimo de' Medici, or at that of his brother Lorenzo, who sits here by my side. They did nothing except that which they were commanded to do by this supreme council. It is too easy to cast blame upon them now, as though the idea did not have the support of all of us – and, I must confess, me above all. Cosimo himself came in person with his brother to speak to me about it. Moreover, it was a decision made to help the lower classes, whom many of you treat with contempt yet who are an integral part of this city and, lacking any real form of defence or protection, are the first to suffer the violence of war. The same applies to the plague which has claimed so many victims from among the poor who don't have the good fortune to be able to flee to the countryside and are trapped here in this stinking hellhole of a city.'

Niccolò paused. All that talking had exhausted him. He was no longer a young man and nowadays debate wearied him, but his opinions were always lucid and even-handed and out of respect the rest all listened attentively to him.

'To tell the truth, it seems to me that this anger against the Medici is dictated by the fact that they are better loved by the populace than the rest of us – and that's because they listen to the people and consider their petitions. The reform of the land registry which Giovanni de' Medici sponsored is much despised, yet we must remember that without the people there would *be* no Republic. Do not forget this, my friends, and use the knowledge wisely. As for the plague, it seems to me that it is now loosening its grip. I therefore believe that this would be a good time to show a little solidarity with the poor rather than to attack their champion for things for which he is blameless. This, I think, would be the first step in the right direction.'

So saying, he fell silent, leaving all present to their thoughts. He had made it clear which side he was on, and it was obvious to Niccolò Barbadori and Bernardo Guadagni that the situation was far from resolved. With Niccolò da Uzzano still alive, the Medici had a powerful ally, and Lorenzo was careful to say nothing, merely to observe them all with a half-smile on his face.

It fell to Palla Strozzi to speak. He knew he must be moderate, but also knew exactly where to strike.

'What Niccolò da Uzzano says is true, and it would be unfair on our part to reproach Cosimo and Lorenzo de' Medici for simply having carried out the decisions of this council. I believe that the real problem is rather Cosimo's recent behaviour. It is well known that in recent days he has commissioned Filippo Brunelleschi to construct a new palazzo for his family which promises to be like no other previously seen in Florence. Of course, I don't criticize a man for wishing to build himself a home, provided that it complies with accepted limits of decorum and size. But from what I have heard about its planned dimensions and decorations, I can't help but feel that Cosimo de' Medici is aiming to build something fit for a king, a palace whose pomp and magnificence will elevate him above the rest of the families in Florence.'

Lorenzo made to speak, but Niccolò da Uzzano grabbed him by the wrist, as Palla had not yet finished.

'Cosimo's behaviour as regards the dome of Santa Maria del Fiore is also a matter of concern. He behaves as though he is the sole funder of the project, which is now being carried out exclusively by Filippo Brunelleschi, even though it was originally commissioned by the Cathedral Works Commission and was to be shared between Brunelleschi and Lorenzo Ghiberti. Ghiberti has effectively been ousted, and it is clear that Cosimo was behind it. I will conclude by saying that apart from his good relationship with the common people, Cosimo de' Medici – unlike his father Giovanni – is anything but a moderate and modest man. He is arrogant and thinks he is better than the rest of us. In my opinion, this is not good for the Republic, and risks turning it into a fiefdom – a Medici fiefdom.'

A chorus of amazement and dismay arose. The other members of the Council were shocked to hear such criticism from Palla Strozzi, who was usually so moderate. His words, initially sober, had gradually grown more incendiary, and had made an impression on the hearts and souls of all present. Some agreed with him while others were openly against him, but that was what he'd intended – he'd subtly devised his speech not to unite but rather to divide. And it was all the more surprising because it came from the mouth of one who had never before displayed such partisanship – a fact which convinced the majority of the supreme council members that things must truly be grim, otherwise he would never have spoken thus. It had had the effect Strozzi wanted.

Lorenzo was red in the face with rage and on the verge of completely losing control. He stood up, adjusted his garnet-red doublet, and replied to Strozzi in kind.

'I am shocked to hear such slander,' he snapped, 'from somebody we considered a friend. Not to mention that it was you, along with Rinaldo degli Albizzi, who incited Fortebraccio to attack Lucca, thus placing Florence in this terrible situation in the first place. And now you dare accuse the Medici of arrogance and a lust for power... Do you not see the hypocrisy?'

But it was too late. His words did nothing but increase the seething resentment which already filled the room. It was clear that from that moment on it would be impossible to pacify the two factions. That was certainly nothing new, but now, more than ever before, the hostility would become open conflict.

Niccolò da Uzzano realized this, and looked at Lorenzo, who was no longer trying to conceal his anger. He placed a hand on his shoulder.

'Today is a sad day for the Republic, my friend. I confess that I fear for its very survival.'

19

The Nightmare

Contessina saw the great mass of Santa Maria del Fiore looming above her. For a moment, the cathedral seemed to be alive and trembling, almost as though it were some primordial creature and, thanks to some obscure magic, had become the beating heart of the city.

Though the sight horrified her, she looked up. Red snowflakes swirled in vermilion arcs through the air.

Her heart was beating so hard in her chest that she was afraid it was about to burst out, and her forehead was covered with sweat. She put a hand to it to dry it, and saw that it was smeared with blood.

The horror was like a noose around her neck that made it hard to breathe, and she felt fear growing inside her like some monstrous child gnawing away at her belly with its sharp little teeth. She wept and wept, but it made no difference: the vision continued to torment her until she saw her beloved Cosimo. He was up on the unfinished dome, as jagged and black as some crown of teeth.

Contessina didn't want to believe her eyes. She shouted, hoping that he would hear her, but Cosimo seemed unaware of her and of what was happening.

She ran desperately towards her husband, the love of her life, her long chestnut hair streaming out behind her like the unruly waves of a brown sea.

Contessina felt her terror mounting until it almost overwhelmed her. She loved Cosimo so much. She kept running, despite the horror of the vision. But however hard she struggled to get to the octagonal base of the baptistery, she couldn't reach it. Cosimo remained out of reach.

She stretched out her fingers in the desperate hope of touching his face: his beautiful, good, intelligent face with its dark eyes, solemn yet dazzling and able to charm all who stood before him.

But despite her efforts, Contessina could not reduce the distance between them. Her mad rush had left her completely out of breath, and the muscles of her arms and legs ached. How long had she been running? She had no idea; she only knew it wasn't long enough. She was racked with guilt at her failure to protect her husband.

Was she so inadequate? Was she undeserving of him? Was she afraid of Florence and that damned cathedral, which seemed to absorb the lives of the city's men, eating up their souls before it devoured their flesh?

Contessina's mind was filled with so many questions that it felt as though it would burst. But whatever spell she was under, only one thing was certain: she was powerless.

Cosimo gazed at her from a distance but once again seemed not to see her – seemed almost indifferent to the upheavals and reversals of fortune of the world. Or, rather, so completely absorbed by them that he was reduced to nothing more than a tiny creature crouching inside that imposing cathedral of destiny, having abandoned the weapons of will and hope.

She saw him fall and screamed, but Cosimo continued to plummet down. Down, down to the ground. Contessina closed her eyes.

When she opened them again, she was lying in a pool of sweat. Her nightgown clung to her body like a second skin, her long hair was soaking wet and the cushions and pillows were as damp as if they'd been at the bottom of a river. And she was shouting: her voice was hoarse and her throat throbbed with pain.

Cosimo was beside her, attempting to calm her. He stroked her head and whispered sweet words, and she surrendered to his gentle hands, letting herself be cradled in his embrace. He had told the servants and maids to remain outside and was taking care of her himself, as always.

Contessina thanked God for having spared her from seeing that nightmare come true.

'I saw you fall,' she said, 'and you were so far away from me and I didn't know how to bring you back to me.'

'What are you talking about, little one? Can't you see that you're here in your room and that I'm by your side? What are you frightened of, my love? Have you forgotten that I would do anything for you, that you're the only light of my life?'

She held tightly on to him.

'My love... What would I do if you weren't there? I had a terrible nightmare: something was keeping us apart, and then you fell from the dome of Santa Maria del Fiore and I didn't know how to save you.'

'Heavens above,' said an amused Cosimo. 'Well, I'd certainly be done for if I fell a hundred yards. I'd better watch where I put my feet next time I go to see Messer Brunelleschi.'

'You can laugh, but it was awful. I'm frightened, Cosimo. I'm frightened that someone wants to separate you from me, that someone wants to divide us.'

'Nothing will divide us, my dearest Contessina. Now calm yourself, and your worries and fears will vanish.'

And so saying, he held her in his strong arms like a little bird, cradling her and covering her with kisses. She could hear his heart beating in his large, strong chest, and while she listened she touched his nipple with her lips, then kissed it harder and harder until she began to bite it.

He gave her an amused smile.

'Go on,' he said, 'don't stop.'

At his words, her skin tingled like ocean foam and she ran her small hands across his broad pectorals. Cosimo was a handsome, strong man with an alluring, slightly astringent scent.

She amused herself by drawing little circles on his skin with her fingers, then she broke from his embrace and kissed him passionately on the lips. One, two, three, ten times until her tongue flickered against his, intertwining with it sensuously.

She began to kiss him on the chest, and then on the belly, and then down, down...

But he was already exploring the most hidden of her treasures. His strong fingers flickered inside her, almost making her swoon, and Contessina felt herself almost overwhelmed by a wave of pleasure. She surrendered herself to his wonderful touch, bending over forward as her voice grew hoarse with pleasure.

When he penetrated her, she had already come twice.

20

The Death of Niccolò da Uzzano

When he'd heard the news, Cosimo had felt death in his heart.

After his father, Niccolò had been one of the few men of honour left in Florence. He had been pure and just and much loved, and his loss was a blow to the whole Republic.

This was on his mind as he crossed the square in front of Santa Lucia de' Magnoli. Niccolò had lived for a long time in the area known as Borgo Pitiglioso. With Cosimo were Contessina and their son Piero, Piccarda, and Lorenzo with his wife Ginevra. When they entered the church, they headed towards the main chapel, where Niccolò's body was laid out for the final farewell. Inside, people were gathered in small groups and many of the rich and lordly had hurried to pay homage to the great man while they awaited the funeral, which would be held the following day.

Niccolò's body had been placed in a coffin of fragrant pine in the main chapel, which was decorated with frescoes by Lorenzo di Bicci. His arms were crossed and a crucifix lay upon his heart. They had dressed him in a silver-coloured tunic encrusted with pearls and precious stones.

Even in death, his face maintained the authoritative composure of the wise.

He reminded Lorenzo of his father.

The chapel glowed with the flames of the burning candles, whose dim, flickering light made the frescoes seem to run with blood.

While Piccarda, Contessina and Ginevra knelt to pray, Cosimo stood looking at the man who had been perhaps their last ally among the nobility.

Only a few days ago he had defended them from the rebukes of Palla Strozzi and Niccolò Barbadori, who had thundered against the Medici and set almost all the Ten of Balia against them.

Cosimo shook his head.

His allies were falling one after the other and the ranks of his enemies were becoming increasingly crowded, eager to overwhelm him and his dear ones. Even the recent failure of Filippo Brunelleschi's clumsy attempt to flood Lucca, which had ended up flooding the camp of the Florentines, felt like yet another nail in his coffin.

Already he could see the resentful, hate-filled glares of Giovanni Guicciardini and Bernardo Guadagni, who looked as though they were ready to stab him at any moment.

He kissed Niccolò on the forehead one last time and gestured to his mother, his wife and the others to leave with him.

Piccarda made the sign of the cross and got to her feet. As always, she was dressed beautifully, her fur-trimmed coat and black robe decorated with pearls and golden embroidery and her dark-grey *gamurra* perfectly suited to the sad occasion.

There was something regal about his mother. She was a tall woman with a proud bearing and beside her Contessina and Ginevra seemed to shine with a special light. It was as though, apart from the Medici's proverbial opulence, Piccarda possessed a delicacy of style that went beyond lineages and families.

The fact must also have been evident to the eyes of the others who were there. Cosimo realized that everyone was treating him with hostility: nobody came to greet him and once he was out of the church and descending the steps leading to the square, someone barged into him with what felt like intentional violence.

He had been expecting something of the kind. He was still telling Lorenzo not to worry about it and to take the family to safety when he heard the unmistakable voice of Rinaldo degli Albizzi, with its undertone of resentment and envy, calling to him.

'What are you here for?' asked Albizzi, his eyes dark and veined with red. He was clad in a crimson doublet and a cloak of the same colour, and his short, black beard gave him a diabolical air.

Disobeying his brother's order, Lorenzo had turned back and his right hand was caressing the hilt of the dagger he had kept on his belt ever since his encounter with the Swiss mercenary.

Cosimo looked at his brother. 'What did I tell you?' he hissed angrily. 'Stay with our mother, Ginevra and Contessina!' He turned back to face Rinaldo. 'I came to pay homage to a great man. Why else?'

Rinaldo spat on the ground.

'You!' – and as he spoke he pointed to him as if he were a leper – 'You have brought ruin upon this city! And the plague! You think you're better than the rest of us but you're nobody – you're just the foolish, arrogant son of a woolman from Mugello! Go back to where you came from!'

Cosimo had no intention of allowing himself be treated this way, not this time. He was sick of the continual provocations of his rivals, and of the way they behaved as though they were the sole custodians of the truth. It was intolerable.

'I'm not afraid of you, Albizzi! I know it torments you, but I'm not going to change the way I live my life. Altruism and decorum have always been my watchwords – and will continue to be.'

It was at this juncture that Schwartz, the gigantic Swiss mercenary with long, lank red hair and thick moustaches, emerged from the church. That day too he wore a dark doublet and a brigadine lined with plates of iron. He went over to Rinaldo. 'Is this man disturbing you, excellency?'

Albizzi nodded.

The man was about to unsheathe the sword that he wore on his belt when Piccarda interposed herself between the two of them. Her eyes blazed with fury and her beautiful, austere features were twisted into a scornful grimace, as though she held not only the life of others in total disregard but also her own.

'You damned windbags with your threats and slanders! I'm sick of you,' she thundered, her voice echoing across the square outside the church. 'If you want to unsheathe your blades then do it now and hack me to pieces, for you're nothing but cowardly curs!'

'Mother!' shouted Cosimo, but Piccarda didn't seem to hear him.

Albizzi was so surprised that he couldn't hide an amused smirk.

'Well, *this* is something I didn't expect,' he exclaimed with a laugh. 'Here, gentlemen, is someone who truly has guts! And as for you two…' he said, turning to Cosimo and Lorenzo, 'your funeral has only been postponed. You should thank this lady, because she's got more courage than the two of you put together.'

'Mind how you talk, Albizzi.' Lorenzo was quivering with rage.

'Go,' said Rinaldo. '*Go!* But remember – your end is only deferred.'

And without another word, Albizzi returned inside the church.

Cosimo and his family walked towards the carriage which awaited them at the centre of the square under the cold gaze of Schwartz, who stared at their backs like a hunting hound.

As he stood there, his sword drawn halfway from its scabbard, Laura Ricci appeared at his side.

She was as radiantly beautiful as ever, her charms enhanced by the obscene luxury of her attire: a white fox-fur stole wrapped around her shoulders and a long vermilion dress with a dizzying neckline which emphasized her full bust. Her green eyes shone like precious gems in the cold spring light.

'You will kill those two brothers one day,' she said in a hoarse, sensual voice.

'You are looking at the backs of two dead men,' said Schwarz in reply.

April 1433

21

The Last Words

Her long, chestnut-coloured hair was now streaked with white and over the last year the proud beauty of her face had faded somewhat. And yet Piccarda Bueri had perhaps never been so beautiful as she was at that moment when she was so close to death.

She sat in her favourite chair in the library, the one near the fireplace. For many years she had enjoyed its warmth, often in the company of a good book and one of the herbal teas that her maids prepared for her. Piccarda was a sober woman of simple pleasures.

She had lived a full life, and now that her time on earth was about to end, she felt neither sadness nor regret, because she had been given much more than she could ever have imagined: above all, a husband who had worshipped her and who had always maintained the love and esteem which, over the years, had taken the place of passion and given her just as much pleasure in the form of tenderness and intellectual companionship. Grateful and content, she was now ready to take the final step. She sensed that the time had come and had called her beloved sons, their wives and her grandchildren to her. In that atmosphere of serenity and peace she planned to close her eyes.

She glanced around her at the room which she had loved so much and then looked each of them in the face as though to warn them that they were about to say goodbye.

She spoke one last time while Cosimo, Lorenzo, Contessina, Ginevra, Piero, Giovanni, Francesco and Pierfrancesco listened to her, their hearts full of love and gratitude.

'Well, children,' she began, 'because I consider you *all* my children, without distinction, because you are blood of my blood or else actually *chose* to become that blood, I feel that the time granted me by God is coming to an end. I have few words to say to you, but they will, I hope, settle in your hearts like grains of gold. What I ask of you – and this is to ensure my happiness even in heaven where I am about to join your father – is to always be united. You will find nothing in life more important than family: it is the cradle of the dearest affections and the source of satisfaction and joy. Believe me when I tell you that in my life I have had much of both, thanks to all of you.'

At that point Giovanni could help himself no longer, and began sobbing. Tears streaked down his little face, and he grabbed a handkerchief from his pocket and tried to dry them off as well as he could.

Piccarda looked at him sweetly.

'Let your tears fall, Giovanni, don't be ashamed of them. There is nothing wrong with showing your feelings, and I welcome them more than silence. People think that it is a sign of great virility not to weep, but I believe that a man who fears emotion is a man who is to be feared, because if he cannot tell someone that he loves them then he is ignorant of one of the marvels of existence. And a man like that, my beloved grandson, is nothing but a coward.'

Giovanni seemed reassured by his grandmother's words and became calmer.

Piccarda nodded benevolently.

'The family is the thing we hold most dear because each day we put it to the test. Every day we live together under this roof and every day we share each other's fears, worries and doubts, but also, and above all, each other's victories, successes, joys and forgiveness. And there is nothing more beautiful than living with those born of you or who have come to you by their own choice, without influence or pressure, and with whom you walk the path of life which, though beautiful, is also fraught with dangers and pitfalls. So try always to love one another. You, Cosimo, remember to use your keen intelligence, your wit and your foresight for the protection of the family. Always look to the future and ensure that the good name of the Medici remains in this city as your father left it to you and your brother. And increase, if you can, its prestige and power, since the latter, if used carefully and wisely, benefits the whole community. You, Lorenzo, who are quicker to act, oversee the business of the bank with your usual passion and diligence, extend our activities where you can and strive always to provide the means for the family to live honest and upright lives. Both of you: love your beautiful wives with all the passion and affection you have in your hearts. And you, Contessina and Ginevra, understand and forgive the weaknesses of your men and be their refuge, without forgetting to demand respect and loyalty. And in your role as confidantes, never fear to express your opinions, because you may be able to lead your men to solutions they have not thought of.'

At that point, Piccarda stopped. She leaned towards the small table in front of her and reached out to pick up the cup filled with rose tea. It took her an eternity to complete the movement but they all knew not to help her – if she had wanted their assistance, she would have asked for it.

She raised the cup to her lips and took a few sips, and Cosimo smiled to see that such a simple thing could still give her profound joy. In some ways it was like looking at a contented child. Over the years she had paid increasing attention to the rich harvest of small pleasures that life was still able to bestow.

When she had drunk enough, Piccarda lowered the cup. Blue steam rose from the infusion and she half closed her eyes as though delighting in the aroma which now filled the air of the room.

'And finally, you,' she continued, 'my beloved grandchildren. Be always obedient and respectful to your parents, and don't forget to express your gratitude and your affection, since the heart of a father and a mother will fill with love at even the smallest gesture from you, and it would be unbearably cruel to deny them the comfort that a kind word or act from you might give them. Learn to know yourselves, and take advantage of that which your family gives you every day. Thanks to the daily efforts of your parents, you live amidst privilege and wealth, so be worthy of them and repay what you receive with application, exercise and study. That way you will become an invaluable resource for the family. And with that, I am done. And now, I think, I will sleep. Thank you for listening to me so carefully.'

And so saying, Piccarda closed her eyes.

They sent the boys out and Cosimo, Giovanni, Contessina and Ginevra watched over her. Her sleep was deep and peaceful. Her face was so relaxed and quiet in that golden silence that it seemed no words could have made her happier.

After a time, Contessina and Ginevra retired to bed.

Hours passed, but Cosimo and Lorenzo remained with her, each holding one of their mother's hands.

Slowly, her skin grew as cold as marble. Her face lost its colour and her breathing stopped.

Piccarda was dead. Cosimo sent for the priest for the last rites. Still sitting by their mother, the two brothers looked at each other and, for a fleeting moment, each saw her gaze in the eyes of the other.

22

Filippo Brunelleschi

The days had passed and the funeral of Piccarda had been celebrated with a restrained yet splendid service. Cosimo's mother was now resting near his father in the sacristy at San Lorenzo. It was the most beautiful thing for two people who had loved each other so much in life, he reflected. He hoped that he would be as fortunate. He missed his mother enormously, and felt a dull ache in his heart when he thought of her. Time would cure even that, he thought. But he promised himself that though he was unable at the moment to take time away from his incessant work, he would preserve her memory and keep it tied by a golden thread that would run from his hand up to heaven.

He sighed.

He was in Filippo Brunelleschi's workshop. Of the many astonishing places he had seen over the course of his life, he could not remember ever having ever seen anything comparable. It was not so much the architecture of the place that took your breath away – it was the endless array of models, devices, machines and wonders of every kind that left you speechless.

His gaze roved between magnificent bronze panels, capitals in pale marble, stone busts, sculptures of classical deities and open books filled with charcoal sketches that covered the floor. And then there were the shards of coloured glass, magnificent figures carved from wood, pieces of frames and preparatory drawings for what might have been a fresco, chisels, brushes, jars overflowing with coloured powders and a scale model of the dome of Santa Maria del Fiore. Filippo was devoting himself totally to the work, as though it were his only reason for living – which perhaps it was. It was beyond Cosimo how a man could dedicate his entire existence to art as though it were a religion, a faith, or a love. It was almost frightening.

As far as Cosimo was concerned, Filippo was a *unicum*. Perhaps it was that which made artists what they were: they did not obey earthly laws because they had been beguiled by a discipline which had about it a whiff of the infinite. It was like a fever, almost – an illness from which they never recovered.

Filippo had ignored the risks of the plague and spent months on end living on the dome, descending only occasionally. But though the construction was proceeding smoothly and approaching completion, a problem of no little importance had now presented itself: how to complete the dome without the entire structure collapsing?

Cosimo had no idea how Brunelleschi would solve that problem. He was more troubled by the fact that he had to inform the maestro that the project for the Palazzo Medici to be built in Via Larga was no longer feasible: the rumours which had been proliferating about the plan were creating bad feeling against his family. For some time, Albizzi and Strozzi had been spreading gossip that the new Medici residence to be built by Brunelleschi would be of such magnificence that it would resemble the palace of a sovereign, in contempt of the good taste and restraint that even the Florentine noble families had to maintain when commissioning private works.

Cosimo knew that his reasoning would sound like madness to Filippo, and this did not make his task easier. While he was still attempting to find the right words, he spotted the maestro crouched on the ground nearby, manically drawing oblique lines – which were completely unintelligible to Cosimo – by the light of a few stubs of candle. So absorbed was he in what he was drawing, Filippo barely noticed when Cosimo laid a hand on his shoulder. He turned around and his appearance froze the blood in Cosimo's veins. Brunelleschi was in a pitiful state. The sunken eyes, intelligent yet evasive, almost like those of a drunk; the emaciated face; the protruding cheekbones. He had lost even more weight. Cosimo wondered if he was eating at all.

'Have you breakfasted this morning?' he asked him.

'I've not had time,' the artist replied. His voice was hoarse, a sort of rattle which was probably the result of not having spoken to anyone for so long.

'May I take you somewhere for lunch?'

'I'm busy.'

'If you're sure?'

'What is it you want?'

'I was wondering if everything was going well.'

'You came to see me for *that*? Come, sir, don't play games with me. I couldn't stand it, not from you.'

Yet again, Cosimo found himself at a loss as to what to say. It always happened to him with Brunelleschi. His clumsy attempts to conceal his confusion left him floundering in vague phrases and half-lies that were worse than the truth. He had to stop doing it.

'The palazzo,' he said.

'Which palazzo?'

'The one you are to build for me.'

'Ah.'

'We cannot proceed.'

'Ah.'

'I will pay you for the project, of course.'

Filippo nodded. He seemed to consider for a moment. 'And why can't we?' he asked.

'The nobles of Florence consider it too magnificent.'

'It is not.'

'You're right, but unfortunately they control public opinion.'

'Including your own?'

'I have to protect my family.'

'So you're giving up?'

'It... it's not about giving up—'

'Yes it is,' interrupted Filippo, 'it is precisely that.'

'I have responsibilities.'

'These are nothing but lies to justify compromise.'

'Is this what you really think?'

'It is.'

'So what should I do, then?' asked an exasperated Cosimo.

'What you had planned.'

'But by doing that...'

'Then we'll call everything off – no problem. I'll only ask you this: why did you come to me if you had already decided?'

'I had not already decided.'

'Don't lie to me again.'

Cosimo snorted. He had fallen for it once more. 'Very well,' he admitted.

'There is no problem.'

'About what?'

'About the building. And I don't want to be paid for the project.'

'But that wouldn't be right.'

'I prefer it that way.'

'I will pay you anyway.'

'Don't you dare,' Filippo said, his eyes flashing wildly.

Cosimo raised his hands. 'Very well, very well... If that is what you want.'

'Messer de' Medici, you must not feel indebted to me. The choice is yours. You are the client. But I have every right to refuse a payment. I'm no parasite.'

'I have never thought for a moment that you were.'

'Very well, then you will respect my wishes.'

'So be it!'

'Is there anything else?'

'No.'

'In that case I will continue with my work.'

Cosimo understood that there was nothing else to say. In the most polite way he knew, Brunelleschi was inviting him to leave.

'Very well,' he said, 'good day to you.'

'The same to you.' Filippo turned his back on him and returned to his drawing, almost as if they had not spoken. For him, that conversation was simply a small bump on the infinite road of his art.

Cosimo was hurt. But what had he expected, after all? It was he who had denied Filippo the job. He had the unpleasant feeling of having somehow betrayed him. Of having put conventions and rules before their friendship.

'Responsibilities,' he had said. What if Brunelleschi was right? What if all that babbling about a sense of duty and respect for the rules was nothing but weakness? Bending to the will of warmongers and thieves? Should he fight? Again?

Cosimo shook his head. He had made the right choice, he decided.

But deep in his heart, something told him it wasn't true.

He left Filippo Brunelleschi's workshop sadder than he had been when he arrived.

September 1433

23

The Accusation

Cosimo knew they were coming.

Since Bernardo Guadagni's name had been drawn as the new Gonfaloniere of Justice, he had known that his fate was sealed. Bernardo was one of Rinaldo degli Albizzi's men, and Albizzi had done everything in his power to ensure his loyalty. Word in the city was that he had even paid him a thousand florins in taxes to ingratiate himself.

It was only a matter of time – or of hours, to be more accurate. He had already warned his wife. Contessina had been frightened at first and then had become furious. She had said that they would take him to prison over her dead body, but Cosimo had shaken his head. Precisely because they knew that it was going to happen they must prepare for the worst and attempt to devise a way to get out of it. Provided, of course, that a way out actually existed...

His reaction was not resignation but simple acceptance of the fact that he was the victim of a grand conspiracy which could only be fought with reason. Rinaldo degli Albizzi was hoping they would be foolish enough to resort to violence and anger: it would be the perfect excuse for him to have them killed.

Cosimo stood looking at the rising sun and the pale shaft of light it etched on the grey-blue sky. That morning he had decided to wear a particularly elegant padded purple doublet: a special colour for a special day. He kept it buttoned up to his neck. It was embroidered with silver and matched the pair of trunk hose of the same colour he wore. He wore no headgear – where he was going, it would only have been in the way. His black hair fell forward in dark, rebellious curls. He was freshly shaven.

He was waiting in the salon, and for a moment he looked up at the imposing wooden ceiling, its coffers arranged in three rows of six compartments each, all adorned with carved acanthus leaves. The candles shone in the wrought-iron chandeliers hanging imposingly from the ceiling.

Cosimo snorted: the waiting was making him impatient. How much longer would it take Rinaldo degli Albizzi to get there?

He had asked Lorenzo to stay with Contessina, Giovanni and Piero.

At that moment, he heard the soldiers' footsteps through the open windows, like a dull bell repeatedly tolling. If that was their way of intimidating him, he would give them no satisfaction.

He left the salon, went down the wide marble staircase and headed for the entrance.

It was then that Contessina appeared. Her face was contorted by pain and streaked with tears, and her dress had fallen below her shoulders, almost exposing her breasts.

'C-Cosimo,' she sobbed, 'what will they do to you, my love?'

He ran over to her.

'Please, my love, be strong,' he told her. 'Difficult days await us, but we will get through them and we will look to the future. Stay close to Piero and Giovanni.'

She threw her arms around his neck and wept on his chest. Without him she felt lost, and she feared she would never see him again.

'Cosimo, I couldn't bear to lose you. I would die if something should happen to you. I cannot bear the thought of living without you.'

Smiling, he stroked her face, and then spoke to her with all the sweetness he could muster.

'Don't be afraid, my love,' he said. 'Before seven days have passed, I'll be back home again. We will be reunited and will continue with our plans. Nothing will separate us.'

'Do you promise me?'

'I promise you.'

While he was saying this, the servants announced the arrival of the guards, who entered with Rinaldo degli Albizzi. His eyes lit upon Cosimo and a cruel smile of feral joy spread across his face.

'Messer Cosimo de' Medici,' thundered the captain of the guards, 'by order of the Gonfaloniere of Justice, I hereby arrest you on charges of treason to the Republic and of tyranny. The accusations will be explained to you by the Gonfaloniere of Justice, Messer Bernardo Guadagni, once you have been taken to the Palazzo della Signoria.

'But,' cut in Albizzi, 'I can informally tell you that the city is sick of your arrogance and your false mercies. We know of the palazzo you want to have built. It makes no difference that it won't be Filippo Brunelleschi carrying out the work – perhaps you will entrust it to Michelozzo or Donatello. You have a long list of artists working for you. We know too of your conspiracies against Florence. And now the time has come for you to pay for your nefarious actions.'

Albizzi must have been waiting a long time for that moment – he uttered the words with such passion that saliva sprayed from his lips like some rabid dog.

Cosimo was silent. He gave Contessina a hard look, because in that moment he wanted her to be stronger than ever. He did not want to give this pathetic creature any satisfaction at all.

His wife understood and, emboldened by what he had said to her, collected herself and went over to kiss him on the lips.

'Do what you must do,' she said.

Upon hearing those words, Rinaldo degli Albizzi, seething with rage, nodded to the captain of the guards. The man put Cosimo's wrists in shackles and he was led out.

It was strange to be escorted through the city. Cosimo tried not to feel downcast, but there was a gloomy mood in Florence. Part of the city seemed incredulous at the injustice of his treatment, while the other part raged against him with all the fervour of those who feel threatened.

When they entered Piazza della Signoria, Cosimo saw that it was crowded with people. The pedlars selling food and wine were doing brisk business. It was a hot morning, and the sun shone in the sky. The air was thick and the oppressive heat hindered his breathing and blinded his eyes. Around him was a sea of people who made the square tremble as though it were a living thing – a Leviathan ready to devour its own children. Ahead loomed the palazzo, the

Tower of Arnolfo di Cambio soaring into the blue of the sky.

A wooden platform had been mounted at the centre of the square. Awaiting them upon it was Bernardo Guadagni.

He was just one face among many, and not a few of them were shouting angrily, their voices full of hatred and envy. He himself had played his part in this madness, thought Cosimo. He looked carefully at them but couldn't see in their eyes the cold determination necessary to stick a sword into an enemy's stomach. For the moment, at least, he did not have to fear for his life. If that had been the case, they wouldn't have bothered bringing him here. And they certainly wouldn't have done it in the middle of the day.

Shouting back at the men screaming insults at him were his supporters. Equally angry, equally ready to fight – with words, at least. In that confrontation, which the guards and the Gonfaloniere, who stood on the platform with his arms stretched out like a mystic, were only barely able to restrain, Cosimo sensed all the fragility and madness of a republic on the brink of the abyss.

He walked forward, trying to ignore the chaos around him.

Someone spat at him, covering his robe with yellowish mucus. He saw women in tears and men vowing to kill him. He saw children, and whores, their make-up smeared. In the blazing sunlight, he stepped through a teeming, roaring sea of bodies; the square was a powder-keg about to explode.

Finally, he arrived at the foot of the platform, and from there was led by two guards to the side of Bernardo Guadagni.

The Gonfaloniere did not deign even to look at him, as though he feared he might be contagious. Cosimo suppressed his anger at the arrogance with which these men, seduced by power and corruption, were treating him, and forced himself to maintain his composure. Losing it at that moment would be fatal.

'This man,' said Bernardo, pointing to Cosimo, 'with his machinations and his agitators, has incited the people against the nobility of the Republic. He did so knowingly, and with malice and shameful arrogance. He commissioned Messer Filippo Brunelleschi to construct a building for himself and his family that was to rise above every other home in Florence. When word of the accusations reached him, he removed Brunelleschi from the commission and asked Michelozzo to take his place. It is not the identity of the artist which interests us, however, but this stubborn insistence upon considering himself better than the rest of us.'

The Gonfaloniere's words echoed like a condemnation before the peasants, commoners and nobles gathered in the square.

'For this reason,' he continued, 'I, Bernardo Guadagni, Gonfaloniere of Justice of this Republic, have summoned the people to this assembly in order to reach a verdict on the sentencing or acquittal of Cosimo de' Medici. Until we do, I order that the defendant be taken to the palace and imprisoned in the Alberghetto cell of the Tower of Arnolfo, where he will wait to discover which fate the institutions have determined for him. Thus have I decided, in the interest of the Republic of Florence.'

On hearing those words, the crowd roared, curses and insults mingling with applause and cries of jubilation. Some voices despaired for Cosimo's future, but many mocked him, calling him a traitor and a Judas.

As the shouts filled the air, Bernardo looked at him with an almost amused expression. He, Albizzi, Soderini and Strozzi had been looking forward to that moment for a long time.

'Take him to the Alberghetto and keep him there until we have decided what to do,' was all he said.

The guards nodded and, taking Cosimo's shackled arms, walked him through the crowd, which parted to let them pass.

24

Contessina

'Have you no love at all for your poor brother?'

Contessina's dark eyes blazed as she glared furiously at Lorenzo. Her voice was filled with rage and in that moment her face possessed a warrior-like beauty. Her long hair was a dishevelled mass of rebellious curls; her bosom heaved under her dress as though her heart were about to burst from her chest.

Lorenzo had never seen her like this before, but he had soon realized that the death of Piccarda and the imprisonment of Cosimo had transformed her.

'Answer me!' Contessina urged him.

'We will take up arms,' he said. 'I will call upon my friends and all those who have supported us so far and will drag Florence down to hell, if necessary. I will drown it in blood—'

'Of course,' she interrupted. 'You will assemble the men, you will call upon those who are faithful to you and you will wage war against the Albizzi. And then? What do you think will happen then? Is it possible that you don't realize?'

'It will be war, my dear sister-in-law.'

'And what *else* do you imagine it could be? And do you imagine *that* will free your brother from the tower? *Think*, Lorenzo! That is exactly what Rinaldo and his men are expecting you to do.'

'It doesn't matter! If that is what they are expecting, all the worse for them! They will fight better, with honour. Perhaps they will face their opponent for once, instead of stabbing him in the back.'

Contessina shook her head. How could he not see that this wasn't the way? There *had* to be another, and she would find it, whatever the cost. She would do it for Cosimo and her children. She would do it for the love she bore them.

'Very well, then,' she said, 'let's do this: you will attempt to use violence but you will leave me the possibility of using more subtle strategies.'

Lorenzo could not believe his ears. What the devil was his sister-in-law talking about?

'What do you mean?' he asked incredulously. 'Do you think we can reason with these people? Did you not see Rinaldo degli Albizzi? At Niccolò da Uzzano's funeral he swore that he would make Cosimo pay. And unless you have completely lost your mind, the best thing you can do is to take refuge in the country and wait for events to run their course—'

The violent slap came suddenly and he immediately felt his cheek burn. His face grew red with shame at having raised his voice against his brother's wife. He should never have spoken to her like that. But it was too late now.

'Do not *dare* tell me to take refuge in the country! Do you think that I could leave my husband to rot in the Alberghetto without doing everything in my power to defend him? I love him more than anything else in the world – you should have realized that at least in all the many years that you have known me! I will not hide in some villa while I wait for Cosimo to end up on the gallows, and neither will our children, of that you can be sure!' Contessina softened her tone. 'This is what we will do,' she continued. 'You will try to gather an army against Rinaldo degli Albizzi and his allies and I will try to bribe Bernardo Guadagni.'

Lorenzo was dumbstruck. Was this what it had come to?

Cosimo stared at the bars.

The Alberghetto measured eight feet by six, and there was single barred window and a bench for sleeping. In a corner, a bucket for his bodily needs. The thick walls of the Tower of Arnolfo made the cell impenetrable. The heavy iron door with its gigantic bolt ensured escape was impossible.

Cosimo dropped on to the bench, which immediately began to torment his back. From the window he could hear the roar of the crowd in the square below. He reflected on his fate. Time was passing and he needed to find a solution as soon as possible. On the other hand, the very fact that time *was* passing might mean they would not impose the death penalty, as everything had previously seemed to indicate they intended to. But apart from Rinaldo degli Albizzi's atavistic hatred for him, nothing was certain, so he had to do whatever he could to influence Bernardo Guadagni, who at that moment held his destiny in his hands.

He had no idea what his family were doing, and could not rule out Lorenzo actually taking up arms. His wife, though, might attempt something subtler.

Contessina was pure and innocent, but that did not mean that she was without resources. It was with her that he needed to talk, and he hoped to see her soon.

He had to find a way out of here. He knew that there were only two possible sentences for the accusation of treason and tyranny: death or exile. Of course, there was always absolution, but as things stood, Cosimo doubted that there was much chance of *that*.

He thought back over the last year, especially to the death of his mother, which had, naturally enough, wounded his very soul. Then there had been the plague, and that absurd ambush, which he had only escaped thanks to his brother, and Albizzi's threats at the church of Santa Lucia de' Magnoli. And finally, Albizzi's diabolical pair of assassins – the soldier of fortune and that woman who was as seductive as she was lethal.

His life had been full of threat and danger, and it occurred to him that he had underestimated Rinaldo degli Albizzi. He hadn't wanted to believe the man could be so obsessed with wanting to kill him. He had always thought, wrongly, that it would be enough to stand up to him, but Albizzi was stubborn. He wanted his head. Badly enough to bribe the Gonfaloniere of Justice.

It was then that he realized what he must do. He had money, men and means, and he had to bribe Bernardo. A man as venal as he, who had allowed himself to be bribed once, would allow himself to be bribed again. Whatever sum Albizzi had offered him, he would offer more. It was said that Rinaldo had paid him a thousand florins in taxes – well, *he* would offer two thousand ducats in exchange for a merciful verdict.

The die was cast, and now all that was left to do was instruct his wife or brother to arrange things.

There was still hope, perhaps.

25

Cruel Beauty

She was sick of Rinaldo and his vacillations. They had used her to instil suspicion and give the Medici a warning, and now, four years later, when they finally had the chance to get rid of them once and for all, they hesitated? Was Rinaldo really so weak?

The situation was driving Laura mad.

She had risked her life: that was certain. Again. If Lorenzo had got hold of her that day, there was no telling how things might have gone. Cosimo seemed harmless enough, or at least less dangerous than his brother, who was a determined sort who certainly harboured a grudge against her. Lorenzo must be eliminated.

At the beginning of it all, she had been a pawn in a game which was far more complex than she had realized.

She had accepted her role, mainly because of the lifestyle that her services to Rinaldo degli Albizzi guaranteed her, but now she found herself a target, and for that reason could not welcome Cosimo's imprisonment. And that was without even considering that the other Medici brother was still at large, and God alone knew what he would do.

The two of them were brothers, of course, but the bond of blood seemed to count more for them than for any other men she had ever met.

It went beyond a simple question of affection: each of the two would happily allow himself to be killed to defend the other, and, once again, Rinaldo degli Albizzi was underestimating them. It was not just about power, interest, money and corruption – there was something far more atavistic at work. The Medici were snakes and needed to be crushed and killed. Uprooted like weeds.

Laura snorted, her red lips curling into a delightful sneer. She sat at her dressing table and looked at herself in the mirror.

She was beautiful. The great mass of black curls framed a face with tawny, almost cinnamon-coloured skin. Her sparkling, cat-like eyes were green and made even more languid by their elongated shape. Extraordinarily large, they were capable of lighting up with a cruelty which could make them seem as hard as diamonds. Her nose, though not small, created an imperfect harmony, giving her face a sensuality that her soft, irresistibly shaped lips only made more seductive. Bare and desirable, her shoulders emerged from the fabric of the magnificent dark-green tunic, and her full, round breasts seemed almost ready to burst out of her bodice.

She smiled. Few men could resist her charms. And now she would have to use them more than ever, or she would be in danger of losing everything she had worked so hard to achieve. It was not easy for a plebeian to get to where she was. Betrayal and lies were arts that must be refined with skill and caution, and God knew she had used them often enough over the years: they had ensured her survival against traps and intrigues in that accursed city where corruption and deception intertwined and flourished.

But poisons and lies were not enough to protect her, and for that reason she had made a tacit alliance with Schwartz. She knew she belonged to Rinaldo degli Albizzi, at least for as long as he guaranteed her what she needed. There was no other way she could have afforded to live in a patrician palazzo in the centre of the city, with servants and guards. On the other hand, though, a *pactum sceleris* made with a man like that was subject to his moods, which made her vulnerable.

Rinaldo considered her simply as a tool for his sexual satisfaction, always ready and available, and that gave her an advantage. On the other hand, despite craving her with a savage, wild desire, Schwartz loved her deeply. He was a violent man who wanted to physically control her, certainly, but once he was sure he had that dominance, she knew he would do anything for her. She had read it in the Major Arcana of the Tarot – and even if they hadn't told her, her own instincts would have.

She put the gilt-edged deck of cards in a drawer of the dressing table.

She needed to be able to exert special pressure on Rinaldo to guarantee herself greater security. She wanted to make him desire the death of the Medici brothers so ardently that he would kill them, or would at least protect her when she did.

In due time, she might even use Schwartz to free herself of him. But not yet.

She detested Rinaldo but above all she loathed the Medici. Unlike Albizzi they were hypocrites: they did not show themselves for what they truly were but rather presented themselves as benefactors and patrons. But the large sums of money they donated to help the common people and the generous funding they provided for public works were for the sole purpose of increasing their prestige and power – and to hide the fact that they were even worse than the rest of them.

There was nothing honest about them. On the contrary, in some respects their behaviour was even more disgusting and revolting than her own. But the nobles who shunned her ways had certainly never known privations and hunger – *real* hunger. Nor would they have been able to imagine the fists of a cowardly, drunken father and his unspeakable attentions. Her father, who had sold her off at the age of ten to a travelling merchant like a piece of meat.

And that had only been the beginning of her nightmare.

The merchant had kept her chained up in a cart like an animal. She slept in the stables next to the beasts, amidst the stinking straw and dung. And she remembered the monstrous men who paid to mount her: rich, poor, false, cowardly and violent. Because, in his own way, each of them had been violent.

And the one that she had never forgotten, the one who had scarred her for life. The one whose eyes, in the dim light of the cart, had seemed to be a terrifying yellow, as though he were consumed by fever. She had shivered at the sight of them.

He was a big, muscular man with a boyish face and pale skin. He hadn't taken her, but he had taught her the real meaning of fear and horror. He had arrived one evening from God alone knew where as though a pack of dogs was at his heels. He must have been a thief. He'd been practically foaming at the mouth when he'd climbed into the cart. Overcoming her terror, she had begged him to free her from her chains, but instead of helping her, he had beaten her so badly that she had thought she was going to die. When she tried to defend herself, he had slashed open her leg with a dagger and then beaten her again. And at that point, Laura had collapsed.

He had rooted around in the wagon for a while, and when he had put on the merchant's old clothes, he had taken off a strange jacket: on it were six red balls on a golden background.

Then he had left her there, vanishing into the nothingness from which he had arrived.

The merchant had been furious when he returned from the village, where he had gone to buy some things, and Laura had spent two months recovering, fearing the whole time that she would be lame and disfigured.

That terrible image had always remained in her mind: the six red balls on a golden background. They had become an obsession, a symbol of horror. Time had passed, and as well as becoming more and more beautiful, Laura had grown taller and stronger, and her will had grown stronger too. Her master had been less and less able to control her and she had frozen her heart, turning it into a fist of hard crystal.

She still remembered the first herbs, the powders and the fungi: shiny, their red or orange caps dotted with white scales, their stalks fleshy and swollen, unspeakably pale. They were so beautiful yet so dangerous, and she was forced to devour them to kill the children that grew inside her. Because men still took her – men like the Medici and like the Albizzis. Men who condemned her to a motherhood she did not want, because raising children in that hell would be even more awful than never giving birth to them.

She remembered the delirium and the nightmares that the mushrooms had caused her – her life had been so shaped by them that they had become the faithful companions of her existence.

But in time she had also realized what an extraordinary effect she had on men – an extraordinary effect that was also a weapon.

And one fine day, when she had grown big and strong enough, she had fed the deadly mushrooms to the merchant, crumbling so many of them into his soup that they had devoured his belly. That night, when she had seen him foaming at the mouth and watched as his eyes swivelled blindly in their orbits, it had been easy to cut his throat so deeply that she had severed his head.

Finally, she was free. And she knew what she would live for.

After a long journey, she had arrived in Florence and put her knowledge of plants and flowers to good use, employing them to make essential oils. And then, one day, she had discovered that the six red balls on the golden background were the Medici family crest.

The crest of the man with the yellow eyes.

When she had first made her discovery, she had thought for a moment that she would die. But after the horror, the anger returned, and she had promised herself that she would do everything in her power to exterminate that family of filthy bastards.

26

The Beginnings of a Plan

The gaoler was a tall man with an open face. Certainly, appearances often meant nothing, but there was something in his eyes that seemed to indicate sincerity, and that was a relief.

Contessina hoped that she was right.

After asking her very politely if he could check she wasn't carrying anything suspicious, Federico Malavolti – for that was his name – led her up an endless staircase of steep, slippery steps. Contessina shivered at the damp cold of the Tower of Arnolfo. The thick stone walls, lit by the flickering red flames of the torches set at intervals along them, were icy, and a draught blew from under the door that gave on to the ramparts. Eventually, they reached the iron door of the Alberghetto and Malavolti detached a large set of keys from his belt, chose one of the longest, and inserted it into the lock, which snapped open with a metallic creak. Malavolti opened the door and gestured to Contessina to enter.

'Stay for as long as you want, my lady. When you wish to leave, just bang on the door. I will be here waiting for you.'

Contessina nodded and, without wasting any more time, went inside.

As soon as she found herself inside that cramped, damp space, she heard the lock snap shut behind her. The cell was dimly lit by several candles, which barely held off the thick, dense darkness that seemed to fill the entire space. Cosimo was lying on the bench, but as soon as he saw her, he jumped to his feet and embraced her. As Contessina allowed herself to be crushed in his arms, she murmured the first words she had spoken since she had come to the tower.

'Cosimo, my love, how are you? I came as soon as I could.'

When he looked her in the face, she saw that he was pale and drawn. Only two days had passed, but prison seemed to have already taken its toll upon him.

'My beloved Contessina, we must act quickly,' he said. 'There's little time and hesitation could be fatal.'

First of all, though, she wanted to know how he could have lost so much weight in only two days and two nights. 'Are you hungry, Cosimo? Because if you are, I know exactly what I shall say to your gaoler.'

Gazing at her, he couldn't suppress a wave of admiration at the sight, in the dim candlelight, of her pugnacious expression, incongruous on such a kind and elegant face.

'I have no doubt that you do, my love. But the truth is that I'm the one refusing the food they bring me.'

Contessina raised an eyebrow.

'The thing is – I'm afraid that it might be poisoned.'

'Really? You think that man...'

'No, not him. He is only my gaoler, but none of us know who prepares the food, and I find it hard to imagine that it is not someone close to Rinaldo degli Albizzi – perhaps even someone in his pay.'

'But you can't go on like this,' she said, her voice breaking with worry.

'Nor can I run the risk of being right.'

'So what do you propose to do? You know I can't bring food into the tower. And even if I did, they would find it, you can be sure of that.'

'That is why we must act quickly, whatever we decide to do.'

'Lorenzo is assembling an army, and intends to attack the city with as many men as possible.'

'What?' asked Cosimo. Knowing his brother's temperament, he had imagined that Lorenzo's reaction would be to take up arms – but not that he would try to assemble an entire *army*. His brother was a man of his word, though, and if he had promised himself that he would free him, he would do everything in his power to keep his vow. Cosimo doubted that it was a wise solution. In fact, he didn't think it was a solution at all.

'Yes,' said Contessina. 'I told him that it was a lunatic idea. As much as I agree that we must get you out of here, I think we need to seek another way.'

Cosimo nodded. Those were his own feelings exactly.

'I agree. We should immediately try to put into action a plan that can guarantee if not my freedom – as I despair of that – at least my exile.'

'Better away from Florence than dead.'

'Exactly. But tell me, how are Piero and Giovanni?' asked Cosimo, changing the subject to less unpleasant matters for a moment.

'Giovanni is well. As well as is possible. Piero insisted on going with his uncle. You know how mad he is about soldiering. That boy will break my heart.'

Cosimo shook his head. 'Another reason to avoid a battle. We have everything to lose and nothing to gain from a war against Florence.'

'I agree, but what do we do?' said Contessina desperately.

Cosimo's eyes wandered the dark space of the cell. It was as though the sparks of a plan were floating in the air – as though he had taken notes on some imaginary parchment. Now he considered it, that was exactly what he *had* been doing in all those hours of waiting.

'I have thought a great deal while I have listened to the shouting of the people down in the square. I know that Bernardo has convened the Council of the Two Hundred and that the Eight of Guard will make their choice, but the final decision is the Gonfaloniere's, since it is he who has the greatest power to influence and address the decisions of the institutions. And so I asked myself, why should a man who has already taken sides for money not do so again?'

'You want to bribe him, then?' she asked.

'I think it's the only chance we have. And I will need you to help.'

'Anything, my love. If truth be told, that was my intention from the very beginning.'

'It shouldn't be too complicated. You see, my dear Contessina, I know for certain that my gaoler, Federico Malavolti, is a good soul.'

'I too felt that.'

'He is, believe me. He is a respected, worthy man who does not have it in his heart to see me dead, that I can say with certainty.'

'For that I rejoice – but how can he help us?'

Her voice came out like a fragile thread about to snap. There she was, discussing with her husband how to save his life, and the idea terrified her. All she wanted to do was take him by the hand and lead him home.

'Well, it so happens that Malavolti knows very well a certain Messer Farganaccio, familiar of Bernardo Guadagni.'

'I think I understand,' murmured Contessina, a smile appearing on her lips. 'You intend to get to Farganaccio, so he can bribe Guadagni.'

'That's right,' confirmed Cosimo, 'and by doing so, to buy my exile.'

27

Nocturne with Fire and Blood

Lorenzo had ridden for two whole days. He had unleashed the agitators in the city and now several hundred armed men, including nobles and soldiers, were camped on the plain outside Florence. He watched the sun melt into the red of the evening sky and the fires of torches and braziers blaze in the darkness.

He stood at the entrance to his tent, aware that in two days' time, he would move against his own city. The situation had escalated and he knew that he had to act quickly. His spies had told him that Cosimo was still alive, but he certainly wouldn't remain that way for long.

The Council of the Two Hundred was split between those who wanted the death sentence and those who were asking for exile. All things considered, the second was not so very different from a pardon. It would be problematic, of course, but the family could continue to run the bank and its many entrepreneurial initiatives even from another city, perhaps from Venice. There was, however, no guarantee that exile would be the verdict.

Lorenzo knew that fighting was the *extrema ratio*. He was a banker, by God! He knew about accounts, writing bills of exchange, keeping a balance sheet, opening a new office: he was certainly no professional soldier, much less a killer. He knew how to defend himself if necessary, but that was as far as it went, so he hoped that the Gonfaloniere of Justice would choose exile when he learned that an army was gathering at the gates of Florence: an army he would have to face if he decided upon a death sentence. And Bernardo Guadagni must already have been informed of Lorenzo's initiative and of the potential consequences of his actions.

The truth was that Lorenzo put more faith in the power of the threat than in any actual battle. It was true that many Florentine nobles had arrived at the camp over the last few hours to give their support to Lorenzo and Cosimo, among them Piero Guicciardini, Tommaso and Niccolò Soderini and Puccio and Giovanni Pucci. Some of them had taken the Medici side out of envy and hatred of their own relatives and therefore with the sole purpose of obstructing them, but this mattered little to Lorenzo – whatever their motives, those who hated Rinaldo degli Albizzi and his friends were their allies.

He was reasoning thus when cries began to disturb the stillness of the night. Lorenzo raced out of the tent and plunged a torch into the brazier at the entrance, sending red sparks up into the black sky. Clad in leather jackets and steel armour, the men were all running breathlessly towards the other side of the camp. A cold sweat ran down Lorenzo's back and he felt a terrible suspicion as he began to run too.

As he approached the point whence the cries came, he realized what was happening. Together with the desperate shouting of the men, there was another sound – the whinnying of horses.

Someone was stealing them.

In that moment, a disturbing spectacle materialized before him. Black-clad men were driving the creatures out from their enclosures so as to leave his men on foot and slow them down, depriving them of much of the impact they would have when they entered the city.

He saw that their enemies had not totally succeeded in their aim: the guards had spotted them just in time. They hadn't been able to prevent the first enclosure from being thrown open, nor the horses from knocking down at least a dozen tents in their frenzied rush, but they had managed to impede the attackers. They had killed those who were trying to open the other enclosures and were fighting with some on horseback who had been about to lead the freed horses away from the camp.

Someone had knocked the braziers over. Bodies lay on the earth, the corpses etched with wide, vermilion ruts. Blood soaked the soil and wherever he looked there were collapsed tents, burned wood and broken swords. He unsheathed the sword hanging from his belt.

A group of horsemen appeared in front of him, one of them swinging his sword. He was dressed in black and wore a doublet and long cloak of the same colour and a tight armet without a visor. He slashed open one soldier's back as he passed. His face was smeared with blood, and his teeth clenched in a grimace: it was Schwartz. Lorenzo saw him choose his target carefully – a foot soldier, whose head he removed from his body with a single gleaming slash. The victim fell to his knees while his head disappeared into the darkness.

Schwartz was as cold and emotionless as the iron of his blade. Until he saw Lorenzo.

He smiled, and saluted him mockingly. A soldier threw himself at him, but Schwartz held him off and, swinging his horse around, sunk a foot and a half of steel into the man's chest. He left his sword inside his opponent's body and unsheathed a second one which he used to deliver a second, diagonal blow.

The soldier brought his hands to his throat as his blood poured out. He fell to his knees and collapsed with his face in the dust.

As the horses galloped away, Schwartz took a last look at him and Lorenzo felt an inexplicable cold invade his limbs. He stood there motionless, as though frozen by the man's eyes. In the light of the torches they were a strange colour.

For a moment, it seemed to him that they were yellow.

He couldn't help trembling. There was something about Schwartz that spoke of an almost supernatural cruelty. He stood watching him as he joined the last of the horses, spurring his mount into a gallop and, unhindered, leaving the camp.

Lorenzo felt like a coward for not having attempted to stop him.

As much as Schwartz frightened him, he knew that sooner or later he would have to face him.

28

To Change the Course of the Stars

Laura had no intention of letting things continue as they were. She had to act right away or it would be too late. And she would never forgive herself for not taking advantage of the opportunity fate had so generously offered her.

She found Rinaldo degli Albizzi sitting at the table, enjoying a goblet of red wine. He loved to dine alone. The man was feared by all and had no friends, only allies, and all of those were terrified of him, which made them unreliable and primed for betrayal.

It was a sorry state of affairs.

She had prepared herself with infinite care, because she wanted to make an impact. She had chosen a pearl-grey *gamurra* with a low and particularly provocative neckline that emphasized her ample, tawny bosom. Her long, well-kept nails were painted a fiery red and the thick black make-up around her green eyes gave them a further note of mystery and seduction. She wore sleeves of black and scarlet braided thread studded with silver coins, which both revealed and hid her beautiful arms.

When she appeared before him, Rinaldo's eyes widened with desire. He said nothing, but stood up from the table and beckoned her over to him, plunging his rapacious hands into her décolletage and grabbing her large breasts like long-sought-after treasures. He took them in his hands, biting greedily at her nipples. Laura was quick to slip her right hand into his breeches, grabbing his swollen member. She uncovered the glans and teased it with her fingertips, and Rinaldo gasped with pleasure. She raised her dress – under which she wore nothing except for her long black stockings – and offered herself to him, kneeling down like a cat and lifting her buttocks towards him. He grasped her long black hair and pushed her head into a cushion until she almost suffocated. He wanted to dominate her. She moaned with pleasure, increasing his desire. She felt the tip of his member against her, the first drops of wetness on her thighs. With his hands between her legs, he lingered with his fingers, and inserted first two and then three until she was soaking wet. Finally, he lost control and penetrated her, making her cry out with wild pleasure.

While he was inside her, Laura spoke to him.

'Punish me,' she said, 'hurt me even more.'

The pleasure was such that Rinaldo feared it might drive him out of his mind. He hissed insults at her, seizing her hips as if he wanted to break her in two.

'Make me happy, Rinaldo,' she murmured between moans, 'kill Lorenzo and Cosimo de' Medici. Promise me.'

'I will,' he gasped, his voice hoarse with desire. 'I swear to you that I will.'

Contessina stared at Federico Malavolti for a long time. He betrayed no embarrassment, and held her gaze.

As soon as she had left the cell, she had felt that she must talk to him about the issue of Farganaccio. Just like the question of the food, the business could not wait, so she decided to go straight to the point.

'Why are you poisoning my husband's food?' she asked him.

Federico was taken aback. His eyes opened wide with surprise.

'Why do you say that, my lady?'

'My husband says his food is poisoned. He doesn't think it's your fault, but he fears that Rinaldo degli

Albizzi is tampering with the meals you bring him from the kitchens.'

Federico shook his head in disbelief.

'That's impossible, my lady.'

'Really?' she asked.

'I swear it to you.'

'And how can you be so sure?'

'Because I have a trusted man who checks the preparation of the dishes.'

'And do you trust him enough that you can be sure he is not lying?'

Federico Malavolti sighed.

'My lady, I can swear to you that I did not want Messer Cosimo to be imprisoned in the Alberghetto. I cannot claim to be a supporter of the Medici but nor am I a supporter of those who oppose him. I am a man of honour, or at least I try to be, and I would never forgive myself if something were to happen to Messer Cosimo. For my part, I secretly hope that the Gonfaloniere of Justice will decide for exile. You must understand that my only intention and purpose is to oversee the imprisonment of Cosimo de' Medici in order that he need suffer no more than he already does, and his refusal of the food I bring him is as much a cause of anguish for me as it is for you.'

Contessina sensed that Federico Malavolti's words came from the heart, and it was with not a little surprise that she found herself touching his arm. After all, she had to trust *someone*. What more had the Medici to lose than they had already lost? But although Contessina might trust him, given the circumstances she could not be content with words alone.

'What would you be willing to do to show me you mean what you say?'

'From now on, I will personally taste each dish that is brought to Messer Cosimo and I will do so in front of him, so that I will die before him if it has been poisoned. I hope this is enough.'

'Would you truly do that?'

'As truly as I see in you a woman in love.'

Contessina was silent for a moment.

'Is it that obvious?'

'There's no reason to feel embarrassed.'

'I'm not embarrassed, not at all – it's just that if it is visible, that makes me weak. Vulnerable. My enemies could use my feelings to strike even more deeply at Cosimo.'

'No, my lady,' said Federico. 'There is no woman stronger than she who is in love.'

Contessina sighed. 'So be it,' she said. 'You, Federico, seem to me to be both wise and sincere. Thank you for what you will do for Cosimo... And in this regard, I have another favour to ask of you.'

'I am listening.'

Contessina searched for the right words. What she was about to ask was no small thing: even though Federico was a good-hearted man, he would have every right to refuse her.

'I gather that you are a friend of a man who has a reputation as an excellent orator and dining companion. I am referring to Messer Farganaccio. My husband knows him well and I would like you to organize a dinner here. It would provide my husband with a pleasant evening and an occasion...' Here Contessina stopped, to allow Malavolti to imagine what she was implying without actually saying it. 'An occasion for Cosimo to start eating again.'

'I know Messer Farganaccio and he truly is a man of spirit. I believe I understand why you are making this request. Especially given that Farganaccio is a friend of Bernardo Guadagni. I will not hinder you. As I said, I am no supporter of the Medici but neither am I a supporter of Rinaldo degli Albizzi, and if I can help in some way to prevent a death sentence, well – I will not hesitate.'

Contessina almost fainted when she heard his words.

'You will do it, then?'

'Why shouldn't I? After all, it's simply a matter of Farganaccio dining with Cosimo de' Medici.'

'Thank you, thank you, *thank* you,' whispered an ecstatic Contessina. 'You cannot know how much this means to me.'

Such was the joy in her heart that she couldn't stop herself from embracing him. Malavolti practically jumped with shock at her effusions. He returned her embrace; then he broke away from her and stepped back a couple of paces.

'It is I who should thank you, my lady, for giving me the opportunity to prove my honour and good faith. And now I should take you back to the tower entrance, so that you may take your leave. Your visit was long – and certainly profitable! – but I would not want to invite complaints from the Gonfaloniere of Justice. We must behave as irreproachably as we can.'

'Of course,' agreed Contessina, 'I understand perfectly. But I thank you from the bottom of my heart for what you have done.'

'I have not done anything yet, my lady, and there's no saying whether our idea will lead anywhere. But let us hope that it helps save your husband's life. I would never forgive myself if it did not.'

So saying, and letting those words of hope drift away through the cold air of the tower, Federico Malavolti descended the stairs, leading Contessina to the entrance and wishing her farewell.

The situation was by no means resolved, but a less gloomy light now shone upon the fate of Cosimo de' Medici. Not to mention that Lorenzo was preparing to besiege the city. That was another reason to hope that her negotiations would bear fruit. Who knew what

Piccarda would have said about what she'd done? Piccarda would certainly have acted in the same way. Would she have been proud of her if she could have seen her in that moment? Contessina hoped so.

One more reason to fight on until the bitter end. Not only for her husband and for the love that bound their hearts, not only for the children who were waiting for her at home, but also so as not to betray the memory of those who had made the Medici great and who had given her so much in the past.

She had acted as she should.

The only thing she could do now was to put her faith in God and his mercy.

But would that be enough?

October 1433

29

The Plot

'Death: that is the only possible sentence for the man.'

Rinaldo degli Albizzi was more determined than ever. His loathing of the Medici was atavistic. He hated what they represented, and even more importantly knew that if they remained alive, sooner or later they would become a threat once more. He had to eradicate them, just as Laura had said. The anger in her had surprised him, but it was just one more reason for wanting to put an end to the Medici.

'I understand why you think so,' said Palla Strozzi, 'but we must tread carefully. Those two brothers are still very powerful. If we condemn Cosimo to death for treason and tyranny, we will have the peasants, the common people and a section of the nobility against us.

As we speak, Lorenzo de' Medici is gathering an army at the gates of Florence. We shouldn't underestimate the threat.'

'And that is why we have to kill them both,' shouted Rinaldo.

Palla Strozzi snorted with annoyance. Why did Albizzi always see that as the only possible solution?

'I am not saying we should not, but let us not forget that several nobles have sided with the Medici. Piero Guicciardini, Tommaso and Niccolò Soderini and Puccio and Giovanni Pucci have already joined Lorenzo. I believe that exile is the best solution.'

'Of course!' exploded Rinaldo degli Albizzi. 'What a *wonderful* idea! Do you think that the Medici will stop exercising their nefarious influence on this city even if they are far away? They have friends *everywhere*! They have them in Venice – the branch of their bank there is so successful that they made an alliance with the doge himself. And in Milan too, if it is true that Cosimo counts Francesco Sforza among his friends – and Sforza seems destined to overthrow the Duchy soon. In this moment, only Rome is perhaps his enemy, and I am not even sure of that, given that the Medici bank is the depository of the Apostolic Chamber – the papal treasure. Do you truly not realize the threat the Medici pose for us? And do you honestly believe that allowing them to live is a solution?'

Bernardo Guadagni had to admit that, though blinded by anger, Rinaldo had listed the dangers with surprising lucidity. But he remained unconvinced that a death sentence against Cosimo de' Medici was wise. The truth was that the Council of the Two Hundred was split down the middle, and was actually slightly in favour of exile. This fact could not be ignored, which was why he was closeted up here with Rinaldo and Palla in the armoury overlooking the courtyard of the Palazzo della Signoria. If anyone had seen them they would certainly have taken them for conspirators, which for all intents and purposes was what they were. The Council of the Two Hundred had adjourned temporarily after their endless succession of meetings attempting to arrive at a clear decision upon the fate of Cosimo de' Medici. For the moment the building was quiet.

'I don't think condemning him to death would be a good idea,' Guadagni said. He saw Rinaldo's eyes fill with rage and immediately added, 'I don't mean that he shouldn't die. But it is important that happens by chance and not as the result of a conviction.'

'Dear Bernardo,' Rinaldo remarked coldly, 'I hope that I do not have to remind you *how* you became the Gonfaloniere of Justice of the Florentine Republic.'

'I have not forgotten, but that doesn't mean I should be imprudent now. I would be very careful about condemning a man like Cosimo to death. The initial aim was to free the city of a tyrant, and I do not believe that capital punishment is the solution. My loyalty to you is not in dispute, Messer Rinaldo, but precisely because, as you yourself pointed out, the Medici have powerful friendships, we must make sure not to invite their wrath.'

'Not to mention,' added Palla Strozzi cryptically, 'that Florence is at war with Lucca at the moment—'

'A war,' Rinaldo interrupted, 'which the skill of our orators managed to make him seem responsible for.'

'I am well aware of that,' continued Palla, annoyed, 'I myself was one of them. But now as well as the war against Lucca there will be civil war if Lorenzo marches on Florence.'

'All the more reason to eliminate the Medici!' said Rinaldo.

'Yes, but some might decide that we were to blame for this second conflict – and, to be frank, they wouldn't be too far from the truth.'

'So be it, then! What do you suggest?' asked Rinaldo. 'Because I warn you that I have no intention of letting an opportunity like this slip through my fingers. We have let him get away too many times in the past.'

'Let's wait a few more days,' said Bernardo. 'We will try to use our men to shift the position of the Council but without giving them the impression that we are attempting a show of force. In the meantime, let's prepare to hold off an attack by Lorenzo. I'll gather the Ten of Balia tonight so that the patrols and guards are doubled. I will put all the available men at the gates and on the walls of the city. That is all we can do: prepare. Two more days and then we will decide one way or another. If face goes against us and the result is exile, we will find some way to make it particularly unpleasant for Cosimo.'

Rinaldo snorted with annoyance, but eventually nodded his assent.

'Very well,' he said, 'but let's not wait too long or I swear to you that I will kill them with my own two hands.'

Cosimo had been awake all night. He had tossed and turned on the bench, but the wood was as agonizingly uncomfortable as the bed of Procrustes. The warm light which came through the window filled the Alberghetto cell with tepid air. He heard the key turn in the lock and barely had time to get up before Francesco Malavolti had entered the room.

As usual, Francesco's frank, calm face made Cosimo feel a little less lost.

'Messer Cosimo, last night I spoke with your wife Contessina. I had not realized that you were refusing the food I brought you because you feared it poisoned, so this morning I will eat with you from the same plate to prove that you can trust me. I harbour no hatred for your faction and I think it is profoundly unjust to hold you responsible for the misfortunes of our Republic. And though I have no idea whether you are guilty of the crimes of which you are accused, I think you deserve at least to have your life spared.'

Francesco stopped speaking and placed the plate on the table. He broke a piece of bread and ate a bite. Then another one. He took the pitcher and poured some water into the wooden cup. He drank it.

He looked Cosimo in the eyes and waited.

Some moments passed; they both remained silent. Francesco Malavolti knew that recent events had left Cosimo absolutely exhausted. Not so much the imprisonment itself, as he had only been in the tower for a few days, but the distress of not knowing what his future held. The people gathered outside every day, and that morning was no exception – they were already crowding the square below. From the cell window overlooking the square they could hear the shouts and the noise. The Council of the Two Hundred had not reached a verdict and the Gonfaloniere of Justice was prevaricating. It was a slow torture, and a man needed to be in a strong fame of mind to withstand it, thought Malavolti.

Without adding another word, Francesco held out his hand. 'Do you trust me, Messer Cosimo?'

'I do,' answered Cosimo, grasping it. 'And I thank you for this proof of your honesty.' He embraced him. 'I do not have many friends these days, unfortunately,' he continued, 'so your kindness is even more dear to me.'

Federico was almost moved.

'It's not true that you have few friends, Messer Cosimo. There are many who support you, both inside and outside the palazzo. You must have faith. Things will come to a peaceful resolution: I have no doubt of it. And in order to facilitate this, tonight I would like to bring Messer Farganaccio to the Alberghetto. He is a courteous and kind man, and I consider him one of my closest friends. I know, too, that he holds you in high esteem. If you are agreeable, we could have dinner together.'

'The opportunity to dine with you both would be an unexpected pleasure,' said Cosimo.

'Very well, then. I will have the cook prepare something tasty to help you recover after your long fast, if not in your soul, at least in your limbs. And who knows, after having restored your strength, perhaps fate will smile on you too,' concluded Francesco enigmatically.

'I really do not know how to thank you,' said Cosimo.

'Do not thank me yet – nothing is certain.'

'I will wait, then. I have nothing else to do, after all.'

'Very well. Until tonight. Let us see what happens.'

30

Reinhardt Schwartz

Reinhardt Schwartz had just awoken and he stretched slowly, savouring every moment of indolence.

He had certainly earned himself a good night's sleep! After a long ride the previous day, he had been kept busy cracking heads and attacking Lorenzo de' Medici's camp. It was par for the course, but he was sick and tired of being Rinaldo degli Albizzi's damned pet. He needed a break. Lorenzo de' Medici was no soldier – how could he be? The man was a banker – but he had guts, you had to give him that. And he kept finding himself face to face with the man.

Albizzi paid him, Schwartz kept telling himself. But when you tell yourself that you do what you do because you are paid and yet still do it unwillingly... well, something's wrong. And Schwartz had been aware of that hint of doubt for two years now. Not to mention that if he continued to work for Albizzi, sooner or later he would find himself with a few inches of steel sticking out of his chest. It was only a matter of time.

He had to stop letting himself be used. Some risk was acceptable, but only if he were given extra protection. And he would have to tell his master that at the first opportunity, because he couldn't carry on like this.

He looked around him. After the sortie in Lorenzo de' Medici's camp the previous night, he had taken shelter at an inn in the Florentine countryside, and his room was simple but pleasant.

That morning, after finally sleeping in a proper bed with clean sheets, he rose without haste when the sun was already high in the sky, washed his face in the iron basin filled with cold water, then dressed and went downstairs to the inn's kitchen.

He found Laura waiting for him. The day was starting in the best possible way.

When he saw her, he bowed and kissed her beautiful hand.

'I can barely believe what I'm seeing. Why this unusual gallantry, Reinhardt?'

Schwartz pretended to be offended.

'Are you really so surprised, *mein Schatz*? Isn't this arm of mine not the one which embraces you in the darkest of moments?'

Laura smiled. That morning she was radiant.

'Very well,' she said with unusual indulgence. 'How much time do we have?'

'There is no need to rush. That looks delicious,' he said, pointing to a magnificent quail pie which sat proudly on the table. Next to it, Schwartz saw a basket of crusty bread, a tray full of seasonal fruit, wild boar ham and cheese. The only thing missing was wine.

'Vernaccia di San Gimignano?' he suggested.

'Wine? At *this* time of the morning?' she teased him. 'How vulgar, my impetuous Reinhardt.'

'You suggest something different?'

'I'm not going to share this sumptuous meal with you, but if I *were* to suggest a wine, then I would choose a Chianti, since that's a quail pie in front of you.'

'Excellent,' he said, smoothing his thick blond moustaches.

He nodded to a serving girl and when she came over to them, asked her to bring a bottle of the best Chianti at once. Laura, instead, ordered an infusion of camomile with honey.

While they waited for their drinks, Schwartz began to tuck into the pie. It was a true delicacy.

'Rinaldo is determined to see it through,' said Laura, 'but he confessed to me last night that his allies don't seem ready to do the same.'

Schwartz raised an eyebrow '*Wirklich?*'

'That's right. After having become Gonfaloniere of Justice thanks to him, Bernardo Guadagni now seems recalcitrant. And Palla Strozzi, as you know, is a born procrastinator. That is the situation in Florence. What about you? Did you carry out your task?'

'In every detail. Thanks to the attack last night, it will be at least another couple of days before Lorenzo de' Medici can move on the city.'

'Very good. That will give us all the time we need to retire to my estate in Veneto.'

'What?'

'Albizzi wants us out of the way.'

'To avoid anything being traced back to us?'

'Precisely. I came to pick you up in an unmarked carriage. When you've eaten your fill, we should get on the road to Padua without further delay.'

Schwartz grimaced. He didn't like travelling by carriage. It seemed to him a very effeminate mode of transport, and he disliked its slowness. A horse was much better. But, on the other hand, a carriage without insignia did guarantee anonymity.

'Very well, then,' he agreed, cutting himself some thick slices of wild boar ham with his knife and relishing their intense flavour.

The drinks arrived and he took a mouthful of the Chianti. It was delicious.

'This wine is nectar. Thanks for the advice, my beautiful friend. Why Padua?'

'A dear admirer of mine dwells there.'

'Naturally. Stupid question.'

'In any case, Albizzi wants us far from here but, at the same time, ready to join Cosimo wherever he ends up – that's if he's spared and exiled.'

'Ah,' exclaimed Schwartz, 'so *that's* his plan.'

'He always wants to have the upper hand, and I can't blame him for that. I confess that I'm sorry I didn't ask you to kill that damned Lorenzo de' Medici for me, though.'

Schwartz couldn't help but laugh.

'That dandy,' he said. 'He was standing right before my eyes last night. If I had known, I would have opened him up like a goat for you, *mein Kätzchen*!'

'If I think about him stalking and spying on me all that time... and he almost managed to catch me... I *hate* him. He and his brother are a plague upon this city.'

'Please, don't speak to me of the plague.'

'Why not?'

'Ach, it's a long story. Perhaps I'll tell you on the way.'

'It's a deal.'

'So why do you hate the Medici so much?'

'That too is a long story, but I doubt I will ever tell you it.'

'*Ach, wie schade!*' exclaimed Schwartz, a hint of disappointment in his voice.

While they spoke, a group of men sat down at a table behind them. They were talking in loud voices and sounded as though they were already drunk even though it was not yet lunchtime. From the tone of their conversation, it seemed that they sided with the Medici.

'If it was up to me I would kill the lot of them,' said Schwartz, lowering his voice.

For a moment Laura stared at him. 'Who do you mean?'

'The Medici *and* Albizzi's allies. Messer Rinaldo doesn't have the guts for it.'

'Are you sure of that?'

'I certainly am! This business of warring factions is tearing apart a beautiful city. Rinaldo would do well to get rid of his opponents. If I were in his place I would chop off Cosimo's head and then annihilate Lorenzo and his ridiculous army. And once the opposition had been eliminated, I would kill of some of his most prominent allies.'

'It would be a bloodbath.'

'Yes, but at least I would turn the Republic into a *signoria* and I would do it by the light of day. I would no longer have to deal with procrastinating parasites and I would seize power definitively. A little at a time, the people would follow me. The plebs need a leader and so do the little people. The rest is just talk.'

'Hardly the subtlest of strategies.'

'Efficacy and refinement rarely coincide.'

'Of course, though I... Why, that *bastard*!' Laura's face grew red with anger.

'What's the matter, *mein Schatz*?'

Laura's eyes filled with hate. 'One of the men behind you just made an obscene gesture to me.'

When he heard her words, Reinhardt Schwartz stood up. He turned around and saw three men seated at a table, who laughed coarsely at the sight of him. The Swiss mercenary looked them up and down: they were just curs, ready to act bold because they ran in a pack. He knew that he was no paladin and that his manners were anything but refined, but he would readily die to defend Laura. He was sometimes hard on her, but over time he had learned to love her and would tolerate no one – apart from himself – treating her with a lack of respect. Not even Albizzi.

'Tell me what you find so amusing, sirs, and we will laugh together.'

The largest of the three rose in turn. 'We are laughing because we can't understand how a filthy mercenary like you can be with such a beautiful woman. And the conclusion we have reached is that she must be a whore.'

The man's friends laughed again.

Schwartz wasted no more words.

'I will await you in the courtyard, sir. With your sword. The offence that you have caused this lady will be washed away with blood, if you do not mind.'

The man shrugged. He didn't look particularly worried.

'As you wish,' he answered calmly.

When Schwartz turned around, Laura looked at him. Her eyes burned with desire.

'Nobody,' she said, 'has ever fought for me.'

'Really?'

She nodded.

'Well, in that case I am happy to be the first. I hope I will also be the last.'

Laura smiled. 'While you take care of that yokel, I will pay the innkeeper – with Albizzi's money! We should be on our way.'

'You'll find me in the courtyard,' said Reinhardt. 'It won't take long.'

The October sun was shining and Reinhardt felt particularly at ease. He drew his sword and dagger and put up his guard.

The man in front of him did the same. And then the duel began.

He made a couple of feints; then he attempted a lunge. Schwartz parried him easily and then he too feinted to the right, only to get in a blow on the return swing. His opponent was not taken by surprise, and their blades clanged again, the impact releasing a shower of sparks. Schwartz did not stop. He made two more lunges, harrying his opponent. He was in no hurry but neither had he any intention of wasting too much time on that peasant. The man parried again, but was now clearly in difficulty. Schwartz feinted a cross and then slashed at him horizontally, catching the man with his guard down. A spurt of blood drew a dark arc through the air and the Florentine raised his hand to his cheek. It was smeared with red.

Laura had come out into the courtyard and her eyes burned as she watched the duel.

Schwartz waited for his opponent to attack, then parried in a high sweep. With a lightning-fast movement, his sword found the Florentine's chest and emerged from his back.

His opponent dropped his sword, which fell to the brown earth; then he collapsed to his knees. Schwartz went over to him and, turning the man's head to the side, sliced his throat open with his dagger. As the blood sprayed out like rain, he drew his sword from the chest of the man, who fell to the ground as a pool of red spread out below him.

Schwartz looked at the dead man's cronies. 'This is what happens to those who are disrespectful to this lady.'

The Florentines stared at him in shocked silence; then they picked up their friend's body and departed.

Laura smiled. In a way, she adored Schwartz, even though she knew that there was something unhealthy about that bizarre mixture of suffering, love and humiliation they shared. She and Reinhardt were hounds in the service of their master, and could give one another pleasure or pain or both. After what she had endured, perhaps, for her, one could not exist without the other.

She also knew that Reinhardt was subject to sudden changes of mood. He was sweet yet violent, refined yet coarse, and within him lived a strange disharmony of opposites very much like her own. In that bizarre see-sawing between extremes Laura recognized her own deepest essence.

In those three years, they had ended up in bed together no more than two or three times, but she had never forgotten them. When she made love to him, she felt both hurt and protected. She was lost in him, and it completely terrified her while at the same time it gave her a thrill of intense pleasure.

And so, as she looked at Schwartz sweating in the heat, the blade of his sword dripping with the blood of the man who had dared to disrespect her, she was overcome with a passion so intense that she wanted to give herself to him then and there upon the death-soaked earth of the courtyard.

In her heart she rejoiced, because for the first time in her life, a man had fought for her. And he had done it to the death. From that moment on, she sensed, he would do anything for her.

Even, if necessary, kill Albizzi.

31

Farganaccio

The pleasant dinner was coming to an end.

Cosimo was surprised how generous Federico Malavolti had been with him: not only had he guaranteed his safety but he had brought Farganaccio to his cell, just as Contessina had asked him to. Perhaps, then, there was still hope.

When he felt that the appropriate moment had arrived, Cosimo had nodded to Federico, who had left on the pretext of getting another bottle of wine.

Once they were alone, Cosimo had explained to his interlocutor what he had in mind.

Farganaccio was a tall man with broad shoulders, ruddy cheeks, bright, lively eyes and a sincere face who had regaled them with many funny tales that evening.

As he had nothing left to lose, Cosimo had decided to speak to him openly.

'Messer Farganaccio,' he said, 'allow me to ask you a question, since you have been kind enough to bring a breath of refreshing, cheerful air into this grim place. So refreshing and so cheerful that I have almost forgotten the reason why I find myself here.'

He paused for a moment to reflect upon how explicit he should be in his request.

Farganaccio, who had apparently been intrigued by this opening, gestured to him to continue.

'Very well. You know perfectly well why I am here,' Cosimo continued. 'Rinaldo degli Albizzi and his supporters claim that I am guilty of tyranny and they obliged Bernardo Guadagni to have me imprisoned and threatened with a death sentence. They think that by doing so they will make Florence a better place. Now, I wish to emphasize that I do not consider Bernardo, whom I know to be your friend, responsible, because it is clear that, in the position in which he finds himself – as Gonfaloniere of Justice – and given the accusations against me, he had no choice but to proceed as he did. On the other hand, even though my conduct has not been free of error, I have never intended to harm my city or my opponents. I have only ever attempted to bring benefit and splendour to Florence. It is no secret that my family enjoys a position of wealth and privilege, but it is also true that we have always tried to use our riches to increase the beauty of the city.'

Farganaccio nodded. He had suddenly grown serious.

'However,' continued Cosimo, 'if I am now considered an enemy of the Republic, I have clearly failed somehow, and therefore I can't say for certain that my desire to make my city more beautiful did not come with an excess of zeal that made me guilty of vainglory. That's why I feel I have no cause to protest and I am ready to accept the penalty that Florence, in the person of its Gonfaloniere of Justice, decides. All I ask is a little clemency, that my life be spared.'

'*Messer*,' said Farganaccio, 'I wholeheartedly agree with your description of events and also with your conclusion. I must inform you that I personally have nothing against you – in fact I too believe that good sense must prevail. The Two Hundred have debated at length over the past few days and their decision, despite everything, remains uncertain. I think that there is plenty of room to tip the balance towards the side most favourable to you.'

'I see. And furthermore, I have no doubt that Messer Bernardo could easily influence the decision, but that, on the other hand, he ought – in the name of the position he holds – to act for the good of the Republic, and I am certain that this is what he will do.'

'Naturally.'

'Since it is also my intention not to be a hindrance to the Republic – rather I want only the best for it at all costs – and because I may to some have seemed arrogant and vainglorious, I have no intention of opposing the sentence. I am perfectly willing to step aside and set off along the road to exile as soon as possible. Therefore I would ask you to report to Bernardo my intentions and my full will in this regard. *Ad adiuvandum*, if the Gonfaloniere of Justice would consider this a solution to the question, I would be delighted to be allowed to pay, as pledge of my good faith, any compensation he sees fit.'

And, at this point, Cosimo looked directly at his interlocutor: the offer had been formulated in a subtle manner, so as not to offend Bernardo's integrity. Cosimo knew that he was all too willing to profit from corruption, but on the other hand could not openly declare himself a man who sold himself to the highest bidder.

'And of course,' he concluded, 'my gratitude would also extend to you for the precious service you would have rendered me.'

Farganaccio had listened to him with great attention. To tell the truth, since Federico Malavolti had offered him that dinner, he had presumed that the reason would be linked to some request from Cosimo de' Medici. He had known, too, that in addition to the enjoyment that the bizarre dinner in Arnolfo's Tower would offer, the proposal would not be displeasing to him. Neither to him nor to Bernardo Guadagni. Moreover, he respected Cosimo, and was enough of a man of the world to know that even though in this moment Albizzi was the favourite in the game of alliances, those alliances were subject to constant shifts.

And after all, what harm could come from a friendship with a Medici?

'And you feel that this compensation might be paid in coin?' he suggested.

'Whatever form Bernardo considers useful, that is the form I will choose.'

Farganaccio sighed and a benevolent sparkle appeared in his big blue eyes. He went straight to the point.

'How much?'

'Would two thousand two hundred ducats be sufficient, so that you may keep the eleventh part of it for yourself?'

32

The Sentence

On 3 October, Cosimo was brought before the Gonfaloniere of Justice. As he stood in front of him, Bernardo Guadagni seemed preoccupied.

In front of Cosimo were the Balia dell Otto – the Eight of Guard, the council which represented the supreme magistracy in criminal matters. Chosen every four months, their task was to decide without scruple or bias upon the fate of citizens accused of crimes against Florence.

They wore beautiful red robes with ermine collars and sat upon carved wooden benches set in a semi-circle at the end of the hall with Bernardo at their centre. His toga, which was of the same carmine colour, was the only one that bore the golden stars testifying to the supreme office he held.

Cosimo knew that his proposal had been accepted so the verdict would now follow a very precise script. On the other hand, there were no certainties in a Florence dominated by warring families – and regardless of the money he had received, Bernardo would certainly have considered the consequences of betraying Rinaldo degli Albizzi.

In any case, they had now reached the point where Cosimo would discover what was to become of him. He looked his judges firmly in the face, ready to accept their decision.

Bernardo raised his hand as though asking for silence, even though no one had, in fact, dared utter a word.

'Cosimo de' Medici,' he began, 'today, the third of October of the year 1433, after repeated meetings of the Council of the Two Hundred to investigate the will of the people, and after carefully examining that conduct which led to your being accused of the crime of tyranny, this supreme council which I have the honour to chair finds you guilty. However, upon consideration of your behaviour before, during and after your arrest, we have decided not to sentence you to capital punishment but to condemn you to exile within the precincts of the city of Padua, whence you may not return to Florence unless thus permitted by the institutions of the Republic. The present sentence extends also to Lorenzo and Averardo Medici and to Puccio and Giovanni Pucci.'

Looking shaken, Bernardo stopped for a moment. The expulsion of the Medici from Florence was now a historical fact. The die was cast, and Albizzi and Strozzi could no longer escape their responsibilities. They no longer had any excuses: now, they would have to govern.

When he heard the sentence, Cosimo nodded.

Bernardo finished proclaiming the verdict of the supreme magistracy.

'In order for the verdict to be respected and to ensure you are unharmed, this evening you will be taken by carriage to the border of the Republic and will be assigned an armed escort to guarantee your safety until you get there. Your family will be informed of the verdict so that they may provide for your well-being, it being understood that the verdict also applies to your brother and the others who conspired with you and plotted against the Florentine Republic. Thus it has been decided, and in the next few hours the verdict will be carried out as stated.'

Piero at his side, Lorenzo rode at the head of his men, seeming to wait only for the moment when they declared war on the city. The messengers they had sent had already returned, reporting that Ginevra and his sons, Francesco and Pierfrancesco, as well as Contessina and Giovanni and all the other members of the family, had already left for the villa in Cafaggiolo where they would remain until a suitable solution was found.

They had set off at the first light of dawn and now saw the walls of Florence in the distance.

Lorenzo had no intention of actually attacking; all he wanted was for them to hand over his brother. He had no desire to sacrifice his friends and all those who had taken his side in his moment of need. He did, however, hope that Florence would see his army and that that cur Bernardo Guadagni would dare show himself. He knew that his brother had tried to bribe him and hoped that he had succeeded.

When they found themselves no more than three hundred paces from the vast St George's Gate he and his men saw the Eight of Guard and the captain of the city guard standing in front of them.

Lorenzo motioned his men to stop and the horsemen formed up in orderly rows. Snorting, their breath steaming in the cold air, the horses took up position, stamping their hooves on the ground.

Lorenzo nodded to Puccio Pucci, who gave his horse a little prod with his spurs and came over to him.

'Well, we've come this far,' Pucci said.

'Let's hear what they have to say,' replied Lorenzo.

'Very well.'

'Give the order to wait and then come and meet me at the centre of the field.'

While Puccio carried out his orders, Lorenzo set off, alone, towards the centre of the strip of land that separated him from the Eight. He spurred his mount forward. It was a cold day: autumn seemed to have come suddenly. The air was freezing and rain had begun to fall, making the earth spongy underfoot. Large, unruly raindrops bounced off armour and helmets, making a dull tinkling sound that rendered that miserable day even gloomier.

Two knights broke away from the group: one of them was certainly the captain of the city guard and the other looked familiar. By the time Puccio had returned to his side, they were very close.

'If Neri de' Bardi of the Eight of Guard is accompanying Captain Manfredi Da Rabatta, something important must have happened.'

'Yes,' said Lorenzo, who barely dared hope for a peaceful solution, even though he had never stopped wishing for it.

They stopped halfway, no more than a hundred paces from the gate. Now Lorenzo could clearly make out the double arch at the top with the bas-relief in the lunette depicting St George on horseback killing the dragon with his spear.

They pulled at the reins to halt their horses and the animals trampled the mud. Lorenzo patted the neck of his mount to calm it. It was being skittish, and kept turning on the spot. He stroked its neck.

'Don't worry, old fellow,' he whispered in its ear. 'Everything will be all right. You'll see.'

As though it had understood his words, the horse snorted and grew calmer.

Neri and Manfredi were now before them.

The captain of the guard wore finely tooled battle armour. In the rain, the steel gave off iridescent glints which mingled with the rays of pale sunlight that had begun to make their way through the clouds.

Lorenzo greeted them with a frank smile, for he had always held both in high esteem.

The captain did not seem to feel the same way about him, but Neri de' Bardi was more accommodating.

'So, Lorenzo de' Medici, you have arrived with your men, I see,' he said, pointing to the lines of knights and infantrymen who formed a dark mass behind them.

'I had no choice,' he replied.

'Well, you will be glad to hear that, despite finding your brother guilty, the supreme magistracy has issued the penalty of exile.'

When he heard those words, Lorenzo felt the ice in his heart begin to melt. It might not be a complete victory but, all things considered, it was still a victory. He thanked God for the decision.

And at the same instant, he realized that those words condemned him too.

'But you should know,' continued Neri, 'that the punishment also extends to you.'

'Just as I expected,' said Lorenzo.

'I can well imagine.'

'The sentence is also imposed on you, Puccio Pucci,' added Captain Manfredi.

'Very good,' said Puccio without batting an eyelid.

'What I would ask of you now is to communicate to your men the decision of the Eight of Guard and of the Gonfaloniere of Justice,' said Neri de' Bardi, 'then to dismiss the troops and surrender yourself to the captain of the guard who will escort you to the border of the Republic. Your brother, Cosimo, awaits you there. From that moment what happens to you is no longer our business. You have been condemned to exile in the city of Padua.'

Lorenzo closed his eyes. They had condemned him to abandon his city. Forever. But it was a price that he was happy to pay if it allowed him to save his life and that of his brother.

'So be it,' he answered. 'I will do as you say.'

And without another word he gave a nod and set off towards his men, Puccio close behind. They couldn't claim to be happy but at least they had ensured that Cosimo's life was saved and that they had not wasted the lives of their companions in fratricidal battle.

Florence, though, was now in the hands of their bitterest enemies.

What, wondered Lorenzo, would become of their beloved city?

January 1434

33

Venice

My dearest, infinite love,
Today the snow has fallen and covers the fields and the bare trees. The cold here in Cafaggiolo is truly bitter and winter seems to have frozen life itself. I miss you as always, just as one misses a piece of one's heart, but today even more than usual. All is silent, all is still, and the countryside seems buried beneath this white blanket. A deathly silence hangs over everything, and not simply because of winter but because the gloomy bark and the twisted branches of the trees seem somehow to reflect the nightmare that has descended upon Florence.

Since you and Lorenzo left, Albizzi and Strozzi have become even more high-handed. The common people suffer the cruellest miseries and the blackest humiliations and the people die of hardship in the streets. The nobles do nothing but tax them to finance their bloody war against Lucca and to maintain a lifestyle that is shamefully lavish and contemptuous of the poverty and pain of those of lower standing. It seems almost that they are pleased with the deep, bloody furrow they are ploughing for themselves, but they do so foolishly, since they seem not to notice the effects it has, day after day, upon their support.

Giovanni de' Benci was here a little while ago to ensure that everything was proceeding for the best. He is a dear man, and seeing him has helped me to bear the pain of this separation a little better. He says that the business of the bank has not suffered in the slightest because of your exile and that, thanks to the trust built up with them over time, your customers hope you will soon be able to return for the good of Florence.

I know that I must be strong, and I do try, as far as I am able, to be an example for everyone, even though – if truth be told – I fear I am not very good at it. Ginevra is much stronger than I and I think that it will be entirely thanks to her if we do not die while we wait for you.

In any case, Giovanni says that the policies of Rinaldo degli Albizzi and Palla Strozzi are perfect for hastening your return. He predicts it may occur within a few months.

I hope that he is right, though the mere thought of not seeing you for the next few months torments me. I know that for my own sake and for the sake of Ginevra we must stay here and wait, but the delay feels more and more like some awful torture.

I hope that everything proceeds for the best in Venice. I know from your last letter that you were working with Michelozzo on the design of a new library for the monastery of San Giorgio. We are all very proud of you and had no doubts about the fact that you would do wonderful things in Venice too.

Sometimes I am amazed at the generosity of your soul and at your willingness to help. I believe these are the virtues which make me fall in love with you afresh with each new day that comes. Yes, you read right, my love: despite the endless days and the cold winter, every morning my love for you continues to blossom.

Stay always as you are and, please, tell Piero not to get himself into trouble.

Giovanni sends greetings and embraces you. He grows better and better at arithmetic and excels at hunting.

I must go now, but I hope to write to you again next week.

I love you.

Infinitely and hopelessly yours,

Contessina

With the back of his hand, Cosimo wiped away a tear. He wasn't easily moved, but Contessina seemed to know exactly which words to use to touch his heart. And who would know them better than she? Her passionate style of writing brought her so close that, even though January seemed to have turned the lagoon of Venice into a single slab of ice, his heart blazed and its ardour burned throughout his body.

He looked at the fireplace: the long orange flames quivered uneasily. Shuddering, he pulled his fur-trimmed cloak tighter around his shoulders, then stood up and looked out of the wide window.

Outside he saw the Grand Canal and the black gondolas that furrowed the cold waters mottled by sheets of ice; the red lights of the boats' lanterns dotted the liquid mirror of the canal, which was now taking on the shades of evening.

The patrician buildings, their awe-inspiring facades towering over the water, left him almost speechless with awe. In the distance, he saw the red roofs of the smaller houses and the narrow streets that opened on to the canal, forming an endless maze all linked together by the humped backs of the bridges and the small squares with their wells.

Cosimo had learned to love that city almost as much as Florence. The doge, Francesco Foscari, had welcomed him with affection and generosity, confirming that the Most Serene Republic was a precious ally for his family and ready to support the Medici in their eventual return to Florence – and was, indeed, hoping for it, so as to confirm an alliance which after their exile had been feared broken. Perhaps forever.

Cosimo turned as Lorenzo came in.

He had let his hair and beard grow and he wore an indigo doublet and a cloak of the same colour edged with fur. His face was red from the cold.

'Good grief,' he said, 'it's nice to be warm again. The lagoon is freezing over. If it carries on like this it will be a serious problem.'

'A letter and a crate of wine arrived for you.'

'Really?'

'Lucky you,' said Cosimo with a smile. 'Ginevra offers you a few bottles of good Chianti as support, not just words.'

'Contessina is more inclined to poetry and news,' said Lorenzo with a smirk.

'You can say that again. There was another letter today. I'm glad to receive them, of course, but I wouldn't mind receiving a few bottles of wine or hams from my beloved homeland once in a while.'

'You're not envious, are you?'

'Not at all, because what is yours is also mine,' answered Cosimo. And so saying, he took a bottle from the crate and set about uncorking it.

'You swine,' laughed Lorenzo. 'What about the party?'

'Which party?'

'Loredana Grimani's party! Don't tell me that you've forgotten she invited us?'

'Of course I haven't, I simply don't want to go. I'd much rather enjoy this good wine...'

'Are you joking, Cosimo? All the Venetian patricians will be there. And so, apparently, will Francesco Squarcione!'

'The Paduan collector and painter?'

'In person.' Lorenzo had mentioned Squarcione deliberately, since he knew that his brother loved spending time with the acquaintances he had made in Padua.

'Very well, then. But first, let us at least *sample* the wine,' insisted Cosimo, who was about to pour the Chianti into two glasses.

'There's no time; we're already late. Come on – put your cloak on and let's get going. It'll take a while to get there. I haven't yet learned to navigate this city.'

'Very well,' said Cosimo, raising his hands in surrender, 'you win.'

'Apparently there will also be beautiful women.'

'You know I don't care about that.'

'I know, I know – you're a faithful husband. Given that it is traditional at parties not to reveal one's identity, though, I shall take the masks.'

'It's as though carnival lasts the whole year around in Venice...'

'You're right, it is,' said Lorenzo, taking two large white masks from a bag. 'Here you are.'

'What are they?'

'They're called *bautte*.'

'They look like the masks the plague doctors wear.'

'For the love of God, Cosimo, you *are* in a grim mood.'

'Never mind. It's just that those things give me a bad feeling.'

'Oh come on, let's get going.'

'Very well.'

Cosimo fastened his heavy cloak around him and followed his brother, who handed him one of the strange and disquieting masks.

'Try it on,' he insisted.

'All right, all right.'

Before leaving the house, Cosimo put on the mask to see how it looked. He didn't like the face that gazed back at him from the mirror at all. There was something distorted and unpleasant about it. He couldn't have said what, but he almost had the impression that the white *bautta* would bring him misfortune.

But, not wishing to spoil Lorenzo's evening, he kept his thoughts to himself.

34

The Incident

Laura was satisfied: the wig with its long mahogany-red curls was perfect and so was the mole she had applied next to her mouth, which highlighted the curve of her smile.

The magnificent aquamarine dress she wore contrasted perfectly with the wig, and she had ensured that its neckline was low and wide enough to leave nothing to the imagination. The tight bodice had an inner lining containing a short dagger which was perfect for what she had in mind.

To hide her face, she wore a *moretta*, one of the small black masks worn by Venetian ladies.

She let her eyes wander across the splendid halls of the building and its beguiling architecture, the tapestry-covered walls that rivalled those of the most beautiful

Florentine residences and the exquisite coffered ceilings in carved wood, decorated in gold.

The room was crowded with the cream of Venetian aristocracy, and echoed with the chattering and vivacious laughter of the ladies and the jokes of the gentlemen, who included some of the city's most illustrious personalities. Francesco Barbaro, Leonardo Bruni and Guarino Veronese had all been invited by Loredana Grimani, a noblewoman who loved to surround herself with the most learned humanists and philosophers. Her salon of intellectuals was well known and, as was already the case with the other arts, had become a remarkable meeting place for Venetian and Florentine thinkers. At that moment, the two cities enjoyed a formidable alliance, and this was another reason why Laura's trip to Venice had to seem not only carefree but also above suspicion.

She must in any case be wary of danger, since that magnificent patina of splendour and opulence concealed myriad political intrigues as individuals sought to increase their own power. The Republic in Florence was being fought over by the Medici and the Albizzi, but Venice was more complex, with a greater number of patrician families engaged in a fight to the death to obtain the doge's favours and take possession of the most prestigious political and judicial positions. Laura would have to be wary of the many spies who certainly crowded those rooms and who were ready to intervene and report to the Ten, the supreme magistrates of the Serenissima – the Most Serene Republic – who were legendary for their cruelty and ruthlessness.

Somewhere, Reinhardt Schwartz was watching over her and would ensure her escape. Or so, at least, she hoped.

'I've forgotten something,' said Cosimo.

They had already gone a couple of streets. Banks of fog floated in the air, adding to the sense of mystery and foreboding in the night, and Lorenzo only half heard what his brother was saying.

'If you go back, have you any idea how to get to the Palazzo Grimani?'

'I'll have Toni bring me in the gondola.'

Lorenzo shook his head.

'What the hell have you forgotten, exactly?'

'A gift for Francesco Squarcione.'

'It's my own stupid fault for mentioning his name,' said Lorenzo. 'Very well then, do what you want. I'll be waiting for you at the party.'

'I'll be there soon, I promise.'

'You'd better be.'

And so saying, Lorenzo continued on to Loredana Grimani's palazzo. He hated arriving late, and the party had already begun.

He couldn't understand why, but it seemed almost as if Cosimo were doing everything possible to ruin the evening. But Lorenzo wanted to enjoy himself, and he was not going to let himself be put off by his brother's gloomy mood. To hell with him. They had worked hard since they had arrived there, and the Venice branch of the Medici bank had taken up all his time. Along with Francesco Sassetti, its steward, Lorenzo had reviewed the plan of investments, had carefully updated and partly changed the cipher and had recovered credit for over four thousand ducats of silver.

That evening he just wanted to spend his time surrounded by wit, good wine and – why not – perhaps a little risqué conversation with some charming lady. Innocent entertainments, nothing too serious or demanding. He had absolutely no intention of getting himself into trouble.

Rebecca had noticed the glasses full of red wine. The two brothers had been so busy teasing one another that they had forgotten to drink it.

She had worked all day and was tired and thirsty. It would be nice to drink something strong. She had been staring at that ruby-coloured liquid in the marvellous crystal glasses for quite a while.

She knew she shouldn't, but if she took a sip from one of the glasses, no one would ever find out – and even if they did, it was a risk she was willing to take.

She approached the table, picked up one of the glasses, raised it to her lips and took one long swallow, then another, and another. It really was exquisite, she thought, licking her lips. She was alone in the house, though, so who would notice? She savoured its heady flavour, but after a few seconds began to detect a strange note in that harmony of aromas which she hadn't noticed immediately – something sharp and crooked and out of place.

A few moments later, the air around her seemed to tremble and she felt dizzy. She gasped and grabbed the table, clutching at the tablecloth of Flanders linen and dragging it along with her as she fell to the floor.

The goblets and the bottle fell to the floor with her and shattered, the sound of breaking glass making sinister echoes and the wine flooding the tiles of Venetian terrazzo. Rebecca stretched out her arms but could not get up – she had completely lost control of her hands, and her fingers found themselves among the sharp shards of glass. Her blood began to flow, mingling with the wine.

She felt her vision dulling just as someone shouted her name and she raised her hands as though to protect herself, because she knew she had been discovered. Something seemed to be biting at her bowels. She felt a stabbing pain and in her mouth there was the bitter taste of blood. It felt as though something dense, something solid, was suffocating her. She coughed and spat and tried once more to get to her feet, but realized that she would never manage it.

Someone took her by the shoulders and embraced her tightly.

Rebecca turned to see who it was but could not distinguish the man's features. Her vision was blurred and even the smallest movement caused her unspeakable pain.

She should never have touched that wine, she thought. It was a just punishment for having failed in her duties.

Tears began to stream down her face. She cried, because for the first time in her life she had been dishonest, and dying with a feeling of inadequacy and guilt made the moment even more bitter.

But now it was too late.

35

Death in Venice

'Rebecca!' Cosimo was shouting.

All around her were fragments of shattered glass and as he watched, Rebecca's eyes glazed over and she clasped her hands to her stomach as though something were devouring her. Bloody from the large splinters which had pierced her flesh, her fingers clawed at the fabric of her dress like those of a blind man.

The wine! The wine from Ginevra! The wine they had never drunk!

The bottle had smashed into a thousand pieces, as had the blown-glass goblets from Murano, and the mess of shattered glass and ruby-coloured Chianti covering the floor pointed Cosimo to the only possible explanation.

'Poison!'

He could barely believe it.

'*Rebecca!*' he shouted again.

He repeated her name one, two, three times, but the woman was no longer capable of answering. Her lips were covered with blood-specked foam and her dull eyes said more than any words.

Cosimo picked her up and placed her gently on the sofa. And in that moment, he understood. He raced out of the door, slamming it behind him.

Lorenzo! They wanted to kill him and Lorenzo!

Albizzi hadn't forgiven him and his brother for being spared and his assassins had followed them here, all the way to Venice. Since he hadn't managed to have them sentenced to death he had decided to snatch their lives away in another manner.

Those two accursed individuals – he couldn't remember their names. That man and that woman. He had seen them at Niccolò da Uzzano's funeral. They must have been spying on them. They knew everything about them. He and Lorenzo had believed they were safe, that no one would venture to Venice for the sole purpose of killing them. But they had been wrong again. They had behaved like fools. How could they have been so naive?

If something happened to Lorenzo, Cosimo would never forgive himself.

He raced down the imposing marble steps, taking the last few in a single bound, and found himself at the door. Once out of the palazzo, he ran towards the pier, weaving like a drunk because of the fog.

'Toni?' he shouted. 'Toni!'

'Here I am, Messer Cosimo.'

Cosimo saw Toni at the pier. He ran over to him and jumped into the gondola.

'To the Palazzo Grimani! And quickly! We have to get there quickly!' he cried, like a sleepwalker trapped in some awful nightmare.

Though uncertain what his master had said, Toni started to row without asking questions.

'My God... Rebecca. Toni. Rebecca is dead! Someone poisoned her... the wine...'

Now *this* was a party!

Lorenzo was in seventh heaven. Those rows of slender and elegant blown-glass goblets on the Flanders linen tablecloths and the mirrors with the gold frames that multiplied the space were absolutely breathtaking. He gazed in amazement at the tapestries, as vast as they were wonderful, which covered the walls with exotic designs woven in the most incredible range of colours, stared awestruck at the shimmering, bizarrely shaped jewellery created by the Venetian master goldsmiths, and watched the glimmers of the candlelight from the vast chandeliers which hung from the ceiling. And with their daring hairstyles, astonishing wigs and clothes made of extraordinary fabrics encrusted with pearls and precious stones, the ladies were the very essence of elegance.

The atmosphere was enchanting, and Lorenzo soon found himself chatting with a pair of Venetian noblemen who were friends of his brother. He found the idea of hiding one's identity behind a mask amusing. The practice of disguise had been developed into a fine art here in Venice, and there were entire shops dedicated to the creation of costumes and disguises. Though not overly strong, the perfectly chilled Ribolla Gialla wine which he had savoured had made him feel pleasantly tipsy.

'You have made it, my good friend,' said one of the two noblemen. 'For months now the talk here in Venice has been of nothing but you and your brother. I am Niccolò Dandolo, a diplomat of the Most Serene Republic,' and he raised his *bautta*, revealing elegant features animated by two particularly lively and witty eyes.

'Really?' asked Lorenzo. He pretended incredulity though in truth he knew perfectly well that the presence of the Medici could not have gone unnoticed. What he could not understand was how the man could have recognized him from behind his mask.

'Oh yes,' added the other. 'And if you will permit me, I am Ludovico Mocenigo, lieutenant in the army of the Republic of Venice.' He removed his *bautta* as he spoke.

'If you are wondering how we recognized you, you should know that here in Venice even the streets have eyes. We knew that you were on your way here and how you were dressed as soon as you left your home. For your safety, of course – Venice is full of the worst kind of spies and assassins. I am honoured to meet you, Messer Lorenzo. I have heard so much about you and your being exiled. I think what you have endured is shameful.'

'It certainly is,' said Lorenzo, raising his mask in turn but unable to stop his face darkening.

Mocenigo must have noticed, because he immediately added, 'But I am sure it will not be for long.'

'I thank you for your concern, but please, don't feel compelled to sweeten the pill. I am managing to tolerate the situation quite well.'

'I have no doubt of it,' said Mocenigo, 'but I also believe that there is truth in what I say. Our informants tell us that Rinaldo degli Albizzi's regime is collapsing in upon itself. I wouldn't be surprised if in a few months you'll be able to return to your magnificent city, to be welcomed in triumph.'

'That would be wonderful,' said Lorenzo, smiling at the thought.

'Do you miss Florence?' Dandolo asked him.

'Immensely.'

'I can imagine. It is a marvellous city.'

'Do you know it?'

'I have been there on business.'

'And, moreover, the alliance between our republics is growing stronger,' added Mocenigo. 'By now, we even share the captains of our armies.'

'I beg your pardon?'

'Sorry, I'm not being clear – the captain of the Florentine army, Erasmo da Narni, has just resigned from his post and enthusiastically accepted the command of the Venetian army. I'm enjoying my last day of peace and quiet before resuming service.'

'Erasmo da Narni... Are you referring to Gattamelata?' asked Dandolo.

'The very same,' confirmed Mocenigo. 'What a curious nickname "Gattamelata" is. They say it comes from the way he speaks: persuasive yet ruthless – some say it reminds them of a speckled cat.'

'That's an odd theory,' said Dandolo. 'I'd heard that it derived from the crest on his helmet – honey-coloured, with a cat.'

'Be that as it may,' said Mocenigo, his green eyes flashing. 'What matters is that he is known for his skill in battle.'

'I find Venice wonderful,' cut in Lorenzo, in an attempt to change the subject. 'A city built entirely upon water – simply incredible. And trade has made it such a melting pot of cultures that it has become a cradle of the arts and of all manner of wonders.'

'Well, I think our cities have a lot in common. And it is thanks to you Medici that the bond between them grows stronger,' said Dandolo. 'I know that Donatello stopped in Padua recently.'

'Another extraordinary city. I am sorry that my brother, who is more sensitive than I to the beauties of sculpture and painting, is not here at this moment. He left something at home and—'

'But he is coming, isn't he?'

'Of course.'

While the conversation proceeded in its polite and diverting way, Lorenzo noticed a woman approaching him. Her coquettish manner contained a hint of mystery.

'Do you wish to spend the whole evening chattering with these delightful gentlemen or are you seeking something more stimulating than conversation?' she asked him in a deep voice which promised delights to come. Lorenzo was shocked by her directness, but at the same time found it inviting.

'Ah,' exclaimed Mocenigo, 'do not let *us* not be the ones to deprive you of such pleasures.' So saying, he nodded to Dandolo, who vanished. 'Good luck, my friend,' he added. 'I do believe that you have caught the eye of the most beautiful woman at the party.'

36

The Red-Headed Lady

'You seem to be the busiest man here,' continued the lady in the magnificent aquamarine dress.

Lorenzo felt almost blinded by her dazzling beauty, which, along with the wine, had completely entranced him. There was a strange light in those magnificent eyes of hers, and for a moment Lorenzo seemed to recognize her, but then shook his head – he couldn't remember whom he was thinking of, he must simply have confused her with someone else. After all, he thought, he certainly wouldn't have forgotten a woman like that.

'Not at all, my lady,' he answered hastily. 'I am at your complete disposal.'

'Are you mocking me?' she asked, her beautiful lips curling into an irresistible pout as she fluttered her long eyelashes playfully.

'How could I?' he asked. 'Only a madman would dare. Your beauty blinds me.'

The woman could not hold back a disarming smile. 'You are too generous.'

'Not at all. Perhaps all Venetian ladies are as beautiful as you, though I can scarce believe it.'

'That I do not know, but Venice is steeped in magic and its women are famous for their talents at bewitching men. I am trying to learn the art, as far as I am able.'

'And may I know the name of the woman who displays so much beauty?'

Laura raised her index finger to her lips. 'Only if you know how to keep a secret,' she whispered.

'I swear it.'

'Are you sure?'

'As sure as I am that my heart beats in my chest. Tell me, I beg you.'

'Not here,' she replied. 'Let us go somewhere less crowded.'

And without another word, she set off towards another room with a great rustling of clothes. Her bearing was so regal and seductive that Lorenzo could do nothing but follow her.

The woman seemed to know the palazzo well. She walked through it confidently and after passing through more salons – these too decorated in the most sumptuous way imaginable – where delicious foods and exquisite wines were being served, the woman reached the foot of a large staircase. She proceeded without pausing and when she reached the first floor, turned right, walked down a long corridor and opened a door.

Lorenzo followed her inside, closing the door behind him, and found himself in a library. Lining the walls were wooden bookcases, their shelves crammed with treasures: rare and precious manuscripts of Greek and Latin classics, the result of a boundless love for humanistic studies. The Grimani family must possess an extraordinary passion for literature and philosophy.

'Incredible, is it not?' asked the beautiful lady, as though she had read his mind. She was perching against a wooden desk, finely carved and decorated with friezes and inlays, and leaned forward slightly, giving Lorenzo a view of her chest, which rose and fell with her breath.

'Have you lost your tongue, sir?' she said.

'N-no. No, truly,' he said hesitantly. In reality, though, despite the confidence he affected, he now felt trapped, as though the fumes of the wine had suddenly evaporated and he had found himself in that room with her without understanding quite what was happening. He realized that the game risked going too far.

But the woman seemed to have no intention of stopping.

'May I ask you a favour?'

'Of course.'

'Would you approach me a moment? Or are you afraid of me?'

Without saying anything, and almost against his will, Lorenzo found himself joining her.

'Oh...' she said, as a gold bracelet slipped from her wrist.

Turning his back to her, Lorenzo bent down to retrieve it from the soft oriental carpet on to which it had fallen, and in that moment, the woman took off her mask and pulled the dagger from her bodice. She raised it above Lorenzo's back, but just as she was about to deliver the fatal blow, the library door burst open.

When Cosimo had arrived at the party, he had greeted friends and dignitaries curtly – there was no time to waste: he had to find his brother.

Cavaliere Grimani had no idea where Lorenzo might be, and nor did Jacopo Tron, *avogador de comùn*, who was also a guest at the party, but when Cosimo encountered Ludovico Mocenigo, the lieutenant was able to show him to the stairs and offered to accompany him. He had seen Lorenzo following a lady of particular beauty with flowing red hair to the first floor.

'I would be grateful if you would be so kind as to come with me,' said Cosimo. 'I'm afraid that his life may be in danger.'

Ludovico nodded. He called over a pair of Sestiere guards who were mingling with the guests in order to oversee security and together they raced up the staircase. After what had happened to Rebecca, Cosimo wouldn't have bet a bent florin on finding his brother alive – and having witnessed the servant girl's agony as she died, the thought tormented him.

When they arrived at the first floor, they found a large empty hall in front of them from which two corridors branched. They split up, the two guards going left and Cosimo and Ludovico going right, and soon found the door which led to the library.

Cosimo immediately recognized the man on guard outside: it was that accursed Swiss mercenary. The one he had seen outside the church of Santa Lucia de' Magnoli at the funeral of Niccolò da Uzzano!

'You,' he said. 'Where is my brother?'

In response, Reinhardt Schwartz drew his sword and dagger and prepared to fight.

'I will deal with him,' said Ludovico Mocenigo. 'You go in and help Lorenzo.'

And so saying, he drew sword and dagger in turn.

'*En garde*, sir,' he cried, adding, 'Men, to me!' to the two Sestiere guards who were now returning from the other corridor.

While Mocenigo and Schwartz engaged one another, the blades of their swords clanging, Cosimo turned the handle – but the door would not open.

He threw himself at it shoulder first, smashing it open, and the scene that appeared before his eyes would remain etched in his memory forever.

He saw his brother intent on picking up something from the floor, and above him a woman of incredible beauty holding a dagger which she was about to bring down on Lorenzo's back.

Cosimo didn't have time to think. He simply cried out with all the breath he had in his lungs and launched himself at his brother, unsheathing the dagger that he always carried with him.

'Lorenzo!'

At the sound of his cry, the woman looked up in shock.

She only hesitated a moment but it was long enough. Immediately afterwards, she brought the knife down on Lorenzo, who, by pure instinct, rolled awkwardly out of the way. He was not quite fast enough to prevent the red-haired fury from injuring him, but the blade of the stiletto struck him only a glancing blow on the shoulder.

His doublet tore open like butter and a crimson arc appeared on his flesh. Lorenzo cried out and Cosimo faced the woman, stretching out his dagger towards her.

There was something familiar about her, though he could not immediately say what it was. The eyes, those green eyes lit by that feverish light – where had he seen them before? The hair... the hair was different... But now that he looked carefully, he could see it was a wig... And at that moment he understood... It was that damn perfume girl! What was she called? He couldn't remember her name, but he knew that she had been tormenting them for far too long!

Laura Ricci. *That* was it... Why she hated them so much, Cosimo had no idea, but he was sure now that she was in the pay of Albizzi.

Her eyes were filled with rage.

'*You*, you bastard!' she hissed scornfully. 'I'll kill you like a dog!'

And without another word she brought her blade down.

Cosimo was faster, though. He dodged to the side and brought up his left hand, blocking the wrist that held the dagger. He squeezed it as hard as he could, forcing the blade of the dagger up to her face.

The beautiful fingers opened and the knife fell to the floor with a clink.

Meanwhile, Lorenzo had climbed to his feet and was holding his shoulder as blood dripped between his fingers. He picked up the stiletto.

'Enough!' cried Cosimo. 'Stop! Or so help me God I will ruin that beautiful face of yours forever.'

'Do it,' she said, and her voice was hoarse and dripping with hatred. 'Isn't that what you Medici *always* do? Ruin *everything*? You disgust me, *messer*!'

Cosimo stared at her in uncomprehending disbelief but also with a hint of admiration: the woman was dazzling. But he mustn't allow himself to be influenced by her beauty – she had just tried to kill his brother.

'You wretch,' said Lorenzo, 'you've been on our backs since our father died.'

As he spoke, there was a sound of shattering glass from outside the door.

'What the hell is going on?' asked Lorenzo.

'I have no idea,' replied Cosimo.

A moment later, Ludovico Mocenigo entered the library, a bloody scratch on his cheek.

Laura could not hold back a smirk of triumph and her green eyes flashed with bloodthirsty satisfaction.

'I see Schwartz left you a gift, my lord.'

Ludovico didn't understand. 'And who are you, my lady?'

'Despite the wig, I can tell you that the person who stands before you is Laura Ricci, a spy in the service of Rinaldo degli Albizzi,' said Cosimo, his voice soft with exhaustion.

A surprised 'Ah' was all Ludovico could manage.

'And almost certainly responsible for the death of Rebecca, our maid. It was you who sent us the poisoned wine, was it not?'

'Poisoned wine?' asked a shocked Lorenzo.

'That's right. And if I hadn't returned home we would never have noticed it in time. It's a miracle we are alive at all. Have you anything to say, my lady?' he asked, turning to Laura.

'You have no proof,' she replied, spitting out the words.

'That will be decided by the Ten!' announced Ludovico Mocenigo. 'My lady, you are under arrest. I myself will ensure that you are brought to justice and thrown into the dungeons of the Doge's Palace.'

'What happened to the man?' asked Cosimo.

'That devil...' said Mocenigo. 'He killed one of the guards and wounded the other. Not to mention that he gave me this scratch. Then he jumped out of the window. He won't be bothering us again.'

'That's what you think,' replied Laura with a cruel smile.

'Before he fell sixty feet into the canal, I made sure to put my sword into his chest. So if he hasn't already bled to death, he will have been killed by the cold of the waters.'

Momentarily, a shadow seemed to cloud Laura's gaze, but immediately afterwards that strange and disturbing light returned to her eyes.

'You will pay for this dearly,' she said. 'In this life or in the next.'

'I doubt it,' said Mocenigo. 'People tend not to come back from the prisons of the Palazzo Ducale.'

September 1434

37

Piazza di San Pulinari

Rinaldo was waiting for him.

The situation had come to a head. Paradoxically, the exile which had been intended to marginalize Cosimo had ended up working in his favour, thought Palla Strozzi as he trotted towards Piazza di San Pulinari at the head of his men. He had chosen a small escort, since he had no intention of staying to fight. All he wanted was to extricate himself from the situation with the least possible trouble.

The peasants were against them.

The commoners were against them.

Even Pope Eugene IV, who these days was at Santa Maria Novella and not in Rome, had done everything possible to avert the looming disaster.

And in the meantime, Cosimo de' Medici was happily enjoying a comfortable life in Venice, where rumour said that he resided in the apartments of Doge Francesco Foscari, studying art and philosophy while his brother Lorenzo expanded the financial network of the Venetian branch of their bank.

In short, everything seemed to indicate that the government he, Rinaldo and their allies had formed had ended in complete failure. They had not been able to take power definitively. They had managed for a brief period, but their victory had proved so fleeting that it would have been better if they hadn't – now they were falling from immeasurable heights to the depths of ruinous failure, and Palla had too much experience of politics not to know that this would be the beginning of the end of everything.

So now he and Rinaldo were there, in the cold, preparing to go to war and get themselves killed. They had gone about it all wrong, thought Palla. Rinaldo's obsessive acrimony had blinded them, preventing them from solving the most obvious of all equations: that without the Medici's money, Florence would sink. And that was what had happened: the war with Lucca, the latest bout of the pestilence and Albizzi's harsh policies were like the plagues of Egypt. So now here he was, trying to extricate himself from the situation. There was no point in Francesco Filelfo, the university's Chair of Eloquence, thundering that Cosimo should have been condemned to death, because the more extreme the position one took, the stronger Cosimo appeared in the eyes of the world. Venice disapproved, the France of Charles VII disapproved, Henry VI of England disapproved. Even the *Pope* disapproved.

They had succeeded in setting the entire civilized world against them. How foolish they'd been.

When he reached the square, he saw Rinaldo waiting for him, his grim troops making that autumn morning seem even darker. Albizzi wore a dark-grey doublet and a long purple cloak edged with fur. He had on boots that went up to his knees and a sword and a dagger hung from his belt. A touch of velvet completed his martial outfit, which looked fit for a parade. Because a parade, and nothing more, was what this was – they were just dressing up as soldiers, and when one pretends to be something one is not, there can be only one possible outcome: defeat.

Rinaldo was deluding himself. He still thought he could get the situation under control, but it was too late.

When Palla saw him, Rinaldo nodded and came over to meet him. The horses stamped their hooves on the ground of San Pulinari Square. The cold wind whistled and the men-at-arms looked like devils waiting to hurl themselves at the enemy.

'So you've arrived, finally,' began Rinaldo. 'Wanted to make us wait for you, eh? Rodolfo Peruzzi and Niccolò

Barbadoro are already here,' he continued, pointing to his friends. 'Giovanni Guicciardini didn't turn up, and I see that you too are in no mood for fighting today! So your promises count for so little?' His words dripped with sarcasm and disdain for the few infantrymen ranged behind Palla. 'What a disappointment, my friend! You have all of my contempt!'

'I understand why you're angry—' said Palla, but he had no chance to finish.

'Shut up! You've already said too much. I warned you that the Medici should be killed, but you and that other bastard Bernardo Guadagni – who filled his pockets with my *and* Cosimo's money – *you* wanted to have them sent into exile. And I made the mistake of listening to you when I should have cut their throats! You have betrayed me three times: first, when you asked for exile for Cosimo, again when you didn't listen to me when I insisted we kill him, and a third time by refusing to come and fight with me!'

Palla Strozzi shook his head. 'You don't understand, Rinaldo—'

'There is nothing *to* understand,' said Albizzi, cutting him off. 'You're all talk, and I've been a fool to listen to you. Scuttle off now, and hide yourself away at home – we don't need you here. And you'd better hope that I don't win, because if I do, I'll be coming to cut your head off and stick it on a pike.'

Realizing that there was nothing to add, Palla Strozzi turned his horse around and, along with his infantrymen, went back whence he had come.

He cut a miserable figure. It was clear to all that, regardless of the outcome of the battle, Palla Strozzi had already lost. And Rinaldo would not forget it. He was so sick of the man, and his broken promises, and his eternal indecision, that, from a certain point of view, it was almost a relief. Better to be free of those who say they are on your side and then behave as though they are not. You might as well just get the troops into formation and go and see what fortune holds in store for you.

Rinaldo degli Albizzi shouted to his men, and they raised their pikes and halberds. They were a fine body of soldiers who wouldn't hesitate to give their all to the attack on the Palazzo della Signoria.

'Let your weapons speak!' shouted Rinaldo. 'They have been silent for too long!'

Upon hearing those words, the men began to advance towards the Palazzo della Signoria like a sea of steel and leather. Animated by murderous bloodlust, they rushed chaotically towards the entrance to the building.

But their advance slowed as terror dawned on their faces.

From the Tower of Arnolfo di Cambio and from the battlements of the palace, a black cloud of arrows soared through the sky towards them. Rinaldo's soldiers watched the shafts rising into the grey sky and heard their fevered hissing, realizing too late that they were completely without cover in the middle of the square. They were the easiest of targets. The men raised their shields overhead in a desperate attempt to protect themselves – many not even having time to do that – and the arrows rained down on them like darts, piercing the shields and biting into their flesh.

Rinaldo watched as his men were mown down. Some raised their hands to their pierced throats while others found themselves looking in shock at the fletchings of arrows sticking out of their faces. Still others clutched at their chests and fell face down on the stones of the square, which soon ran red with blood.

How in hell was it possible? Had he wasted so much time waiting that the enemy had barricaded itself in the Palazzo della Signoria and organized its defence during the night? He had no idea – but the fact was that the archers were firing volley after volley at his men.

He saw them fall, and, hearing the whistle of an arrow nearby, managed to duck out of the way just in time. He shouted out, but by now the scene in the square was carnage. He'd been convinced that he would be able to take the palazzo with ease, and it had never occurred to him that those who wanted Cosimo's return could have organized themselves so quickly and so effectively.

He gritted his teeth.

'Men, to me!' he yelled. But his soldiers were now backing away in an attempt to get themselves out of firing range of that hail of arrows that was pinning them, one by one, to the flagstones of the square.

Rinaldo felt a cold wave of surprise flow through him. He hadn't expected anything like this.

He saw Cambio Capponi running towards him and then suddenly throwing open his arms and slumping to the ground, pierced by a shaft.

The volleys rained down again and again until the men had finally managed to get out of range of the archers. The square was filled with corpses yet it had all happened as quickly as a flash of lightning: groaning men lay on the ground, which was covered with missiles, dead horses and the wounded, screaming in agony. Rinaldo kept well back: he had no intention of being killed before he had even fought. He had made a fatal mistake, he realized – the long-awaited battle was already almost over, and at great cost to his forces. They had thought it would be child's play, but they had found themselves marching straight into the mouth of hell. He had sent them to slaughter.

The men of the Republic glared down at them defiantly from the battlements. At that point, what the hell could he do?

Niccolò Barbadoro got off his horse. His hands were covered with the blood of his fellow soldiers who had died in his arms, begging him for help. He spat on the ground while his black horse, foaming at the mouth, pawed the ground.

'And how do we get out of this?' he said.

'We attack!' shouted Rinaldo. The words came out in an impulsive reaction to his frustration and impotence, but even as he spoke, he knew that what he was suggesting was utter madness: another *ten* charges wouldn't change the result by an inch.

'Are you insane?' cried Niccolò Barbadoro. 'Do you want us all to be slain like dogs? And to what end? In the name of your blind ambition, which has already damned us all? I'm starting to think that Palla Strozzi was right.'

Rinaldo was about to reply when he realized that, as if by magic, the arrows had suddenly ceased to fly. Astride a white horse, his hands raised, someone was coming across Piazza della Signoria towards them.

'Are they surrendering?' asked Niccolò Barbadoro incredulously. Rinaldo waved a hand to silence him. He knew the man well: it was Giovanni Vitelleschi, his good friend and one of the most esteemed patriarchs of Florence.

The old sage eventually arrived before them.

'My son,' said Giovanni in a calm voice when he was before him, 'I come to you on behalf of Pope Eugene IV who, as you know, is in Santa Maria Novella, where he has withdrawn because of the events which forced him to leave Rome.'

'I am listening,' Rinaldo murmured, uncertain what Giovanni was about to say.

'Well, you have seen how hard Florence fights, and how Palla Strozzi and Giovanni Guicciardini have abandoned you. I come to inform you that Pope Eugene IV would be happy to negotiate honourable conditions for you with the palazzo if you and Niccolò Barbadoro would be kind enough to put down your weapons. He has faith in you and knows that you have been wronged; yet he believes that there would be greater profit for all if you were to enter the palace and talk rather than fight your brothers. The choice, of course, is yours but, in faith, I do not think you will take the palace easily, and it will cost you many more men even if you try to do so. Is that what you want?'

Rinaldo looked him in the eye. He knew that Giovanni was right and that the soldiers inside the palace were ready to hold him off.

His men were peering at him with a mixture of fear and uncertainty in their eyes. He knew that if he carried on, he would lose his credibility and their trust – which, given the catastrophic outcome of his first attack, he perhaps no longer deserved anyway. And anyway, what Giovanni Vitelleschi had said was irrefutable: how could they force their way into the palace after the men had been weakened in spirit more even than they had been weakened in number? And would he be able to save them from what looked like a certain massacre?

The situation was weighted against them, to put it mildly, and before his own men had managed to cover even fifty paces, they would be slain by the archers on the battlements.

It didn't take a genius to realize that the men would mutiny – and probably lynch him – rather than let themselves be slaughtered under another hail of arrows. That was perfectly clear from their faces.

Rack his brain as he might, Rinaldo could think of no way out: he was no strategist, much less a courageous leader. He had always used other people's swords to advance his plans, and his inadequacy proved so much more shocking in that moment because it had arrived so suddenly and ruthlessly, jolting him out of his dreams of glory.

He shook his head. It cost him dear to admit that all was lost, but life sometimes offers no choices.

'Tell Pope Eugene IV that I will consider his offer,' he concluded, 'and that if I should follow his advice, I expect him to safeguard me and my men.'

And there he stayed, waiting to decide what to do while the pale sun shone high in the sky.

38

Reversal of Fortune

My beloved Cosimo,
After a year of your absence, life becomes tiresome and the wait interminable. However, the time has come for your return and my heart overflows with more joy and love than ever before.

Giovanni de' Benci has confirmed the events of recent days. Not only did Rinaldo degli Albizzi fail to take the Palazzo della Signoria, which was strenuously defended, but, following the Pope's intercession, he agreed to withdraw his men. The nobles who oppose him, however, exploited his uncertainty by calling the people to council and ordering your immediate return to Florence, condemning Rinaldo degli Albizzi, Rodolfo Peruzzi, Niccolò Barbadoro and Palla Strozzi to imprisonment, along with all their acolytes. It seems that Rinaldo attempted to refuse and remonstrated with Eugene IV, as it was he who – all unknowingly – betrayed him. But to no avail: his properties and lands have been confiscated and Rinaldo has left the city and taken refuge in Ancona.

In any case, the Republic awaits you, Cosimo.

We have returned home to Via Larga and I long only to welcome you into my arms. I have missed you so much. I am trying to decide what to wear so that I shall be beautiful for you when you arrive. It is said that you will be proclaimed *Pater Patriae*. In the end, all knots come to the teeth of the comb, as they say: who would have thought that this exile would have actually made your position stronger?

And yet that is what has happened.

And so, my dear Cosimo, I await you. Hurry back, because Florence acclaims and demands you.

As do I.

Always yours,

Contessina

Cosimo put the letter back in the pocket of his doublet, right above his heart.

It was as though his wife's words were a balm for the wounds of his soul.

After galloping ceaselessly for hours, they had stopped at a fountain to water the horses, but now it was time to get back on the road. Florence was not far away and if they continued at that speed, it wouldn't be long before they would see it.

He climbed back into the saddle, turned his mount around and spurred it into a gallop once more. Lorenzo, Giovanni and Piero and all his men followed suit.

As he went, he reflected on Venice and the friendships he had left there: Francesco Foscari, and Lieutenant Ludovico Mocenigo – and through him, Gattamelata. Venice would be a precious ally for Florence, and so would Francesco Sforza, who longed to take the Duchy of Milan for himself. Cosimo thought he should take advantage of these happy times to extend his hegemony over Florence and establish a new relationship with the Pope and with Rome. It was a way he could bring peace to his city by defeating Filippo Maria Visconti and the current Duchy of Milan, who did nothing but incite Lucca against them. Now, the time of stability, or at least of rebirth, had come. How was construction of the dome of Santa Maria del Fiore proceeding? How much money was left in the city's coffers? Had the plague finally died away? These questions filled his mind. He must never again underestimate his enemies but he had no desire to be forever accompanied by an armed guard. He would not let what had happened change his way of life or that of his family.

He gazed confidently ahead and his smile returned: around him he saw the Florentine countryside with its green meadows, and a sky so intensely blue it gleamed above them; and the air was fragrant with the perfumes of flowers and freshly cut hay.

Suddenly, Cosimo and Lorenzo saw Florence appear in front of them in all its hauteur. Surrounded by walls and bristling with towers, it was beautiful enough to take your breath away.

Cosimo felt his heart leap in his chest. As he grew older, he was finding it increasingly difficult to hold back tears in moments like this. Perhaps it was because of the distance from his beloved Contessina, perhaps because he had suffered for so long and had risked death only a year before, perhaps because he felt that the city had not yet granted him the ultimate triumph – and he could not stop himself from wondering if, when that moment came, he would be equal to the task.

Or perhaps it was because when he looked at it, he once more saw his father and mother, whom he had loved so dearly and who were now gone.

There were many reasons. No longer asking himself why, he let the tears fall.

And he realized that, as his mother had once said, there was nothing to be ashamed of in tears – that it is only possessing the strength to show his feelings, be they happy or sad, which makes a man a man.

Months had passed but Laura knew that she must be patient. Her cell was tiny but her gaoler, Marco Ferracin, was a good sort. Better yet, he was attracted to her. She knew it, just as she knew that she had to continue to talk him round. It would take a while, but she mustn't lose hope. She would wear down his resistance as water wears away rock: she had only to persevere. She had faced worse in her life and needed to concentrate on one thing alone: survival.

To do so, she would deceive, lie and manipulate. They were the arts in which she had always placed her trust, and they had never betrayed her. She had grown used to living with the worst of the world – with thieves and traitors, executioners and turncoats – and vice and crime had become such a part of her that she couldn't have rid herself of them had she wanted to. She couldn't imagine living a normal life – and perhaps wouldn't even have wanted to.

It was too late for her. Her soul had been tainted when she was nothing but a girl, so what did she expect? To be able to go back to being a respectable woman? That would never happen. And she was certain that not even Schwartz would come to save her. She didn't believe he was actually dead, but she knew that she had to look after herself.

Therefore, there was no alternative. She had to use her charms upon her gaoler.

She was absorbed in these gloomy thoughts when she heard the iron door of her cell creak open. Laura watched Marco Ferracin enter with another person and, at first, she didn't understand why her gaoler was trembling and as white as a ghost. A moment later, a blade burst through the man's chest, drenching him with blood.

Ferracin dropped to his knees and collapsed face forward.

The man behind him was wrapped in a dark hooded cloak and dressed in the uniform with blue-striped sleeves of gold of the guards of the Palazzo Ducale. He wore long boots up to his knees and a steel breastplate bearing the Lion of San Marco – the symbol of the Most Serene Republic. But when he lowered his hood, Laura recognized him immediately: those icy blue eyes, the thick blond moustaches and the reddish-blond hair left no doubt.

'You're here...' she murmured. 'You're alive... Have you come for me?' Her voice trembled, because she could scarcely believe this miracle was possible.

'I would die for you, *mein Schatz*.'

Laura burst into tears and, for the first time, Reinhardt embraced her.

'S-say it...' she murmured. 'S-say it again...'

'Later,' he replied, 'there isn't time now. Put this on, quickly. If we are discovered, it's all over.'

From under his cloak he pulled out a bundle that he unfolded on the wooden bench of the cell, revealing a pair of boots, a guard uniform and a hooded cloak.

'With a little luck,' he said, 'it might even work.'

She dressed quickly, tying back her hair and lowering the hood over her eyes.

'Damn it all,' muttered Reinhardt.

'What is it?' she asked.

'You look beautiful even like this...'

Laura smiled. She wiped away her tears and said nothing.

'Now,' continued Reinhardt, taking a large set of keys from Marco Ferracin's belt, 'follow me and make sure you stay by my side. Let me do the talking and keep your face down. And let's hope we don't meet anyone.'

'What if we do?'

'I'll take care of it, *mein Schatz*.'

So saying, Reinhardt opened the door and they left the cell. They found themselves in a long corridor on to which the other doors of the many cells in that wing of the building opened, the torch flames providing a path of flickering light. They were in the dungeons on the ground floor of the Palazzo Ducale, very close to the waters of the lagoon. They climbed a short narrow staircase at the end of the corridor and emerged into the main courtyard where guards were stationed in pairs.

Laura at his side, Schwartz moved quickly. They strode forward boldly, as though perfectly at ease, towards the two soldiers guarding the main door. As they approached, the guards began walking to meet them.

Schwartz positioned himself in front.

'What are you doing here?' one of the guards asked.

'We've been told a cargo's arrived. We need to check it.'

'Ah, really?'

'Lieutenant Ludovico Mocenigo of the Venetian army asked me to see to it personally.'

'Are you sure of that? Do you have written orders?'

'No I do not. But I have no intention of being taken to task for doing my duty so I ask you: would you kindly come with us? The boat is waiting for us at the pier, just out there.'

And as he finished speaking, Schwartz continued to walk towards the door, trying to reduce as much as possible the distance that separated them from freedom.

He knew that his fate and that of Laura depended on how brazenly he was able to lie. Of course, he could engage in a duel, but within a few moments a whole garrison would be upon them, not to mention that it wouldn't take them long to figure out who the person beside him actually was once her hood was taken off.

He therefore decided to carry on pretending, at least until they were on the deck of the boat waiting out there to rescue them.

He proceeded through the Porta del Frumento, Laura by his side and the two guards behind them. They walked out on to the jetty that gave access to the pier and from there Schwartz quickly boarded the boat.

Laura and the guards followed him. The more talkative of the two soldiers was about to reopen his trap, so Schwartz decided to silence him.

'Isaac,' he said, clapping his hands, 'please show us the goods that Lieutenant Ludovico Mocenigo of the Venetian army has asked us to inspect.'

A black-eyed man with an aquiline nose – a Jewish merchant – came out to meet them, holding a canvas sack in his hands.

'Let's see,' said Schwartz as he pretended to inspect the sack; then, turning to the two guards, he added, 'See how wonderful it is, my friends.'

More out of curiosity than anything else, the two bent forward to see what it contained, and Schwartz pulled out two daggers hidden under his cloak and, with a double upward slash, slit both their throats.

Silent and sudden, the blades flashed and both guards gave strangled gurgles. Schwartz grabbed them as they collapsed and lowered them to the deck of the boat, ensuring that it looked as though they were all sitting together, leaning against the gunwale. Meanwhile, Isaac had untied the mooring line and was using the oar to push the boat away from the mooring dolphin and the small pier.

On the pier, someone raised a lamp. 'Who's there?' shouted a voice.

Schwartz stood up. 'The guards of the Most Serene Republic,' he shouted back. 'We are accompanying this merchant to the arsenal. He has weapons for the Venetian army aboard.'

'Very good,' came back the voice of the other.

After that the voices were silent and the only noise to be heard was the slow lapping of the lagoon waters against the side of the boat.

As soon as they were far enough from the Doge's Palace, Reinhardt pushed the dead guards overboard.

The boat's lamp lit Laura's face, and Schwartz saw that it was glowing.

'I love you,' she said, 'but I don't know where the feeling will lead me.'

He stared into her beautiful eyes and could see she had decided to trust him. He knew that wherever they were going would be no land of milk and honey, but it was also the only possible way for them to start a new life. He cared too much for her to keep the truth from her.

'I'm sorry, but a future full of uncertainty awaits us. Can you ever forgive me for this?'

'As long as I am with you, Reinhardt, I can face anything.'

'I promise you that I'll stay by your side. But I can't promise to protect you from suffering.'

'My life has always been a mixture of pain and pleasure – I don't understand why and I can't escape it. Yet I doubt I would be able to enjoy it if it were not.'

He smiled bitterly, thinking how he too had accepted that cup, and every day drunk from it a dose of bitter poison that over time had drained his soul. Yet again, he had lent his services to a lord who was even worse than the previous one because, in his heart of hearts, he feared he had no other choice.

'I'm a coward,' he said as the swaying boat crossed the black waters of the lagoon.

'You're no coward,' she said with an assurance that sounded almost like a pardon for his past behaviour. 'Who else would have come to free me?'

'I don't know,' replied Reinhardt, 'but your freedom is already curtailed by a new slavery, my dear: we are now both the property of the Duke of Milan.'

There, he thought – he had said it, and the confession made him feel better. For the moment at least.

She did not seem particularly upset.

'Is that all?' she asked. 'Did you really think that would frighten me?'

'No, not really,' he said, 'though the man *is* a lunatic.'

'I have no doubt that he is. But people like us find the source of our lives in lunacy. Pleasure and pain are the very essence of our life – we cannot give them up, because the absence of one or the other would deprive us of the energy to feed our sick need for self-destruction.'

Reinhardt said nothing as he contemplated the truth of her words.

Without another word, he took Laura in his arms and kissed her, savouring her soft and fragrant lips and the accursed innocence that lodged within them. In spite of everything, there was a candour in her that bewitched him, and made him a slave to her beauty and to the long, dark shadow in which she had chosen to live.

Just like him.

He kissed her again, hungrily; then he gazed at the irresistible sweep of her neck, her high cheekbones and the wonderful cleavage of her bosom. He bared her shoulders and covered them with kisses, abandoning himself in the hope it would erase for a moment the guilt that devoured him.

Could they have both fled at that moment? But where? The duke's men were hidden below deck – men who were to escort them on this escape from Venice but who would hunt them down and kill them if they reneged on their word.

He smiled ruefully.

Being Rinaldo degli Albizzi's man had deprived him of his freedom to decide his own future, which was all the more peculiar given that he was a mercenary.

Soon, Laura too would discover how difficult it was to serve Filippo Maria Visconti, to whom Rinaldo had entrusted his life and with it that of his precious possessions: Reinhardt Schwartz and Laura Ricci.

Rinaldo had sold them to save his life, and in the hope of constructing an uncertain future for himself – one which also contained Laura and Reinhardt's hopes.

Reinhardt shook his head mournfully; then he put aside his dark thoughts and surrendered, once again, to Laura's caresses.

Sooner or later he would have to tell her everything, but for the moment he found he couldn't summon up the courage.

September 1436

39

Filippo Maria Visconti

Lying comfortably in the huge stone basin, his flabby white flesh rendered translucent by the veil of clear water, Filippo Maria Visconti looked at him in that hateful, infuriating way of his.

Rinaldo degli Albizzi felt as though he might vomit at any moment, but made a supreme effort to suppress his nausea. How could the Duke of Milan have been reduced to this? With that jutting forehead and that neck wrapped in rolls of rosy fat, he looked like a pig that had been washed for slaughter. What a disgrace the man was!

And while *he* had been abandoned by all, that giant ball of lard dominated the Duchy of Milan and had the power to grant him the men and weapons which could change the course of history – if he only chose to.

Filippo Maria looked at him with his porcine eyes and laughed.

Rinaldo knew that his position was a desperate one. Two years ago he had escaped to Milan in an attempt to win the support of the duke, as everybody – even those fanatical Florentines, who had vowed to see him dead at all costs – knew.

He had also known that if he was hoping for the duke's help he would have to give him something in exchange, because the man was as greedy and shrewd as he was awful to look at. Rinaldo had in mind a pair of assets which were of extraordinary importance to him: what money that he had left and two people who, given the man's depraved nature, might be worth their weight in gold to him.

The duke's perversions were as well known as his sexual appetites, which encompassed both women and men. The orgies held in his apartments were as legendary as the fits of rage which were surely the result of the hereditary illnesses that had marked his life since childhood.

For that reason, he had needed Reinhardt Schwartz and Laura Ricci.

Rinaldo had known that if he handed them over to the mercy of Visconti he would have nothing left, but if he waited – or, worse still, refused to let the duke *take* his best people – what exactly would he have achieved?

Nothing at all.

And so he had decided he might as well risk it.

When he had fallen into disgrace, his Swiss mercenary had been forced to make the same choice. Schwartz had wound up injured and covered in mud in the waters of the Venetian canals, and had only survived thanks to Rinaldo's men. He could have offered his services to another gentleman, but once you had accepted the Albizzis' coin, it was no small task to find another employer, even less so when you had been seriously injured.

When Rinaldo had been expelled from Florence and had settled in Milan, Schwartz had willingly agreed to put himself in the pay of Filippo Maria Visconti to aid his lord. The choice was certainly not the worst available, and had allowed Rinaldo to leave with a handful of gold and a few soldiers. Schwartz had immediately made an impression upon Filippo Maria, who appreciated above all else a man who knew how to handle a sword – even more so in a period like those last two years, when he had found himself fighting for the succession of the Kingdom of Naples and at the same time the Republics of Florence and Venice.

Schwartz's worth on the battlefield had soon been proved when he had gone to fight under the colours of the Visconti viper – the *biscione* – and he had found a way to finance his sortie to Veneto to free Laura. The mission had not been without costs, though, and the noble Visconti had thus adopted the role which suited him best: that of the usurer.

As pledge for funding her release, Filippo had imposed the *conditio sine qua non* that Laura become one of his favourites.

Rinaldo had made sure to describe her in detail, praising her skill as a whore, a perfumer and a poisoner, and this mixture of talents had ignited Filippo Maria Visconti's passion. Laura, though, had used her diabolical feline intelligence to carve out a different position for herself. She had remained a courtesan but to the role of court poisoner she had added that of fortune teller, and the duke never failed to consult her and her cards about any important questions concerning his future.

Rinaldo had sold his two most precious assets because they had been all he'd had to trade with, but both Laura and Schwartz had come out of the transaction remarkably well. Although they had each in their way become Visconti's property, they were much better off than Rinaldo. So there he was, like a prisoner in the duke's palace, imploring his help in the war against the Medici.

And there was the duke before him: a man immersed in his own blubber and swimming through the water with lazy strokes while he waited with distaste to hear him beg.

Rinaldo shook his head.

'Your excellency,' he said, the word feeling like blasphemy in his mouth, 'I was wondering when we might consider attacking the Medici and Florence so as to bring my city back under the aegis of Milan.'

Filippo Maria pursed his lips and spat out a jet of gurgling water. He said nothing for a long time. He was resting after the labours of the day; why should he hasten to answer that inept exile who had managed to lose himself a city? Visconti did not hold Albizzi in high esteem – as soon as the fool had arrived with his handful of rags, he had started asking for favours. Yes, he had brought a little gold with him, and was so consumed with rage and envy that, with a few horsemen and a hundred infantrymen, he might perhaps actually succeed in doing something useful – something, for example, like taking back control of Florence. If, of course, the mercenaries were led by Niccolò Piccinino and that bloodthirsty man of Albizzi's... What was his name?

He considered the question while the warm water caressed his soft white skin. How wonderful it was. He would have liked to float there all day watching the columns of blue steam rising from the surface of the water... What the hell was the man called? He had a strange name, something Swiss...

Schwartz! That was it. With those two at the head of a handful of men, even that fool Albizzi would be able to bring Florence – full of perverts and swine – back under the Milanese yoke. And that would certainly be helpful.

He took another couple of strokes before finally deciding to be charitable and answer Albizzi's question.

'My dear Albizzi,' he said distractedly, 'I will see what I can do. For the moment my main concern is the Genoese question. The Republic has not looked favourably upon my unsuccessful alliance with Alfonso of Aragon and therefore, as you well know, if I don't ravage Liguria I shall end up finding the Genoese on my doorstep. Fortunately for me, Niccolò Piccinino knows what he is about.'

'Very well, excellency, but you did promise...'

Heavens above, the man was *intolerable*! What on earth did he *want*? He didn't have a penny to his name, he was devoid of men and means, he came asking for his help and then wanted to dictate the times and the ways in which he, the Duke of Milan, was to give them to him? Had the world gone mad? He had no intention of allowing that spineless nobody to vex him. What a cheek, insisting like that, he thought, puffing in annoyance. To hell with him. But then suddenly he smiled – why let his day be ruined by that pathetic man?

'Patience, my friend, everything in good time! Perhaps you do not like my hospitality?'

If Albizzi were critical of his conduct, let him say so. He would make him regret having been born.

'Your excellency, that is in no way the reason for my question.'

I should hope not, Filippo Maria thought.

'But I am sure you can understand how eager I am to return to Florence.'

What a bore, thought the duke. That was all he seemed able to say. If that was the case, perhaps he would have done better to avoid being thrown out of his city in the first place.

He shook his head again.

'My dear Albizzi, I understand perfectly, though it was certainly not *my* idea for you to lose control of a city which you held in your fist. My God, you had even managed to rid yourselves of those accursed Medici! And now, instead, we find ourselves here.' Filippo Maria approached the edge of the large stone basin and attempted to lift himself above the rim. To his frustration, he failed.

'By God, what hellish tub is this? What are you doing standing there?' he shouted to Albizzi, a flash of rage lighting up his face. 'Call that idiot Ghislieri and give me a hand, otherwise I will be stuck here soaking until morning. What are you waiting for? By God, my skin is all wrinkled!'

Filippo Maria looked at his hands in terror. How would he manage with his fingers in that condition? They were horrible to look at. Damn it, he had stayed in the water for too long again.

Albizzi would have liked to drown him in that tub, but he concealed his embarrassment with a cough and called for Ghislieri. Tall and lanky in his dark-blue tunic, the duke's secretary appeared on the instant.

'Hurry!' thundered Rinaldo. 'Call two guards and help his excellency out of the water.'

Ghislieri wasted no time and, a moment later, two guards were grabbing Filippo Maria Visconti by his arms and hips and hoisting him with superhuman effort over the stone edge of the tub.

Ghislieri in the meantime had taken care to welcome him into the soft embrace of a bath towel. The duke slipped his dripping feet into comfortable velvet slippers and then spat, making sure he displayed all his disgust.

'You could have helped, Albizzi. Acting so superior despite being little more than an exile does not become you, my friend. And then you demand that I help you. I advise you to show a little more solicitude in the future if you truly want my support. For the moment, I will say only that the road which leads to Florence is long and your behaviour is doing nothing to shorten it. You're a fool – and a haughty one at that. True, you once brought me two excellent servants, but what they have accomplished these past two years is due more to their merit than yours. Indeed, it remains a mystery to me how you managed to choose them so well in the first place.'

'Your excellency, I called for help immediately—'

'Of course, of course,' interrupted the duke. That unpleasant grin appeared once again on his fat face. 'And thus, instead of holding out a hand to help you, I will do as you did: I will speak to your servants – who, moreover, now belong to me. I am sure they will be able to further your interests, which may, incidentally, also be mine. But they will do so as and when I tell them. Until then, my advice is to start getting your own hands dirty or I swear you will remain in Milan until the end of your days.'

And without another word, the duke shuffled off, dripping and pale, leaving Rinaldo standing alone by the large stone basin.

Albizzi stared at the furious face which glared back at him from the water and watched its eyes fill with rage. His hands clenched into fists until the knuckles went white.

It was so frustrating. How much was he supposed to humble himself to get the man's support? He, whose name alone had once been enough to terrify all Florence. He, who belonged to one of history's most noble families. He, who had put Volterra, Lucca and many other cities to the sword. He, who had driven the Medici from the Palazzo della Signoria.

And now here he was staring into the water, filthy with the sweat of that degenerate who ordered him about.

How he would have liked to slit Filippo Maria's throat. But then where would he find the soldiers he needed to return to Florence? No, damn it, he couldn't allow himself to do that, and the sooner he got that through his head, the better.

He had to put his pride aside and concentrate instead on appearing contrite and obsequious to the duke in the name of a greater project: the reconquest of his city. With Piccinino, Schwartz and a thousand men, he could do anything, and although Filippo Maria openly mocked and despised him, he too had an interest in modifying the status quo. Venice and Florence held Milan in deadlock: installing Rinaldo in the Palazzo della Signoria would guarantee the alliance necessary to expand and consolidate Milan's hegemony and escape the threat of the Most Serene Republic. Not to mention that Cosimo de' Medici was plotting with Francesco Sforza to take the Duchy from the Visconti.

He had to be cunning and appease the duke to ensure he got what he wanted. But it was so difficult. Losing power was far worse than never having had it, and he found it practically impossible to accept.

He clenched his fist again, so hard that the nails cut into the flesh of the palm, and by the light of the flickering torches he swore to himself that he would do whatever was necessary to recover what had been taken from him.

And if that meant kneeling before Filippo Maria Visconti, he would not hesitate.

Sooner or later, he would have his revenge.

40

The Dome Completed

The work was done.

Cosimo still could hardly believe it, and yet here they were in the cathedral to finally bless the completed structure.

The roof lantern was still missing, of course, but Santa Maria del Fiore was now almost done. Filippo Brunelleschi had made the impossible possible.

When he looked upward, Cosimo was overcome with something that felt like dizziness and his mind swarmed with questions that distracted him from the words of Eugene IV, who was conducting the consecration ceremony.

It was said that Filippo had used a rope which was stretched from the centre of the dome to its circumference in order to guide the laying of the bricks, and that this cord could be rotated three hundred and sixty degrees around the dome which was being constructed by the skilled hands of the master builders. Progressively raised and shortened as new layers of bricks were laid, the rope had become the principal tool for determining their inclination and radial position, meaning that it must have been at least ninety yards long.

This extraordinary construction had been created from the materials of mystery and miracle themselves, thought Cosimo. How could Filippo have made such a long rope without it sagging in the middle and distorting the measurements? Was it covered with wax? Had Filippo used one of his incredible contraptions? And above all, how had Brunelleschi managed to attach it to the centre of the structure? They would have needed a wooden pole at least a hundred and twenty yards high to reach the summit. Not to mention that the bricks used were of the most unusual and disparate shapes: rectangular, triangular, dovetailed, edged, shaped to fit in the corners of the octagon. It was even rumoured that at one point Filippo had run out of parchment upon which to draw the plans and had been forced to note them down on torn pieces of old manuscripts.

None of Cosimo's queries were destined to receive an answer though. And much less from the architect himself. Cosimo glanced over at him and saw that even in that moment he was there in body but wore upon his face the absent expression that betrayed how deeply his mind was absorbed in other projects. After God, he was the day's chief protagonist, and yet he behaved like a mere spectator who had been passing by. He hadn't even bothered to dress suitably: he wore a threadbare jacket of rough leather, his hose were mottled with wine and his manic eyes made him look like some crazed bird. His smooth bald head gleamed, and when he smiled he displayed awful black teeth.

Cosimo would never understand why Filippo was the way he was. It almost seemed that the care he took of his person was inversely proportional to the energy he dedicated to the planning and realization of his works, leaving nothing for his appearance. It was as though his art absorbed all his energies, including those needed to choose a garment or wash his face.

Cosimo looked up at the dome again.

He remembered what the workmen and carpenters had told him: apparently, the builders had discovered pigeons and blackbirds by their hundreds nesting in the interstices and narrow spaces. They had been thrown into the pot and cooked for dinner on the scaffolding arranged between the inner and outer dome until an order had been given forbidding their capture for fear that hungry workers might end up falling to their deaths.

As he let his gaze drift upward, Cosimo breathed in deeply, savouring the aromas of the various materials from which the incredible building had been constructed. The astonishing architecture of the place had the same effect on him every time.

As though guessing that his mind was wandering, however delightedly, Contessina took his hand.

The sun blazed in magnificently through the eight windows set around the tholobate, over which thin sheets of linen had been stretched to prevent the cool wind from damaging the interior of the cathedral.

The Pope, who for some years now had used Florence as his residence, smiled from the high altar at the centre of the great drum. Giannozzo Manetti had just finished celebrating the grandeur of the dome through the recital of the prayer 'Oratio de secularibus et pontificalibus pompis,' written specifically for the occasion.

The cardinals lit the candles set before the twelve wooden apostles composing the choir, which were also the work of Filippo Brunelleschi. As soon as the twelve tongues of fire began to dance in the air, fragrant with the perfumes and aromas of flowers and incense, the Pope nodded to the choir to sing the motet composed by Guillaume Dufay to celebrate the consecration: 'Nuper rosarum flores' – 'Here Are Rose Blossoms'. Their voices clear and magnificent, the choir sang the melodies of that daring composition while Eugene IV arranged upon the altar the relics, which included the finger of St John the Baptist and the remains of St Zenobius, the patron saint of Santa Maria del Fiore.

The motet continued, the voices seeming almost to chase one another through those beautifully designed spaces beneath Arnolfo di Cambio's vaults.

Harmony was finally descending upon his beloved city, thought Cosimo. Beneath the vaults and dome of the cathedral, Florence found itself united for the first time in over 140 years. Cosimo saw a unifying of intentions that he had experienced before.

For a moment his gaze halted on the whiteness of the lilies, garlands of which decorated the aisles and the altar. They seemed to have bloomed early, as though even nature was participating in the triumph and joy of that day

Lord of the city and friend and favourite of the Pope, with whom he had managed to form a solid and sincere friendship over the last two years, Cosimo could finally say that he was confident about the future.

In her ivory-coloured gown, Contessina looked wonderful, as did Ginevra and the boys. Lorenzo watched over the family with him.

The melody carried on. Something about it captured his soul and his reason, and he closed his eyes, transported by the notes.

How he would have liked to know how to compose music of such beauty – he would have given up the entire wealth of the bank to write a motet of such elegance. He felt his heart soar above the aisles, up to the tholobate and then even higher, towards the top of the dome. His thoughts floated through space and all fears and worries seemed to melt away as though by magic.

He looked at Giovanni and smiled. He had great plans for the boy. He loved Piero dearly too, but the younger of the two brothers studied and worked hard, and instead of wasting his time imagining foolish feats of derring-do, he put his lessons to good use and was already revealing himself to be a careful treasurer. Cosimo sensed that Piero's desire for action was a reaction to the delicate health and frail physique which continued to torment him – he was certain that the boy's emaciated, sickly frame troubled him, and felt a secret pity for the lad. Yet, despite his melancholic character, Piero had travelled widely and proved himself to be an excellent student of languages. However, Cosimo had to be realistic, and he would be lying to himself if he denied investing most of his hopes in Giovanni. He planned to put him in charge of the Ferrara branch soon. Then, with time, he would have a political career. Giovanni was handsome, strong, tall and slender. He was a confident young man, and witty to boot, his only weakness consisting, perhaps, of a certain taste for excess. But people liked him very much, and the girls all made eyes at him. That day he wore a light-blue doublet, his hair was short and well combed, his eyes large and sincere, his demeanour bold and shrewd: in him, all was brilliance and vivacity, and many were the looks his person attracted.

Cosimo finally felt safe, protected, loved, and with excellent prospects ahead of him: what more could he desire?

And it was exactly at that moment that he opened his eyes and realized that he couldn't have been further from the truth. He had let himself be carried away by the music, but when his gaze returned to the crowd and he looked for a moment behind him, he seemed to glimpse something both luminous and unwholesome.

At first, he couldn't say what it was, but then he saw at the rear of the nave something splendid but sinister – something that glowed with malign light.

When he managed to bring it into focus, he felt all his certainties collapsing within him – falling one after the other like the playing cards of a castle built by some king's fool.

Because right next to the great portal of the cathedral, he saw, with absolute certainty, the wonderful and terrible face of Laura Ricci.

For a moment he was unable to move, an irresistible force seeming to bind him to the earth. How could it be her? He recalled that long ago Ludovico Mocenigo had written him a letter telling him that the accursed woman had escaped from the prisons of the Palazzo Ducale, but he had never expected to see her suddenly appear there, during the consecration of the cathedral. It must be some kind of hallucination – there was no other possible explanation.

Feeling feverish, he turned to his brother.

'I'll be back in a moment,' he said and, trying not to draw too much attention to himself, walked silently down the aisle towards the great portal where he had seen – or *thought* he had seen – Rinaldo degli Albizzi's accursed woman.

But he found no trace of her.

He certainly couldn't have imagined that she would wait for him. And besides, *had* he really seen her or had it been some unsettling fabrication of his mind? Perhaps a projection of his most deeply hidden and unconfessed fears?

He halted, and peered around the interior of the cathedral. He saw the poor people crowded in front of him in the empty pews at the back: the front rows were reserved for the nobles, those in the centre for the rich, then came the lower classes and, after them, the commoners. Barefoot children and men dressed in rags, mothers with hollowed faces who clutched their children to them like puppies. There was, in that vision of poverty and destitution, such dignity that even the most cynical and indifferent of men must see it. Cosimo knew some of them – he tried to help them whenever he could.

He looked out through the open doors of the cathedral, which were crowded with other poor families, hoping to bring into their lives some spark of the blessing the Pope was dispensing in the consecration of that magnificent house of God. Hard as he looked, though, Cosimo could not see her. Was it possible that he had only imagined her?

He peered into the square. It was crowded with people all the way back to the bronze panels that made the door on the eastern side of the baptistery shine with golden light.

And in that sea of ecstatic faces, their mouths wide open in amazement, Cosimo suddenly saw the green flash of those feline eyes.

It felt as though he had been struck across the face.

41

Towards a New War

Four men stood at the centre of the monumental hall. The high wooden ceilings inlaid with gold friezes, the braziers and the solid silver candlesticks filled the space with light, and brightly coloured tapestries covered the walls, including a particularly large one bearing the Medici coat of arms: six red balls against a golden background. Finely crafted furniture, marble busts and racks bearing halberds and spontoons crowded every corner of that refined place, and there were four tables loaded with all manner of foods: roast lambs and pheasants, game pie, sweets and cheeses, fruit, grapes, walnuts and pastries. Cosimo had dismissed the servants, since he did not want indiscreet ears overhearing what he and his guests had to say to one another.

'I tell you that we are heading for a new war, there is no doubt of it. Lucca was not enough, Volterra was not enough: Rinaldo degli Albizzi wants this battle; he wants it more than he wants anything else. It is all he has ever sought. And now Cosimo sees that woman! Venice and Florence have established ties and Milan wants to break what it thinks can only be an alliance!'

Lorenzo's angry words poured out like molten lava. He was sick and tired of all the subterfuge, banishments and machinations that never actually solved anything, and all the exasperation of the last few years was audible in his voice. Things had certainly changed since their return, but now the suspicion that they were being spied upon by Laura Ricci had rekindled their fears. They knew all too well what that woman was capable of. She *and* that devil Reinhardt Schwartz, because where one of them went, the other was almost certainly lurking.

'There's no point hesitating,' he continued. 'For ten years now Florence has been dragged into this war against Lucca without concluding anything. Niccolò Piccinino has proved superior to all his opponents: Niccolò Fortebraccio, Guidantonio da Montefeltro – even Filippo Brunelleschi failed against him and ended up flooding our own camps. I believe that only you, Francesco, can lead us to victory.'

Sforza looked Lorenzo in the eye. He was struck by the courage and passion with which the younger Medici brother had spoken. He was totally unlike Cosimo, who was observing him to study his reactions.

In a corner of the room, the lieutenant of the Venetian army gave a cough.

'If I may,' he said, 'I believe that the idea of a league against the Duke of Milan is the only possible way to contain Milanese power. After all, *rebus sic stantibus*, Filippo Maria would be encircled: by Venice and Florence, without even counting Genoa, who are keeping him busy at the moment. And it is no secret how close the pontiff is to you,' continued Ludovico Mocenigo, looking over at Cosimo. 'Am I mistaken or did he not consecrate the cathedral of Santa Maria del Fiore just a few days ago?'

'You are not mistaken,' said Cosimo. 'And that's when I saw our mortal enemy.'

'Are you alluding to Laura Ricci? The woman who escaped the dungeons of the Ducal Palace and made me look a fool?'

'I'm sorry to remind you of that regrettable fact, but it was she, in person,' replied Cosimo. 'There is no doubt that at this moment she is in the service of Rinaldo degli Albizzi. And according to what our spies tell us, she is also the favourite of Filippo Maria Visconti.'

'That man is a fool.' Francesco Sforza spoke impulsively and there was a fatalistic note in his voice as though he were surrendering to incontrovertible evidence.

'Perhaps, but there is method to his madness,' insisted Lorenzo. 'And at the moment he holds us in deadlock on several fronts, not counting his recent support for Alfonso of Aragon in the war of succession for the Kingdom of Naples.'

'Which did not stop him losing,' pointed out Mocenigo.

'And therefore,' said Sforza, looking at the elegant man with the thin moustache who represented the Most Serene Republic, 'what do you suggest doing?'

'Captain, I shall be frank. We know how close you are to Milan and to Filippo Maria. It is no secret that a few years ago he offered you his daughter Bianca Maria as well as the fiefs of Castellazzo, Bosco and Frugarolo. I'm not trying to interfere in your business but to point out that what matters most at this moment in time is clear and consistent conduct. The truth is that Filippo Maria must be stopped as soon as possible. Before it's too late. If this alliance of ours holds, we will be in a position to exert a hegemony over the entire peninsula. On this I believe you have no doubts whatsoever, or am I wrong?'

'Not at all,' answered Sforza.

'But above all, my friend,' Cosimo pointed out, 'you must aspire to that which you have so far been unfairly denied. You don't mention it because you are afraid to speak its name, and I understand why, but I am not afraid to say that it is to you I look when I think of the Duchy of Milan. I told you a few years ago and I'll tell you again now: my brother and I will always be at your side if and when you want to try and take what is rightfully yours.'

Lorenzo nodded.

'My friends,' continued Cosimo, 'I believe that the time has come for us to stop fighting wars so that we can finally focus our attention on the peace and beauty which are the foundation of prosperity. After the removal of Albizzi and Strozzi, Florence is once again on the rise: the consecration of the cathedral of Santa Maria del Fiore is only the first step along a road which will be lined with wonders of art and advances in knowledge. For this to happen, though, the political situation must be made secure and Lucca placed under our control. Captain Sforza knows only too well how long this war has been dragging on, seeing that around six years ago we met in his tent and he inaugurated our friendship by abandoning his camp. By so doing, he allowed us the conquest of a city that has still not been tamed. On the other hand, it is obvious that Venice needs to consolidate its dominion on terra firma, as Gattamelata is fighting the Visconti troops near Padua and Piove di Sacco. And finally, Pope Eugene IV, who was forced to flee Rome, still hopes to be able to return to the Eternal City, despite the warm welcome we have given him in Florence.'

'Let's assume that we all agree with what you've said,' said Mocenigo. 'What's your point?'

'The point is that each of us has a clear objective but is too weak individually to take on the Duchy of Milan. But if we accepted how much more productive it would be for all of us to act together, I believe it would provide the solution to all our problems. In short, are we ready to put aside our differences and use everything at our disposal to create a league against the duke which, working in turn for the benefit of one of us and then for the benefit of the other, strengthens us all?'

That final question hung in the air until Francesco Sforza broke the silence. 'Cosimo, I thank you for your words. I'd like to take the perhaps excessive liberty of asking you this: how would you commit yourself to supporting my claims to the Duchy?'

'I will be frank with you, Francesco, since I want no misunderstandings between us: with every instrument necessary. *Apertis verbis*: the Medici bank would be at your disposal. We would give you all our financial support.'

Francesco Sforza's eyes glinted for a moment with a cunning light: Cosimo had managed to arouse his interest. Not that it took a huge amount of imagination but, as he had said, that was the direction in which the alliance could and should go. The Medici were not fighting men but they did have their own financial empire, and he and the Venetian army could be an important military wing of it – Venice had access to the sea while Rome, with Eugene IV, would guarantee the spiritual superiority of the alliance, as well as a good number of soldiers.

Wasn't that the way a monarch was supposed to think?

Francesco Sforza stood there with an expression of amazement on his face. But then, he thought, how could the Medici ever have got where they were and made Florence their *de facto* seigniory if they had lacked the vision Cosimo had just displayed?

'Very well,' he said eventually, 'you are right. Just like six years ago, today we seal a pact, an alliance, and – like then – the bonds that unite us grow stronger still. I will be ready to come to your aid and I expect that you will do the same for me. Together we can bring equilibrium to these lands and remove them from the control of a man who is as greedy as he is mad. Let us dare, let us fight until the bitter end and let us try to bring peace back to Milan, Venice, Florence and Rome. Together, we cannot fail.'

Cosimo de' Medici's eyes sparkled.

'Let it be so,' he said, 'and woe to any who try to stop us.'

42

Poisons and the Major Arcana

Laura was sitting at a table, arrayed upon which were the cards of the Major Arcana.

Filippo Maria Visconti watched her beautiful tawny fingers, their nails painted carmine red, as they moved rapidly over the backs of the tarot, as though weaving a web of invisible lines in the air.

The duke was completely under her spell. It was not just her beauty – though that entranced him – it was also her indefinable aura of damnation and sorcery. When he had seen her for the first time, he had immediately been hypnotized by those dark-green eyes with their hints of gold and had decided then and there to make her his favourite. But in a very special way.

It was not only his bodily senses that trembled under her gaze, or the blood which burned in his veins or that unspeakable sinful desire which inflamed his limbs, but a fascination with the arcane and unspeakable power which emanated from her and which somehow made him her slave.

He would never have been able to explain the tangle of emotions he felt within him when he saw her. There was something of the spider about her, some dangerous and perfidious seduction. And yet it was precisely for that reason that he so desperately sought her out.

Like every time they met, Filippo Maria let his eyes lose themselves in hers, ready and impatient to listen to her prophecies and to follow her advice, for he believed that the woman had the power to predict the outcomes of battles and influence earthly matters. This, as well as knowing how to extinguish lives with the potions and concoctions he commissioned her to create so as to carry out the wicked acts his black heart devised.

The cards were at the centre of the large round table. Thick and decorated with magnificent patterns, they were edged with gold and exquisitely designed. Around them were countless bottles and jars of various shades filled with coloured powders, dried flowers, herbs and liquids as transparent and odourless as they were lethal.

Laura was clad in black, her long dress decorated with silver and precious stones. Sleeves of light-blue brocade, woven with pearls and tied with leather laces, left her shoulders naked, revealing her beautiful arms. Her eyes were dark and her long lashes a like bird's feathers. Her full lips, painted a red so dark it was almost purple, looked livid and ready to take possession of men's minds.

She was a vision, and she was there for him alone. Filippo Maria looked at her for a long time while she regarded him in silence. He said nothing, but inside him his heart cried out with lust.

'First of all,' said Laura, 'I wish to remind your grace that what I read in the cards is not the future but simply what I have learned from the study of the tarot over the years. An interpretation of what the cards tell us, without any pretence of being truth. I say this to advise you to adopt the detachment befitting a moment like this – I know you believe that I see in them what is yet to happen, but I must warn you that it is not so.'

Still looking at the duke, Laura raised the first card.

'Do you see this man hanging upside down, bound to the branch by one foot, my lord?' And she pointed to the figure with the index finger of her right hand. The carmine fingernail flashed in the light of the candles and braziers that illuminated the room and, for a moment, something in the fireplace seemed to roar.

Filippo Maria nodded in silence.

'The hanged man holds his hands behind his back. As you can see, his face is calm and reveals no fear or uncertainty. Although the image makes us think of torture, we must not stop at a reading based purely upon what we see first. We must look closer – at the young man's expression – and think again. He undoubtedly represents the value of sacrifice, but also the acceptance of a choice that leads to imminent and radical change – a renewal of oneself. The card came out the right way up, so there is no doubt as to what it suggests.'

'Could it allude to our meeting? To the fact that I've changed since I met you, my lady?'

Laura seemed to reflect for a moment. 'That could certainly be, your grace, but only if you believe that our meeting has changed you as a man and in the way you make your choices...' Laura hesitated, then went on. 'May I speak freely?'

'Not only may you, you *must*,' thundered Filippo Maria. 'I demand it!'

'Very well. I believe that this card indicates that you should take a different approach during the war that awaits you. We know how fleeting alliances are and how easily they can change, and it is in these continuous shifts that your grace has always tried to build his fortunes, often by suddenly changing side. But in the long run, this constant volatility might cost you. So make a choice. You have finally found men capable of guaranteeing you victory.'

'Niccolò Piccinino? The commander of my army?'

'Not only him.'

'Who else?'

'Think of the man who helped you most of all in the recent campaign against the Genoese and the Venetians.

A man who was brought before you not so very long ago.'

'Reinhardt Schwartz?'

'Precisely, your grace. It is he and Niccolò who will lead you to victory, provided that you make the choice to abandon Sforza and prepare to face your enemies, who, however well organized they may be, cannot defeat you. This, at least, is what the hanged man suggests to me. But let us see...'

Laura raised the second card.

Filippo saw a young girl with golden hair, dressed in dark blue, her head crowned with a wreath of flowers and her dress strewn with petals. The girl's delicate hands rested upon the stubby muzzle of a lion, its long teeth clearly visible and its mane thick and flowing. But far from appearing dangerous or ferocious, the beast seemed tame, almost affectionate, towards the young woman.

'Strength,' said Laura. 'This time, though, the card came out upside down. As you can see, your grace, the unusual combination of girl and beast does not suggest conflict but rather harmony, as though to advise in the use of force a balance of reason and ruthlessness where necessary, as long as the second is governed by the first. Because excessive trust in anger and cruelty would mean you would be lost. This implies that you must advise your men also to be merciful and stop them indulging in rape and looting. Let their wages be their compensation. Losing the support of lands conquered by greed and avarice always proves a bad investment.'

'So I should limit the bloodthirsty temperament of my men?' asked the duke with a hint of disappointment in his voice.

'Precisely.'

'Are you certain this is necessary?'

'As I have already told you, my lord, there is no certainty in the cards. In this regard, poisons are much more reliable. There is always a component of chance, especially as I am not making predictions. But there is no doubt that the cards speak their own language; what they communicate in their messages benefits those able to interpret them. My purpose is certainly not to deceive you. I simply tell you what I know and try, together with you, to adapt that to reality. You are under no obligation to comply. You should simply decide whether there are aspects of these reflections that you feel strike the mark.'

Laura's words sounded very sweet to Filippo Maria. There was a seductiveness about the woman's throaty voice that he found immensely alluring, and he spent the whole week awaiting the moment when he would meet Laura to have his cards read.

'So you must decide what you feel is the most appropriate way to behave. However, you should also know that if the warning contains truth – and there is no way of knowing this before the fact – then not respecting it may determine your defeat. Pay close attention to the choice you make, especially as the card was upside down, which confirms that you are often unable to curb the violent part of your temperament. The insecurity and brutality that lead to impulsiveness can only make you lose. Perhaps for good. Aggression too can have a negative effect upon your relationships with others, and the upside-down Strength card indicates an inability to experience positive feelings, which might push some people away from you.'

'Let's continue,' begged the duke, his trembling voice growing annoyed and high-pitched, like that of a capricious child.

Laura turned over the third card.

Death made its appearance.

The duke's eyes flashed with terror. The chilling vision was horrible to behold: a yellow skeleton sat astride a horse whose coat was as shiny and black as coal and looked as if it had galloped straight out of the mouth of the underworld. Death held a long-handled scythe whose long blade raked the severed heads under the horse's hooves.

Sensing the duke's fears, Laura reassured him immediately. 'Death, your grace, is not a negative card in itself. Think again of the message of the Hanged Man: Death too should be understood as an end that brings with it the seeds of change and regeneration. Especially since the card came out the right way up. Its meaning is, of course, obscure and ambiguous, and thus it remains a symbol of a fragile balance – of a violent change that is difficult to overcome. Especially in light of what we have said about Strength. Personally I think that a very important battle is approaching.'

'When will it be?'

There was madness in Filippo Maria's eyes. Laura knew all too well the mood swings that made him behave like a frightened little boy – the hysterical weeping, followed by sudden fits of anger. Yet he wanted her to continue, so she decided to do as he bade her, regardless of the consequences. She knew that her privileged life in the court inevitably depended upon the happiness of the duke who, precisely because he was perverted and sick, lived for those tarot readings and for watching her preparing her poisons. Life had taught her all too well not to create problems for herself. She would manage him, just as she always had.

'I cannot say, your grace, but I feel that when it arrives we will know it: it will be a supreme moment, and when it comes, you and your soldiers must make good use of the virtues of which we have spoken.'

'Show me the last one,' the duke croaked, his voice now breaking with emotion and the pupils in his huge eyes as small as pinheads.

Laura turned over the final card.

'The Devil,' she said, and as soon as she had uttered the word, she felt a twinge in her heart, for she sensed something strange in the silence. She could not have said what it was, yet a gloomy, creeping something had suddenly drowned the calm, replacing it with a chilling feeling of emptiness.

'Fortunately,' said the duke, 'he came out right way up.'

'Alas, your grace, the Devil is the only card of the Trumps which obeys the opposite rule. This means that if it is drawn right way up, as in this case, the meaning can be one and one alone: darkness, weakness, submission to the fear of taking responsibility. The Devil announces a great tragedy on the horizon, represented by our fears and our inability to face the events of life.'

The duke began to tremble. He rose shakily to his feet; then he collapsed to the cold marble of the floor. He burst into tears and his shoulders heaved with sobs like a slapped child suffocated by shame.

Laura got up and went over to him.

'Your grace,' she murmured in a soft, warm voice. 'Come to me. Be brave; do not be afraid.' His chest still heaving and his shoulders shaking with sobs, Filippo Maria Visconti turned around and crawled over to Laura and embraced her; soon afterwards he began to calm down. In that marvellous woman alone did he see salvation. She was the only creature capable of understanding and forgiving him – of standing by him and giving him what he so desperately needed.

He clung to her, letting himself be cradled against her soft body. Slowly, the tears ceased to fall.

'Kiss me, my angel,' he whimpered. Laura put her beautiful lips on his, and Filippo Maria kissed them, gently and then with increasing fervour until finally he was filled with raw lust. His frightened, quivering mouth fixed on Laura's, his huge tongue flickering between his lips. It searched and found hers.

The poisoner stroked his head and the duke surrendered to her, trying to drown in pleasure the words he had heard.

Fear, pain and pleasure: the recipe for the most powerful poison of all. Laura knew its characteristics well, as she had experienced its effects first-hand.

His fat hands began to undress her, as though by taking off her clothes he could fill his empty heart, and his eyes lingered on the curves of her body. His tongue inside her, his breath reeking of his broken teeth. The wounded moans of a frightened and perverse child; the tears that still fell, wetting her tawny skin; the fingers that explored her, squeezing and kneading in a madness of anger and terror.

Laura let him do it. It didn't hurt. It was no worse than she had already endured.

She lay on the ice-cold marble while the duke unlaced her bodice. His gasps, the creeping rise of his lust – everything about him was disgusting and repugnant but no more than she was herself. She who had accepted every compromise, even the most squalid, in order to keep hidden away in a corner of herself the scrap of a feeling that resembled love.

She felt lost without Reinhardt. She would do anything to remain beside him.

Long, long ago, something inside her had broken, so the duke's drool, his semen, his rotten smell felt like nothing but the bizarre pranks of a jester who never missed an opportunity to mock her. Laura let her right arm fall to her side while, above her, Filippo Maria began to thrust.

She looked over at the closed door and smiled. She knew that nobody would come in.

And then she stuck her nails into the duke's back and matched his mad, furious movements with her own hips.

February 1439

43

A Difficult Choice

Lorenzo stared at his brother in disbelief.

'Do you realize that we have footed the bill for seven hundred Greek prelates and intellectuals to travel from Ferrara to Florence just so as to transfer an episcopal council? I hope you have a good explanation, because I tell you, I am struggling to understand. In my opinion, we've shown our hand too clearly this time.' Lorenzo's voice betrayed incredulous anger. 'And for what? Don't tell me that you really believe in the reunification of the Churches of Rome and of Constantinople!'

'It's not what you think,' said Cosimo.

'Don't talk in riddles! I went all the way to Ferrara to petition the Pope and conduct negotiations which were bizarre to say the least, with an offer even a madman would have accepted: tell me that you have a more serious project in mind than *that*! Let me in on your secrets, even if I am only your *brother*!'

Cosimo sighed.

'Lorenzo, I beg your forgiveness. I didn't explain more clearly for the simple reason that I felt it was important to act as quickly as possible. We couldn't risk wasting an opportunity like this, don't you see? We are talking about uniting the Catholic and the Orthodox Church – bringing Greek doctrine and culture closer to the Roman Ecclesia. And yes, you're right! Men like Bessarion are the last intellectuals at the gates of the Eastern Roman Empire, and Constantinople risks falling into the hands of the Ottoman infidels, so this meeting of Churches will be an attempt to bridge the gap between cultures and allow us to save the history of which we are all children. At least in part.'

Lorenzo shook his head.

'Sometimes I think you have too much faith in culture and art. Even this madness of collecting manuscripts, ancient codexes, lining our shelves with parchments and rolls of paper, creating a library larger than any ever seen – I don't understand it. You seem to love studying and art more than anything else. I'm not saying you should give it up, because I know how much prestige and power the restoration and conservation of buildings and churches have brought our family... But damn it all, Cosimo, *seven hundred people* – seven hundred people is an *army*!'

'Well said, my brother! So why spend that money on financing a war and lodging soldiers? Must we invest our florins only in death and destruction? Why not make Florence home to something which will go down in history? Have you any idea how much closer this initiative will bring us to the Pope? You know that Martin V never made the task an easy one, but our relations with Eugene IV are excellent.'

'Of course they are – look at what we have given him!'

'Should we have left the council in Ferrara after the plague had broken out there?'

'I never said that! I'm not an imbecile – don't treat me like one!'

Cosimo raised his hands. 'Very well, very well. You are right. So, think about this…' he urged. 'Do you have any idea of how much the money spent now will multiply in benefits over the next few years? Try to think not only about the indulgences but about how important it will have been, in a year, or maybe two, to have welcomed not only the Pope to our city but also the highest officials of the Greek Church, and to have facilitated the meeting of these two cultures and the peaceful carrying out of the council! Do you know what that will mean? I'll tell you, brother! When it is time to wage war against the Duke of Milan – who, let me remind you, has set Niccolò Piccinino and Rinaldo degli Albizzi to burning and looting the countryside

– not only will Sforza be with us, not only Venice, but so will the pontifical troops. And given the state to which that accursed Filippo Maria Visconti has reduced our Republic, the support of Pope Eugene IV will be essential. So forgive me if I was cryptic, for that I apologize – but as you can see, there wasn't a moment to lose.'

'I doubt it will be enough...' replied Lorenzo.

'You are right, and in fact that is only the first advantage it will bring us. Try and imagine who at this moment derives most benefit from the routes that lead to Byzantium and therefore from trade with the East.'

'Venice and Genoa,' said Lorenzo without hesitation.

'Exactly! Merchants. Or rather, pirates. Men so cunning and unscrupulous that they bleed the entire *region*! And are we going to just stand there and watch them do it? No, we are *not*. Our city exercises sufficient hegemony over Pisa that we finally have the opening on to the Mediterranean we have struggled so hard for. Do you think that connections with the Far East will harm our business? And do you think that leaving Byzantium in the hands of the Ottoman Sublime Porte and allowing the Muslims to take control of the straits is the right way to preserve the world we have worked so hard to create? The real problem is that the kingdoms, lordships, duchies and monarchies of the West are fragmented, and that is why we need unity.'

And so saying, Cosimo looked into his brother's eyes, challenging him to disagree.

Silence fell in the library.

For a few moments Lorenzo said nothing. He saw now that what his brother had done had been not only for the benefit of the family but had also required great promptness. One thing struck him especially: France and England were emerging from a war that had lasted a hundred years, Germany was so broken up into kingdoms that it did not represent a force upon which it was possible to rely, and all Genoa, Milan, Venice, Florence, Rome and Naples did was fight for supremacy among themselves without ever actually succeeding. In short, they were all so committed to waging war that they hadn't even considered that the Ottoman threat could sweep them all away if it managed to break down the walls of Constantinople.

'So?' he asked his brother. 'What are you going to do? Support a crusade?'

'If that turns out to be necessary, yes. But for the moment I simply want to guarantee the Pope's support in the war against Milan and the appointment of a friendly bishop in Tuscan territory: someone who can represent a spiritual link between Florence and Rome. Do you have a better idea?'

Lorenzo took a deep breath.

'Very well. I understand,' he said, smiling and holding out his hand. 'You acted well. It's just... I like being involved in our decisions. You know how much I believe in what you do and how hard I too work to increase our fortunes, so please – keep me informed of your plans. I trusted you while I conducted the negotiations and I would trust you again, but next time, explain your motives to me more clearly.'

Cosimo embraced him.

'You have no idea how relieved I am to receive your forgiveness,' he said. 'It was never my plan to exclude you from the decision. Things just happened so suddenly that I simply didn't have time to speak to you. You did an excellent job in Ferrara – I know very well how great your commitment has been in this affair.'

'Even when you have been off talking to your favourite artists,' said Lorenzo with a smirk.

'Even when I have been off talking to my favourite artists,' agreed his brother.

'And now?' Lorenzo asked.

'What do you mean?'

'Well, now that the council is going to be held in Florence...'

'We will attend, when possible.'

'B-but... I know *nothing* about this kind of thing!'

'That's not true. And anyway Marsilio Ficino will be with us. His knowledge of Greek and Latin is little short of extraordinary.'

'If I remember, you too know Latin.'

'Certainly not as well as he does.'

'Very well, I give in. I understand – I'll be watching.'

Niccolò Piccinino rode as if he had the Devil at his heels. His sword gleamed in the air as, a cruel grimace on his face, he struck his opponent, sending him crashing to the ground to be trampled under the hooves of his horse. The man was a true soldier of fortune, thought Reinhardt Schwartz, watching.

What struck him most was the readiness with which his men obeyed him and the dedication they showed. After he had escaped from the siege of Verona, Piccinino had managed to make his men build a bridge of boats connecting the Veronese shore with the Mantua shore of the Adige over the course of a single night. That way he would more easily be able to escape or, alternatively, await reinforcements and supplies.

And now he was slaughtering the Venetian sailors who found themselves at the mercy of his company because of the ice banks in the river. With their short-range cannons, the galleons, stranded further back and unable to manoeuvre, had no hope of setting up covering fire for their men. *Luck?* Luck smiled upon the audacious, and Piccinino was nothing if not audacious. When necessary, he was the kind who jumped straight in and stared death in the face. And his men stayed with him, sated by the spoils their captain often managed to get his hands on.

The lead shot of the culverins was exterminating the sailors in the boats and now Piccinino intended to use the cavalry to finish off the others on the banks of the Adige. He had ordered a few of them to be left alive while the cold waters of the river grew red with blood.

Reinhardt heard the hiss of an arrow near him. He saw the archer who had tried to catch him with his guard down and, swinging his sword, rode at him and severed the arm with which the man grasped his bow. A fountain of blood gushed from the stump as the Venetian shrieked in desperation. Schwartz raced on, and then yanked on the reins and halted his horse. The beast reared up, kicking out with its forelegs, and as soon as they were back on the swampy shore, Schwartz turned it around and spurred it into a gallop.

The Venetian was on his knees holding the stump in his left hand when he saw Schwartz coming back towards him. He closed his eyes, waiting for death.

The horse increased its speed until it was alongside the kneeling man, and Schwartz swung a diagonal blow that opened up a gash in the man's neck.

The Venetian soldier fell forward, spraying more blood into the frozen, clear waters of the Adige. Around him, the desperate cries of the dying made an obscene contrast to the bloodthirsty yells of the men flying banners bearing Filippo Maria Visconti's *biscione*, which flapped horribly in the cold wind of the February afternoon.

44

The Archbishop of Nicaea

Cosimo had set off early in the morning. In those cold winter days, the streets of Florence buzzed with a special energy. Only a few weeks before, on 21 January, the pontiff had arrived from Ferrara with a part of his retinue, and the day had been declared a public holiday so as to allow all citizens to participate in the sumptuous celebrations.

For Eugene IV, it had been a grand return to the city that for years had been his second home. Florence had given the Pope a triumphal reception and was now preparing to acclaim Joseph, the Greek patriarch who would be arriving a few days later escorted by thirty bishops and the entire papal court with over five hundred knights. After him, it would be the turn of the *basileus* to arrive: John VIII Palaiologos, the Emperor of Constantinople. Leonardo Bruni was composing magnificent welcome speeches in Greek to ensure them an appropriate reception.

Thanks to the Pope's intercession, though, Cosimo had managed to obtain an appointment with one of the illustrious Greek scholars of religion already in town, and was thus at that moment hurrying towards San Lorenzo.

He entered the church and went straight to the sacristy, where his father and mother lay at rest. Whenever possible, he always held discussions there, because he felt he could hold on to the past despite the wearying passage of time.

A few years earlier, Cosimo had feared that the passing of the days would weaken his recollections, making his memories of his father and mother grow fainter, but he could now say with certainty that they had not. He had not forgotten them, not at all, and the sacristy and the family tomb beneath the altar had played an important role in preserving their memory.

When he reached the sacristy, he saw that the person he was to meet had already arrived.

Cosimo was surprised by the appearance of the man before him. He had been expecting a refined intellectual, a man of the Church, and had therefore imagined someone tall and thin, but Giovanni Bessarion was an imposing man, strong and muscular, with broad shoulders. He wore a dark robe, edged with embroidery in gold and precious stones. A long, thick beard ending in two sharp points like knife blades adorned his chin, and his eyes were as black as shards of onyx, and flashed whenever something captured his interest.

Pope Eugene IV had brought Cosimo to the high priest, introducing him as a lord of Florence, a man of letters and patron of the arts, and emphasizing how it had been his generosity that had allowed the council to be held in one of the most beautiful cities in the world.

For Cosimo de' Medici, this man represented one of the last heralds of the Byzantine knowledge and culture of the Eastern Roman Empire. Bessarion was the Archbishop of Nicaea and he had come to Ferrara the year before, accompanied by Cardinal Cusano. He was said to be one of the proponents of the so-called party of union, that handful of men of faith who still dreamed of a reconciliation between the Latin and Byzantine Churches, even though, back at home, the monks and much of the Greek Church took a dim view of the idea.

The moment had arrived. Since the archbishop seemed perfectly willing to stare him in the eye without saying a word for the next two hours, Cosimo attempted to break the ice.

He spoke in Latin.

'Your grace,' he began, 'your presence here is an immense honour for me and for our humble city. I am a passionate supporter of the cause that is so close to your heart and I hope very much that this council will bring our two Churches closer together.'

Bessarion smiled and there was a sincere light in his dark eyes.

'My friend,' he replied, 'I am happy to meet a Latin supporter of this union. Unfortunately, I regret to say that reunification between Rome and Byzantium still seems distant.'

Cosimo was sorry to hear the hint of bitterness in the Archbishop of Nicaea's words. Perhaps if he could learn more it would be possible to find a thread of hope.

'Why do you say that, if I may ask, your grace?'

'In truth, the issue of separation is not so closely linked to matters of doctrine. The problem behind the dispute is not the *filioque* – the expression added by the Romans in the *Credo* to that *qui ex Patre procedit* which confirms that the Holy Spirit proceeds from the Father and the Son.'

'Really?'

Cosimo knew little about it but through his informants had followed all the proceedings of the council of Ferrara, and had understood it was *precisely* the Holy Spirit proceeding from Father and the Son and the inclusion of that double origin in the Creed that represented the principal cause of the dispute between the Latin and Greek Churches.

'The truth is that nobody actually intends to contest that point, provided that the formal conciliar expression of the Nicene-Constantinopolitan symbol is not violated. The real causes of the conflict between the two Churches, my friend, are the underlying political and cultural questions which are rooted in the oceans of time.'

Cosimo was confused, and expressed his bemusement openly.

'I had thought the reasons for the dispute unrelated to politics.'

'My friend, it is evident that the doctrinal dispute has its own weight. Especially since there is another question: if the Church of Rome can unilaterally modify a common *Credo* which has been approved by ecumenical councils by inserting the expression "*filioque*", it thus affirms a *de facto* primacy, which is clearly intolerable. But what should we say about the abandonment and the massacres that the West, and especially the crusaders, have committed in Byzantium over the centuries, without even managing to save it from the clutches of the Ottomans? Is that not, in your opinion, more than enough reason to justify the feelings of anger if not outright hatred of many of the monks, prelates and archons of our land? And he who speaks to you now is among those who most ardently desire a return to union. Certainly, Byzantium has made mistakes: isolating itself and claiming an autonomy which over the centuries became presumption, without even mentioning the unbridled corruption that has pervaded the place in recent times and the ineptitude of some of its emperors. These are no small failings. But when the crusaders repeatedly stripped her of her treasures and when the Genoese and Venetian merchants plundered her for their commercial trafficking, well, autonomy and isolationism looked like the only way to survive. And despite this, the *basileus* of Constantinople has today arrived in person in your city to ask for help from the West, which for centuries has abandoned and robbed us, and stripped us of our dignity. As you can well imagine, my heart bleeds to tell you this. And therefore the hope of a reunification is also linked to ensuring the survival of an entire culture which risks being lost under the Ottoman yoke.'

As he listened to Bessarion's words, Cosimo sensed the great archbishop's profound sadness and realized that this council was not simply a question of unification for ecclesiastical communities but was also perhaps the only means of keeping alive the last spark of Christianity in the East. Otherwise it would not only mean the end of Rome, but also the destruction of a memory – the annulment of a thousand years of history.

'Your grace, what you say is so sad that I struggle to find words. I acknowledge how great our failings have been, and I know that the many divisions into which the West is split, the many lordships and duchies which compose it, certainly do not help in the construction of a single, shared vision which might bring about a reconciliation. Yet such is the purpose of this council and I am committed to forging an alliance that, through our good pontiff, can bring together the two sides so that, together with the Christian sovereigns and lords, he can despatch a new crusade – one to bring Constantinople under his protection and guardianship and to preserve the roots of a culture which is so much more precious because we are its children. Look at our churches, our palazzos; visit our libraries. God is my witness as to how deep our commitment here in Florence is to reaching such a goal. Like that of the many other intellectuals who have come to our city, your presence here will be a precious guide to promoting this belief and this sensibility.'

For a moment, Cosimo saw that Bessarion's frown had eased and his eyes – no longer lit with a grim, grave light – held a flicker of hope.

'My dear Cosimo, your words give my heart wings. Pope Eugene IV puts great trust in your abilities and I can say what I have heard confirms his beliefs. As you may have intuited, union is possible only through a political and cultural rapprochement of our worlds. I will try to take advantage of the opportunity that has been given me and I undertake to discover as much as possible about your city while I am here. In fact, I hope that you will guide me in learning of its wonder. I cannot imagine better days than those I feel await me.' With those words, Bessarion suddenly came over to

Cosimo and embraced him, and the lord of Florence was so taken aback by this gesture of affection that it took him a few moments to reciprocate – but when he did, he did so with all of himself.

When they separated, Bessarion looked him in the eye. Cosimo saw not only friendship and indulgence but also a firmness of spirit that he knew he would never want to disappoint.

45

Council of War

'We must wipe out Florence, your grace, we can wait no longer,' insisted Rinaldo degli Albizzi. 'The Medici are becoming too powerful. Bringing the ecumenical council to the city was a masterstroke. Cosimo is trying to consolidate an alliance with the Pope.'

'Yes, your grace,' confirmed Niccolò Piccinino, 'and if I were you, I wouldn't trust that snake Francesco Sforza. The man is treacherous and always ready to change sides. As God is my witness, if you continue to protect him, he will turn against you, my lord.'

'Silence!' cried Filippo Maria Visconti.

He rose from his wooden bench and crossed the room in great strides. He and he alone was the Duke of Milan, and he certainly did not need the advice of those who were unworthy to polish his boots. How dare they? They only existed at all because he willed it. He had only to click his fingers and they would disappear, to be replaced by others. Not to mention that that idiot Albizzi was entirely at his mercy, even if the fool did keep forgetting the fact. His eyes flashed and his gaze fell upon Reinhardt Schwartz. Now there was a man that he liked. A skilled soldier who had plenty of guts and the estimable habit of never speaking unless spoken to. He was standing in a corner, slicing an apple into segments with a large knife.

'And you, Schwartz?' said Filippo Maria. 'What is your opinion?'

'Mine?' asked the Swiss mercenary, seemingly surprised by the question.

'Yes, yours – do you see someone else near you? I wish to know what you think.'

As was his habit, Schwartz took his time. That it had been the duke who had asked the question made no difference to him. He chewed a piece of apple and swallowed it and then spoke.

'My opinion, my lord, is that Rinaldo degli Albizzi speaks the truth. As does my captain. It is no secret that Francesco Sforza is considering lending his support to Venice, and we all know how close the friendship between the Serenissima and the Medici is. I believe that in life a point comes when the definitive battle, the one that ordains the victory of one side and the defeat of the other, can no longer be postponed. The moment, excellency, when one kills or is killed – when one wins or one loses.'

'And do you think that moment has arrived?'

What was the duke asking him? How could he imagine that he had an answer to that? Filippo Maria must have completely lost his mind, thought Schwartz. And to look at him, it certainly seemed that he had.

'That I can't tell you with certainty.'

'So what good are you, then, Schwartz? You've started to talk like my poisoner: in riddles! You're a soldier, damn it!'

Reinhardt ate another quarter of an apple. Filippo Maria grew even more agitated, and when he glanced over at Rinaldo degli Albizzi, he realized that the man was about to start asking questions again.

'What is it now?' he shouted in exasperation.

'You see, your grace…' Albizzi began, 'with the council of Florence, Cosimo de' Medici is aiming to promote the unity of the Churches so he can obtain favours from Eugene IV, and despite the recent disputes with Basel and the Emperor Sigismund, the pontiff is rapidly regaining power and prestige. The day will come when that man will sit once more in the Eternal City; it is only a matter of time. And when he does, that bond of friendship with the Medici will be even more disadvantageous for you. What I would like to suggest is that we strike now, before they reach that position of strength.'

Rinaldo had spoken carefully, with circumspection. Over the years, he had learned to measure his words. His life was now that of an exile and conspirator, and as such he could not allow himself to appear impertinent. The years of waiting had not yet bent him, but his bravado was muted and his demands now resembled more the supplications of a desperate man. He had not abandoned his dream of returning to Florence, but weaving his plans with the calm of the spider waiting for its prey had tested him to the limit. He was tired, and the more he tried to grasp his dream, the more it seemed to slip away from him, leaving his fingers closing on empty air. Even his eyes, once hard and brash, were now shadowed with gloom.

'My dear Albizzi,' said the duke, suddenly calm, 'whether you believe it or not, I share your concerns, and you will be happy to learn that your time has finally come. You will have your revenge, you can be sure of it, but you must never forget to whom you owe your loyalty and gratitude. In these years you have learned temperance. I remember when you first came here with your tail between your legs, passing judgement on all and sundry, and I must confess that I much prefer this new manner of yours. That said, if you – and you too, Piccinino – believe that you can tell me when and how to attack, you are wrong. That decision is mine and mine alone. What I *can* tell you is that we must leave nothing to chance. Now,' he continued, 'my soldier of fortune and Gian Francesco Gonzaga will go to Veneto to attack Gattamelata and Bartolomeo Colleoni, in order to halt the progress of Venice. The Serenissima is moving too far inland. And immediately afterwards, Captain, I order you to cross the Po and descend upon Florence, and I want you and Albizzi and the men that he assembles to take the city. This, of course, also concerns you, my dear Schwartz. I realize that all this will take some time, but it is for this reason that I want you to set off now.'

The Swiss mercenary nodded.

'I will need money, my lord,' said Piccinino.

'As regards money, Captain, you are well equipped. Feed your men with what you loot. Loot, rape, kill – I want your name to sow terror. Some time ago, it was suggested to me that I be merciful to the vanquished, but I think that an unwise strategy. I would rather be feared than pitied.'

Piccinino didn't like the answer – he had hoped to get a few ducats from Filippo Maria. He pressed his case.

'You are right, of course, my lord. But the men are tired. This bitter winter has frozen fields and rivers, and the condition of the roads makes the transport of supplies for the troops uncertain and often impossible. My men are devoured by disease and the hardships of the winter encampments on the Salò riviera, but are nevertheless fighting to hinder the movements of the Venetian fleet. I need to offer them something to give them a reason to continue. Unfortunately, staying still kills even more of them than the cold. So I beg you, help me. Otherwise I cannot answer for their loyalty.'

Filippo Maria snorted with irritation. His men were becoming increasingly greedy and continued to plunder his already depleted resources. But he also knew that if there ever was a man hungry for the spoils of war, it was Piccinino, and so his request must be sincere. It was not impossible to believe that the situation was exactly as he had described.

He turned to Schwartz.

'You, Reinhardt... Can you confirm what my valiant captain says?'

Of course, it was absurd that the duke did not trust Piccinino, who fought for him under his insignia, but on the other hand, Filippo Maria was notoriously consumed by suspicion and the fear of betrayal. He lived practically barricaded inside the fortress of Porta Giovia, which he rarely left, and had set up such a dense network of spies to watch over his men that on several occasions it had emerged that two men were each spying upon the other. Everyone informed on everyone else, and one of the duke's favourite occupations was sitting in the tower listening to his spies telling him what those in his employ were up to. It was no easy task to climb the steep staircase of his favours, which were few and secretive, yet all tried to show themselves loyal and accommodating towards him. And those who did were the ones Filippo Maria mistrusted most.

Schwartz had learned that the best way to navigate his web of obsessions was to say exactly what he thought in as simple and direct a way as possible, since there was no point trying to deceive the man.

'What my captain says is damnably true, your grace. I do not remember a harsher winter than this and those men who were not injured or killed in the recent clashes with the Venetians are now falling victim to the frost and snow. They are soldiers, and knew what they were signing up for, but this forced inactivity caused by the winter and the cold, together with the lack of booty that results from it, is putting a strain upon their spirits. The fear is that many of them may abandon your grace's armies, despite the powerful sway the captain holds over them.'

'By God, Reinhardt, they are nothing but mercenaries!' shouted the Duke of Milan in exasperation. 'We can replace them!'

'Of course, your excellency, but do not imagine that substituting the men would be straightforward: a company has its own rules and codes, and when that breaks down it is almost impossible to heal the fracture by adding new men. I believe that giving them something today would be a good way to receive much more in exchange tomorrow.'

'Then so be it, damn it. I will let you have five thousand ducats to cure this rampant despair, and not one ducat more! But mark you, snow or not, I want you to leave as soon as possible for Verona and Soave to drive those damned Venetians back to their lagoon, after which you will head for Florence. Have I made myself clear? And take Rinaldo degli Albizzi with you! Since he is so keen to leave this castle, I think that a taste of the fray while he waits to enter his city can only be of benefit to him. And now off with you!' thundered the duke, eager to be free of the three bloodsuckers.

Without daring to answer, Albizzi, Piccinino and Schwartz lowered their heads and left in silence. And while his captain and his previous master huddled together in discussion outside the door of the chamber, Schwartz set off towards Laura Ricci's apartments.

As he walked down the stairs leading to the central courtyard and then proceeded to the eastern wing where the woman lived, Reinhardt's thoughts grew gloomy.

The times he spent with the duke's personal poisoner had become more infrequent and melancholy since they had been in the pay of Filippo Maria Visconti. Reinhardt had long harboured a secret that now often seemed to be on the tip of his tongue. He couldn't have said why it was happening in that moment – perhaps because he had kept it inside him for too long and because, although he didn't want to admit it, he truly cared for Laura.

How else to explain his having gone to save her? He still didn't understand why he hadn't run away with her then. In a way, he almost felt as though he was imprisoned by what he had become. He had grown to hate being a professional soldier, and yet it was all he knew how to do, and Laura had not penetrated his soul deeply enough to make him abandon all of them and devote himself to her.

Perhaps he was just a coward?

Or perhaps, in his heart of hearts, he felt that he didn't deserve to be happy. Because he had no doubt that it was only with her that he felt a real sense of peace and joy.

He didn't want to wound her with the secret that he kept locked inside the deepest part of him, but the struggle between the need to tell her and the fear of hurting her was so violent that he took refuge from it in battle, fighting for the sole purpose of having an excuse to see her as little as possible, however much it tore at his heart. Once, he had been convinced that he had managed to erase those memories, but the violence of the recent battles had made them emerge anew, as though regurgitated from deep within him and rubbing the broken edges of his soul in his face.

And so the days had become ever grimmer and their rare meetings and moments of passion had become imbued with sadness.

In a way, it seemed as if time itself had simply been waiting for that moment which, sooner or later, would arrive. Perhaps even that day.

Since she had arrived in the Visconti court and had learned her destiny, Laura had accepted without demur what life had reserved for her. As far as she was concerned, it was nothing new. And yet, even though life grew grimmer and darker with the passing of the days, she had clung to him almost suffocatingly.

And now when he saw her, the violent part of him, the part he had never been able to keep under control, came back overpoweringly, just like that night many years ago.

He suddenly decided not to go to her apartments. He would see her another time. He wasn't ready for it yet.

Would he ever be? Of course he would be; he *must* be. But not that day. He turned around and retraced his steps. He would go to his men and bury his thoughts in the ice of the camp.

July 1439

46

The Meeting of the Churches

The cathedral was crowded. On the right side were the Catholic cardinals and bishops, on the left, the high priests and monks of the Greek Church. All wore long robes, the first of red and gold and the second of black and silver.

Clad in his papal habit, Pope Eugene IV stood at the main altar beneath Brunelleschi's dome. Before his eyes, written upon the finest parchment, was the text of the reconciliation and union of the two Churches: Western and Eastern.

At his side, Cardinal Giuliano Cesarini read the decree, drawn up by common agreement, which sanctified the reunification. It sealed an alliance that could pave the way to a political and military agreement aimed at protecting the Christian world from the fury of the

Ottomans, while breaking down the last walls which still separated Byzantium from the Western kingdoms.

Cosimo, who had been allowed to attend the solemn occasion, listened. He had managed to obtain himself a place in one of the front pews. Eugene IV's words sounded grateful and unequivocal. They were the result of negotiations which – even the final part held in Florence – had taken months, in addition to the years previously, first in Basel and then in Ferrara.

'The Greeks state that by claiming that the Holy Spirit proceeds from the Father they had no intention of excluding the Son; the Latins, on the other hand, reiterate that by claiming that the Holy Spirit proceeds from the Father and the Son they in no way wish to deny that the Father is the source and principle of any divinity, and therefore of the Son and of the Holy Spirit; nor do they believe that there are two principles or two spirations for this. The Holy Spirit has one principle and one spiration. From this derives a single and identical sense of truth, so that the following formula of a holy union pleasing to God is clear and unassailable.'

All present were aware just how crucial that passage was, especially Cosimo, who recognized it as both opportune and magnificent – particularly in the light of what Giovanni Bessarion had confessed to him a few months earlier.

A plan began to take shape in his mind, and it was so vast that he almost feared to give voice to it, though, after hearing those words, he knew that anything was possible.

He was aware that he had great responsibilities and knew that, at this point, expectations were running very high. And from such heights, one risked a terrible fall. Yet the league against the Duke of Milan could easily become the secular body that guaranteed that union.

Was he just a crazed idealist? Lorenzo, who had been at his side in this, didn't seem to think as he did, and had repeatedly stated that the alliance was so fragile that it would fall apart with the first gust of wind.

And yet dreaming had never hurt anyone. Cosimo knew that it was from the most grandiose visions that the most extraordinary achievements were realized.

'In the name of the Holy Trinity, the Father, the Son and Holy Spirit, with the approval of this sacred and universal Florentine council, we ordain that this truth of the faith must be believed and accepted by all Christians; and so all must profess that the Holy Spirit descends eternally from the Father and the Son, and has ever done so, as from a single principle and from a single spiration; and we declare that the holy teachers' claim that the Holy Spirit proceeds from the Father through the Son tends to affirm that the Son, like the Father, is cause, according to the Greeks, and principle according to the Latins, of the subsistence of the Holy Spirit...'

As he listened to those words, Cosimo closed his eyes. The miracle of the union of the two Churches had been accomplished, and now all the hard work carried out over all those months would bear fruit. He smiled at the thought that, once again, such an important event had taken place in Santa Maria del Fiore.

Perhaps its wonderful architecture would become a temple of achievements and success. He sat for a few moments with his eyes closed, letting himself be lulled by the closing words of Cardinal Giuliano Cesarini.

'Is it true what people are saying?'

Cosimo looked up from the letter he was reading.

Contessina's face was dark, and an angry pout tugged at her lips. For the entire week, Cosimo had had the feeling that there was something on her mind, and – as he tended to do in those circumstances – he had waited for Contessina's anger to fade. But this time, evidently, that was not going to be what happened.

'And what are people saying?' he ventured.

Contessina shook her head in disbelief.

'I don't know you any more!' she said bitterly. 'Once, at least, you would have confided in me, you would have deigned to whisper your doubts, speak to me about your decisions. But not any more. Do you deny it?'

Cosimo didn't know what to say.

'Piccinino has taken Verona and marched on Padua. His men have reached Venice and even though your dear friend Francesco Sforza, with whom you have long conspired, seems to be holding his own, Piccinino appears to have every intention of arriving, sooner or later, at the gates of Florence. Lorenzo has divulged that apart from all the promises and agreements aimed at promoting the union of the two Churches, this whole business of the council is actually a plan of yours to bring the Pope and the papal troops over to our side. So I ask you: when exactly were you intending to tell me?'

Should he have? Cosimo raised an eyebrow, but the gesture only had the effect of making Contessina angrier.

'Does such a request surprise you? After all I've done for you over the years?' she continued, without giving him a chance to answer. 'Always, *always* remaining by your side, even when everything conspired against us? And now, after exile, corruption and separation, I am to remain silent and demure, only to discover that one day you will leave me to go off and fight, and perhaps die, withholding the truth from me until the end? Oh no, my love. If that is what you think of me...'

'I think of you only the best of which my mind is capable. Since the day that I first saw you, I have wanted with all my heart to be a better man, and such I have hoped and tried to be, for you and for our family. I have not always succeeded, perhaps. And as regards the reasons that led me to host the council in Florence, well... The plague broke out in Ferrara: what was I supposed to do? And yes, it is true: I intend to guarantee the alliance with the Pope and the necessary indulgences... You and my brother are exactly alike sometimes. Am I a bad husband because I care about my family? I should have involved you both in my decisions, at least the most recent ones, but there are situations where discussion does nothing except slow everything down. And I don't understand why an occasion as important as the reunification of two faiths must be reduced to a simple political strategy to guarantee allies in war. The question is much more complex than that and I would ask you to believe me when I tell you that what I do is aimed solely at guaranteeing the well-being of you and our children!'

Contessina took a step towards him. Her expression had grown imperceptibly sweeter. It wasn't much but it was something. Cosimo looked her in the eye. Several years might have passed but she was still beautiful. The green gown embroidered with silver and decorated with pearls and gems enhanced her luminous skin. She looked glorious.

He took her hands in his.

'I did not mean to exclude you, my love,' he said, 'only protect you. Is there something wrong with that?'

'No,' she said, keeping her gaze steady, 'but you also know that I don't need protecting. No more than you do, at least. I am afraid, Cosimo, can you understand that? This continuous shifting of alliances, these political calculations, the reforms you have made, your men who sit in the Palazzo della Signoria, the relations you have with Eugene IV, the meetings with the officers of the Venetian army… all this puts you at great risk, and your enemies have become countless and plot against your life. And despite this, you seem to constantly seek other opponents, as though the ones you already have weren't enough! There are days when I am frightened of you, truly. And can you, in all honesty, tell me that I'm wrong?'

He placed his lips on her perfect forehead. So delicate yet so strong, she was like a flower that had resisted the wind and the cold of the last winter. And he loved her so very much because there was such pride and rare composure in her. Even when she became angry, it was always for a good reason. He was a truly lucky man.

He smiled.

'Very well, I understand. You're right about my agreements and pacts with our allies, but I believe that it's better to act instead of waiting. Just look at what happened the last time we waited… I ended up in the Alberghetto cell and we were only saved by a whisker. And even then, we had to spend a year apart.'

'And I have no intention of going through anything like that ever again,' said Contessina.

'Nor do I. And it is precisely for that reason that I intend to put an end to this exhausting checkmate.'

'What do you mean?'

'I will tell you the truth, because what else could I do with the woman I love? Rinaldo degli Albizzi has always been a coward. He betrayed the very city that years before had raised him to the highest of ranks, but he will never forget the humiliation of having been exiled from Florence and for years has been plotting to return like the snake he is. Filippo Maria Visconti, the Duke of Milan, yearns for an opportunity and has entrusted his captain, Niccolò Piccinino, with planning an attack. This is what our spies tell us. But Piccinino has made a mistake that is as serious as it is fatal – and it is the same one that I myself made all those years ago. He's waiting. For too long. It doesn't matter much that he continues to conquer – and then lose – castles of little importance in an attempt to annoy or threaten Florence, because by doing that, he only gives us the opportunity to prepare ourselves. And you're right when you say that my desire to strengthen relations with Pope Eugene IV is part of that preparation. But what you must understand, my love, is that this final confrontation can no longer be avoided. The moment comes when a destiny must be fulfilled and therefore, sooner or later, it will happen, and neither you nor I can prevent it. So I ask you to be strong one last time. I don't know how long it will take, but that day will come, and when it does, I hope you will be at my side.'

'As always,' she said, tears streaming down her flushed cheeks.

Cosimo embraced her.

'As always, my love. I beg your forgiveness. I know I ask a lot of you, but try to understand that this will be the last time, the final obstacle that separates us from peace and prosperity. Fate has not always been kind to us and I know that I have made my mistakes, but destiny is something that a man builds for himself and his loved ones. I have a feeling that what is about to happen will bring us fulfilment and that once it is over, peace and harmony will finally reign over our beloved city.'

'I hope so, my love,' said Contessina, 'but I'm frightened of the day when our destiny will be fulfilled, because things don't always go as we have hoped or planned. If I'm honest, I hope that day will never come.'

Cosimo said nothing and simply embraced her harder.

'I'd like to stay like this for the rest of my life,' said Contessina, 'but that cannot be. Hug me again, Cosimo, because fate will once again come to separate us. I feel it.'

And even though she was now calm, Contessina remained in his arms. He felt a strange and gloomy apprehension in his heart, but tried not to dwell upon it. Everything would be all right, he said to himself.

Even though he knew he was lying.

47

The Confession

She had waited for him all day. He had arrived in the heat of the newly begun summer, while the flaming July sun blazed down on the walls of the castle and the air around it.

Reinhardt had been covered in dust, sweat and blood. Laura had helped him remove his armour and had drawn him a bath, with the water not too hot, just the way he liked it.

When he had stepped into the tub, savouring the water's heat, she had undone her dress and stood naked in front of him. Her cinnamon skin was lit by sunlight filtering through the large windows, a faint scar stretching out like an irregular thread along her tapered, muscular leg.

She had looked him in the eye and saw, in that moment, something in him that had changed forever. A sense of anger and torment gnawed away inside him like a cage full of rats, and perhaps not even she could pacify him.

She had decided to confront the issue directly, the way she always had done in life, and had climbed into the tub next to him, but he hadn't even given her time to touch him, hadn't been able to wait a moment longer. Silence was a pain that he could no longer bear, and the truth lodged in the bottom of his heart had come flooding out.

Finally he had found the courage to talk and confess his shame – a shame she knew he had nurtured all those years.

And now it was as if the Devil had come to ask him to settle his account for his life – as though by hiding the man he really was, he had stolen it from someone else.

He had begun to tell Laura what she had thought she had already guessed.

But none of it was what she had expected.

Reinhardt spoke in a voice breaking with torment, each sentence another step along that journey through evil and deceit.

'I knew I had them on my heels,' he said. 'I started running, but it was too late.'

He stopped again. For a moment he seemed to hesitate while Laura looked at him as though she could guess what he was about to say. In a sense both of them had always known that the strange spell which bound them together would one day break. And that when it did, they would suffer savagely.

'Poaching wasn't the brightest idea, but I was hungry. I'd been wounded in an ambush and then bitten by a fox. How it managed to bite me I've no idea, but as tiny as it was, its teeth had sunk into my flesh like razors. After it happened, I didn't feel like myself. For a couple of days my head kept spinning. I kept having strange spasms, and I felt incredibly hot, as though I were being consumed by fire.'

'Like now?' she asked.

'It wasn't a sense of guilt, it was physical – a disease, something eating up my mind. In any case, I was wearing a Swiss mercenary uniform, which wasn't going to help my chances. I was starving and I needed shelter, and there I was running through the woods with dogs on my heels and voices shouting from the darkness of the trees. I kept the deer on my shoulders. But I couldn't run any more. I was exhausted. So I decided to stop and wait.'

'Why are you telling me this?' she moaned. 'Why must you take everything from me?' She said it softly, as though saying it any louder would make the pain even more intense.

But it could never have been worse than that moment.

'Because I want you to know what kind of a man I am,' he continued. 'As soon as the hounds appeared in the clearing, one of them broke away from the rest and leapt up at me, trying to rip out my throat. I managed to keep a cool head. I dodged to the side and stuck a dagger in it, and then kept stabbing. I got rid of a second dog with a kick and pulled out my sword, but then two gamekeepers appeared. They couldn't have been alone, but I couldn't see anyone else. And they were dressed in bright colours – leather tunics with six red balls on a gold background.'

Laura began to cry. She went back to that night and to the yellow-eyed man, and suddenly felt with absolute certainty that her entire life had been a lie. That she had become the woman she was by a simple whim of destiny. She said nothing though, simply weeping so hard that it seemed it would break her in two.

'When they saw the dog with its belly ripped open at my feet and the other yelping – I think its leg was broken – they drew their swords and flung themselves at me. But things didn't go as they had imagined. I heard the first blade whistling through the air and managed to duck out of the way just in time. The sword went over my head and the man was left defenceless. His abdomen was exposed and he was unsteady from the lunge, and my blade found his belly and slashed it open. He fell to his knees and dropped his sword, and when he saw what had happened, the other man hesitated for a moment. That moment cost him dear. I brought my dagger down on his foot, pinning it to the ground, and then I slit his throat with my sword. The other dogs had retreated, whining – they must have been frightened by the fury in me. At that point, I took the tunic off the man I had just killed and put it on. I took his boots too, and rummaged through their bags and stole a dozen florins.'

Laura felt as though she was dying. She had hoped to the last that he wouldn't say those words. Slowly, she climbed out of the tub. Just the idea of being near him at that moment made her stomach turn. She didn't blame him for what had happened but could do nothing to prevent the instinctive feeling of revulsion that his presence was causing her.

Schwartz, unable to stem his torrent of words, cut her more deeply than a thousand swords.

'Desperate and half-mad, I put the deer back on my shoulders and ran until I collapsed at the mouth of a cave. I staggered inside and fell into a faint. I don't know how long for – I was in the grip of a fever. When I was at least able to crawl, I lit a fire, butchered the deer, roasted the meat and ate it. By the end of what must have been the third day I was feeling better, even though I was still delirious and having muscle spasms. My eyes were burning terribly. When I felt as though I could walk, I put a little meat in the bag and set off.

There was a fire devouring me from within – a thirst, drying me up. I couldn't quench it – it was agonizing. I had to unburden myself somehow, but I didn't know how to do it. The day before, when I had come out of my delirium, I had also felt that excruciating need. Once out of the woods, I came across a road and from there I continued on foot until I saw a cart. It was dusk. I discovered a pair of horses, untethered. The owner must be away. I climbed into the cart. I was looking for clothes to replace that tunic – it was torn and too showy – but inside I found a beautiful girl with black hair and green eyes. What happened next... you know all too well. You still bear the scars.'

Laura stood there immobile, saying nothing. She looked at him one last time and was filled with a depthless bitterness. Her tears had dried and she felt an indescribable emptiness overcome her. She remained silent. She heard him climb out of the tub, dry himself and then get dressed.

'Get out,' she said, 'and never seek me out again. And if by chance you happen to encounter me, you would do well not to look at me, because I might kill you.'

He did as she said. He would never see her again.

June 1440

48

Towards the Battlefield

Contessina had noticed how tired he was. In fact, he seemed more exhausted than merely tired. Cosimo had given her a sweet, reassuring smile, as he always did, but this time she felt that the danger at their doorstep was so great that it might overwhelm them. Contessina had an ominous feeling that the war against Milan might prove fatal.

'Swear to me that you'll come back,' she had said with tears in her eyes. 'There was no need for this war. Why did you do it? Why did you and Lorenzo decide to cause us this new pain? Was exile not sufficient for you? Was it not enough to know you were at the mercy of your enemies, a step away from death, while you were locked up in the Alberghetto? Why must you Medici always seek to challenge fate? Try and shape it as you wish, as you yourself said, without succeeding?'

Questions, just questions. They had come to her lips like some ungovernable army, a storm of questions that rose up from the depths of her heart demanding explanations for this new vigil that was being imposed upon her. She would wait, of course, and she would honour her husband with fasting and prayer. But why should their lives always be hanging from a thread that threatened to break at any moment?

She knew that nothing would stop him, though. Not this time. Not after what had happened over the last decade. How could he tolerate another attempt by Albizzi to take back Florence?

He would go to war, and with him Lorenzo. She had long known that, in spite of everything, the moment would arrive. It didn't matter how many churches he built, how many works of art he funded or how many offices of the bank he opened through hard work and self-denial: as long as Rinaldo degli Albizzi and Filippo Maria Visconti were strong, there would be no peace for Florence.

'I have to go, my love. I cannot avoid it this time. I must be on the battlefield. Together with my brother – and with my cousin Bernardetto. He will lead our men. I want to show that I am not afraid to face the responsibilities that leadership imposes.'

'But it's ridiculous! Let the soldiers do the fighting!'

'I am not so mad as to go rushing to the front line; I'm no man-at-arms. But I intend to be there and be close to the soldiers who are fighting for us. Don't you understand: they have to see me and know that I believe in the league and support this alliance against Filippo Maria Visconti? Otherwise all my promises will ring hollow. And that is something I cannot allow.'

Contessina lowered her head and embraced him; then she wiped away her tears.

'Promise me that you will keep yourself away from the fighting,' she said softly.

'I care too much about my family to let myself be blinded by anger. I know my limits, as does Lorenzo.'

And with that, Cosimo had kissed her on the lips, mounted his horse and was gone.

Contessina had watched as he joined his brother and they set off for the city gates. She had watched them until they disappeared from sight.

She turned to the wonderful David that her husband had commissioned from one of his favourite artists, Donatello, to embellish the courtyard of the Palazzo Medici. She stared at the figure with its sleek muscles and angelic features. There was something ineffable in that face, she thought. As though you could never fully understand the nature of the thoughts that had animated the artist as he created it, and even less those of the figure that stared boldly from the pedestal.

Just like her husband's eyes that morning when he had left. His usually serene gaze had been defiant.

Cosimo and Lorenzo were on their way to meet Bernardetto de' Medici, Micheletto Attendolo and Ludovico Mocenigo. They would face the men led by Niccolò Piccinino, who had been quartered at Borgo Sansepolcro. Piccinino had seemed invincible over the last few years, and the fact did nothing to reassure her.

She prayed. It was the only thing there was to do.

Reinhardt Schwartz understood perfectly what Niccolò Piccinino's intentions were. He had been fighting alongside him for long enough to know the way the soldier of fortune thought.

No one was more devious than Piccinino, and that was perhaps the key to his popularity among the mercenaries. He had gone to Perugia with the permission of the papal governor, had entered the city by the Porta di Sant'Angelo at the head of five hundred men on horseback and had dismounted from the saddle in front of the Palazzo della Signoria. There he had arrested the treasurer Michele Benini on charges of embezzlement and had persuaded the governor, the Archbishop of Naples, to leave the city with a message for Eugene IV. He had received – or perhaps it would be more accurate to say had confiscated – eight thousand ducats, and had returned to his troops far richer than when he had left them.

He had then gone on to plunder Mugello in a surprise attack and devastate the surrounding countryside until Filippo Maria Visconti had asked, or rather, ordered him to attack Florence. The Duke of Milan was furious that Piccinino had waited as long as he had and now he demanded an exemplary victory.

A victory of the cruellest and most prestigious, but also the most difficult, kind.

Piccinino had decided to quarter with his men that evening in Sansepolcro, on the slopes of the mountains that divided the upper Tiberina valley from the Chiana valley.

His company of a thousand horsemen had been joined by another two thousand men from the surrounding countryside, all hoping for easy loot, Piccinino's reputation for ruthlessness and bravery being a guarantee of success. As always, he had relied on hatred and envy, feelings that the people of Sansepolcro nurtured in abundance for their neighbours in Anghiari, a town a little more than two leagues distant.

The plan was to overrun the town and then swoop down like a flock of crows upon the city of the Medici. But they knew for a fact that the men of the league were camped out there waiting patiently for Piccinino to mobilize – the slopes of the hill of Anghiari were dark with their tents. They were all present: the Genoese and Venetians, the papal troops and even the Florentines had arrived. It was a battle whose outcome would determine a new geometry of power between states.

But the real issue was that the Milanese were going into that battle without any real strategy. All that wandering around Tuscany like a swarm of locusts was no way to engage in battle, especially because they had now lost the element of surprise and, despite the two thousand new men gathered together from around Sansepolcro, were clearly outnumbered.

And now the rascal Piccinino was looking at him and seemed ready to come up with some marvellous solution for obtaining a victory.

Only a fool could be optimistic in a situation like this, especially when stirred up by Albizzi, who over the course of the last month had revealed all his limitations. Schwartz had always known Albizzi was a great conspirator, but hadn't realized quite how depraved he actually was. Over the last few days, however, he'd had the opportunity to discover the worst sides of his former master. Frustrated and disappointed by the many defeats he had suffered over the years and made insecure and angry by a wait that smelt of death, Albizzi had become a shadow of the man he had once been. He would have inspired pity if it hadn't been for his cowardice and violence.

In any case, they would attack, despite everything promising the worst possible outcome. Schwartz had been riding all day and had hoped to be able to get a few hours' sleep in. His ears still rang with the desperate screams of the previous nights, when Niccolò Piccinino had massacred the population of Monte Castello di Vibio: the cries of the men killed in the streets, the sobbing of the children, the screams of the women raped on the tables of their looted houses, which were then burned to the ground. And the crazed expression on the face of Albizzi, who had enjoyed the slaughter.

They had even stolen the cattle.

But he had the feeling that Niccolò still nurtured some other impulse he wished to satisfy.

The presence of the league was the perfect excuse – the ideal justification for going on the attack the next day. There was, in Niccolò, a longing for glory that seemed to increase the more difficult the undertaking at hand.

'My dear Reinhardt,' he said – and as he spoke, his thick moustaches could not conceal the shining tips of his unusually long, fang-like canines – 'it is my intention to attack the village of Anghiari tomorrow, where I count upon collecting many spoils. Furthermore, the Duke of Milan believes that Anghiari is the gateway to Florence and I confess that, for once, his theory seems to me both lucid and accurate. That, therefore, is what we will do. I want you to lead the men on the attack. I will trick them into thinking I am returning to Romagna but when you reach the Forche bridge, while the light cavalry is proceeding along the road to Citerna, you, at the head of the heavy cavalry and the foot soldiers, will cross the river and attack Anghiari, catching the troops of the league altogether unprepared.'

What wonderful news, thought Schwartz.

'I know you would have preferred something simpler but there is a surprise awaiting you in your tent. Partial compensation for what I owe you. And, if I know you well, it is the most agreeable kind of compensation possible.'

'I imagine that Rinaldo degli Albizzi and the other gentlemen will be holed up well away from the battlefield.'

'You imagine right.'

'I also imagine that I cannot question your orders.'

'Your insight is second only to your courage.'

'Then, if that is the case, I'll go get some sleep.'

'Rest your limbs. The alarm will come well after dawn – we attack during the hottest part of the day, when the sun is at its zenith – right when those scoundrels least expect it. Only a lunatic would think of attacking at that time.'

'Yes,' said Schwartz laconically, resigned now to the inevitability of tomorrow.

And, so saying, he headed towards the tents.

He had a good idea of who might be waiting for him, and in his heart he was afraid. Of himself and his own cowardice, of course. Of how he had forever ruined the life of Laura, to whom life had given little enough. Only lies and violence, and he was the principal cause of both.

The weight of the guilt that had been preying upon his mind would finish him off during the battle if the men of the league didn't do for him first.

After what had happened, he wasn't ready to see her. Because she was certainly the person waiting for him in the tent: Reinhardt had no doubt of it.

He hated himself, but, drawing on all the determination of which he was capable, he decided not to go to his tent and headed instead for an abandoned barn. He would be able to rest better with his mind free of irksome thoughts. If he survived the battle, Laura could say whatever she wanted to him, even kill him if she thought he deserved it. And he certainly did. But until then he had no intention of allowing any thought to occupy his head other than that of preserving his own skin.

The next day would be a bloodbath, and he would need all his skills to still be standing at the end of it.

49

The Bridge at Forche

From the walls of Anghiari, Cosimo observed the plain below. There was something odd about the torrid calm of that morning: it was too quiet. At the first light of dawn, Sansepolcro had been feverish, the town a wasps' nest of activity, and now, after all that clanging of metal and weapons, it seemed to doze in the placid calm of the sun that was flooding the sky with golden light.

He had spoken about it with Lorenzo and Ludovico Mocenigo and especially with Micheletto Attendolo and Bernardetto de' Medici, his cousin. He couldn't be sure but he would have wagered that rogue Piccinino was plotting something. His fame for cunning and butchery was legendary, and Cosimo had decided to go out with a few hundred men to the bridge at Forche in order to safeguard their troops and Anghiari itself.

There were several miles of fields between Anghiari and Sansepolcro but Cosimo had the feeling that the enemy commander was planning some trick to shorten the distance his infantrymen and cavalry would have to cover in the open: he would want to guarantee himself the benefit of surprise and catch Cosimo and the troops unprepared.

Thus he had asked the Venetians to come with him through the June heat towards the road that in one direction led to Citerna and in the other led straight to Anghiari

In all likelihood he was mistaken, but he'd rather return to the camp on the slopes of the hill of Anghiari after some time sweating in the saddle than discover that the Duke of Milan's men were swooping down upon them in a surprise attack to raze the city to the ground. A defeat caused by negligence would throw open the gates for an attack on Florence.

The sun was high in the sky and its rays beat down upon the fields. The hay had just been harvested and its dense, heady perfume floated through the humid air. They had advanced cautiously and after less than an hour had stopped near the Forche bridge.

Cosimo snorted with discomfort. Sweat poured down his neck, drenching his chest and hips under the jacket and armour. He tried to cool off in the shade of a tree that, standing alone, projected a tiny shadow upon the ground, and his eyes burned in the light of that torrid day as he raised his flask to his dry lips.

The water was warm, but at least it calmed the fiery torment that burned in his throat. He remained on his horse. Hidden behind the treeline, the men were tired and wanted to rest but Cosimo and Lorenzo and even more so the captains urged them to keep their eyes open and stay alert. A flock of ravens swept across the blue sky, croaking a macabre chant.

As time passed, Cosimo and his companions gradually began to realize that they must have been mistaken. And yet there was something about that scorching calm which rang false.

It was when they were about to turn their horses around and return to Anghiari that they discovered they had been right. In front of them they saw a dark cloud of dust, which was drawing closer. Soon, Cosimo was able to distinguish the helmets and cuirasses, the swords and armour, the banners with the black Visconti viper and the coat of arms bearing Niccolò Piccinino's crouched leopard.

'They're heading this way,' said Cosimo.

'There is no doubt of it,' confirmed Mocenigo.

As the column of men approached, the situation became clear. Part of the ranks continued to head off towards Citerna and Romagna, but the bulk of the soldiers, infantrymen and heavy cavalry began to run silently towards the bridge.

Piccinino had enlisted a noticeable number of lancers in his surprise attack. It was an impressive plan: to launch a disruptive initial strike would guarantee control of the battlefield right from the start; and reducing the length of the battle was certain to affect its outcome.

'It was just as you said, Cosimo,' whispered Micheletto Attendolo. 'They trusted in the heat of the day and our laziness to reduce the distance across the open ground – cut across the bridge to surprise us with the sun high in the sky while we were locked up indoors waiting for evening. What a son of a whore Piccinino is!'

'He always has been.'

'True. But now we have a problem...' continued Attendolo.

'There are too few of us,' said Lorenzo bitterly.

Mocenigo nodded. 'Someone has to go back and tell our army to hurry here or we'll be overrun,' he said. 'Cosimo: you and your brother take two of my men with you and bring the reinforcements.'

'And what will you do in the meantime?'

'We will do everything possible to defend the bridge. Come, there isn't a moment to lose. Make your horses fly if you want to get home in one piece.'

Without waiting for him to say anything more, Cosimo and Lorenzo turned their mounts around and, escorted by the two Venetians, galloped off towards Anghiari.

As soon as the infantrymen began to run, Reinhardt realized that something was wrong. He thought he'd caught the glimpse of a ray of light glinting off steel on the other side of the bridge – a helmet? It hadn't stopped the men from running, through, proceeding with long strides even though they were dripping with sweat under the blazing sun. This had not been a good idea. It was clear to him now that sacrificing strength and energy for surprise was a mistake. The men would arrive at the gates of Anghiari exhausted, and the manoeuvre, however well thought-out, felt like a gamble. After all, the entire operation was based on the belief that no one suspected that the larger part of Piccinino's army was not actually retreating but was pouring out on to the plain.

The captain had wagered on distracting the enemy, but what if he had been mistaken? They would be sending the men off to be slaughtered, which was exactly what Schwartz was afraid might happen.

And that was without even considering the night he had spent, which had tested him more than he thought possible. To hide his black heart from the only woman – worse yet, from the only living *creature* – for whom he had ever cared had been an experience which had mortified his very soul. He felt a pain within him so deep that he was certain he would die, despite having avoided seeing her the night before for precisely that reason. It was thus with little conviction that he sat astride his horse, sweating like a pig and trying to figure out what the hell awaited him on the other side of that damn bridge.

He didn't have to wait long to find out.

Even before the first men could cross it, dark clouds of arrows filled the warm air with their flickering, lethal shadows. Their fletchings as colourful as decorations, the arrows embedded themselves in the chests of his men, their iron heads finding lethal passage through the fissures in their hardened steel armour. There were screams of pain and shock. Bodies slumped to the ground and on to the yellow grass of the field, some falling into the waters of the stream with dull splashes.

He saw a pair of infantrymen attempting to pull the arrows from their necks while another threw his arms up, gasping for air: he had tried to escape but an arrow had hit him in the back. He dropped his sword and collapsed to the ground, his face a mixture of anger and amazement at his absurd and unexpected death.

The bowstrings of the enemy archers were again pulled taut and once more launched their awful volley with a deadly hiss, and the entire front line of cavalry and mounted infantry was mown down by another hail of arrows. The bridge was acting like a hellish funnel that made the men huddled helplessly at the entrance the perfect target for the archers on the other side, who had clearly been waiting to ambush them. Worse still, the Milanese were trapped under their dying horses, creating a wall of flesh and cuirasses which made things even easier for the archers of the league.

It was slaughter.

The waters of the small river reddened with blood.

Reinhardt could hide no longer. He decided to lead his vanguard in an attack and see what happened, but to have some small hope of success he ordered the infantry to fan out and wade the stream on foot, so as to circumvent the enemy and attack their flanks.

He didn't know if he would be able to turn the outcome of the battle around, but at least in that way the Milanese wouldn't be the easy targets they were now.

He hoped in his heart that he was right.

50

The Duel

The horses were foaming at the mouth, their glistening muscles contracting in the sunlight. Cosimo and Lorenzo galloped like madmen, certain that the result not only of that first skirmish but of the battle as a whole depended upon their speed.

Cosimo knew that the number of troops the league had managed to assemble far exceeded those of Piccinino – but as they were by the walls of Anghiari they were completely useless. Attendolo certainly wouldn't abandon his position, but neither could he allow his few men to be massacred with impunity, leaving the road open for Visconti's forces.

At that moment they were facing the advance guard, but when they had left the Forche bridge the bulk of the Piccinino's troops had yet to arrive – and as the number of opponents increased, the Venetians would certainly find themselves in trouble.

Cosimo could not allow that.

He spurred his horse on harder still, and the creature responded, increasing its pace. Such was the speed of the noble animal that Cosimo felt as though he were riding some mythological beast.

He dug his heels in again.

Fields flashed past his eyes in an iridescent yellow blur. Lorenzo was at his side and Cosimo thanked God that he had his brother with him. He thought of how much they had been through together. It was only a moment, a fleeting image of what they had done, and yet it put a smile on his face and renewed his confidence and energy.

They soon came in sight of the league's camp outside the gates of Anghiari. Cosimo signalled to the sentries and the Venetians waved the standards bearing the Lion of San Marco while the Medici's men did the same with theirs.

'Quickly, men, hurry!' cried Cosimo. 'There's fighting at the Forche bridge! Follow me!'

While he shouted, his horse had already reached the centre of the camp and spun about in great agitation, its eyes huge and its hooves pawing at the beaten earth, until, suddenly arching its back, it reared up and came crashing furiously back down to earth. Cosimo called to Simonetto from Castel San Pietro and his papal troops.

'Simonetto!' he shouted. 'Take your men to the Forche bridge. And hurry, otherwise there'll be nothing left of Micheletto and the Venetians!'

The situation was rapidly deteriorating. After an encouraging start as the archers had mown down the enemy's front lines, the Visconti armies now seemed to have regrouped, their ranks filled out by the arrival of Astorre Manfredi's men, and had begun returning fire and undertaking sorties. The action had soon shifted to the centre of the small stone bridge. Neither side was willing to concede ground and Ludovico Mocenigo, who had no intention of allowing the defensive line to be broken, was at the centre of the battle.

Drenched with sweat and gore, he swung his sword downwards from right to left, severing an opponent's limb, then pirouetted and swung again, horizontally this time. A trail of blood sprayed through the air. It was becoming impossible to move because of the corpses crowding the floor of the bridge, which was covered with a streaming broth of blood and bowels. The stench – of death and of excrement of those whose intestines had emptied themselves in terror – was repulsive. The fiery disc of the sun beat down relentlessly.

Ludovico dodged a sword and at the same moment an arrow whistled by a few inches from his eyes and stuck into the chest of one of the duke's men who had been sneaking up behind him.

In his attempt to hold off the enemy, he had unwittingly ventured from his half of the bridge. He dared not hope to force Astorre Manfredi's men back – especially now that he saw a face as familiar as it was terrible appear in front of him.

It belonged to a man wielding a halberd whose razor-sharp blade was plunging between the hardened steel plates of his opponents' armour. The warrior manipulated it with incredible skill, whirling it through the air like the vanes of a windmill and smashing his way through the defences as though it were a ram, taking advantage of its length to shred his opponents.

At first, Ludovico did not realize who it was, but then that face, with its thick blond moustache and light-blue, almost liquid, eyes took him back to a few years earlier: to a party in Venice – and to the man who had defended the woman who had tried to take Lorenzo de' Medici's life.

And in that moment, when Ludovico understood for certain whom he was facing, the Swiss mercenary was already upon him.

When Schwartz saw him, he smiled and threw the halberd aside, drawing another sword – a gigantic *Zweihänder* which he swung through the air with superhuman strength.

When their blades made contact, Mocenigo had to summon every ounce of strength he still possessed not to relinquish his grip on the hilt and be thrown over the parapet of the bridge.

A murderous rage blazed in the man's eyes.

'You!' he shouted at him when he recognized him. 'Curse you, Mocenigo! You will fall by my hand today, or my name's not Schwartz.' And so saying, he swung the gigantic sword upwards. Both hands tightly grasping the grip of his own weapon, Mocenigo parried. His face was dripping with sweat and his arms trembled under the impact of Schwartz's blade. He knew that this duel would require everything he had – and he was already exhausted.

He tried, though, to show contempt for the risk and for his adversary.

'We'll see about that!' he shouted, and swung twice at him. Schwartz parried easily and responded with a flurry of rapid slashes. Mocenigo was forced to retreat and realized that it was not only he who was retracing his steps – so was the entire company of Attendolo, who was leading his men in an attempt not to cede too much ground. The ranks were thinning and there were now more dead than you could count in the ranks of the Venetians. But looking behind him, he saw a river of iron and leather flowing from the camp towards the bridge.

'Hold steady!' he shouted, knowing how ridiculous his order was, since the Visconti militias far outnumbered them and were wading across the stream to cut them off at the same time as they were crowding the bridge. They were a ring of armour, blades and leather that threatened to crush them like a pincer.

It was only a matter of time. And Mocenigo knew that there was very little of it left.

'You have no hope,' shouted Schwartz, as though reading his thoughts. Illuminated by a cold light, his terrible face was covered with blood, and saliva sprayed from his mouth as he swung the deadly *Zweihänder* down upon him once more.

One parry, then another. Their blades clashed and Mocenigo found himself with one knee on the ground. Schwartz was wearing down his resistance. His strength almost entirely gone, Mocenigo attempted a final, desperate thrust, which he seemed to rip from his very soul.

But the Swiss, who now towered over him, parried it with ease, knocking his sword out of his hands. It flew through the air, spinning like a pinwheel until it landed blade down, sticking out of the soft, sodden earth and vibrating like some ribald cross. Mocenigo threw open his arms and waited.

The blow came soon afterwards.

*

Cosimo galloped desperately towards the bridge. Bernadetto de' Medici and Simonetto of Castel Pietro were racing ahead, their horses fresher than his. He was tired, and barely lucid now. The men of the league were approaching the Forche bridge and he saw the vanguard collide with the enemy, their swords clanging against those of their adversaries, the cavalry in a fierce melee cutting down the infantry and engaging Astorre Manfredi's men in battle.

All around was only blood, dust and sweat.

Suddenly, he heard a shout that froze his soul. He looked around him, searching for the source of that cry. It echoed across the battlefield as though emanating from some god of war.

Then Cosimo saw him.

With one hand, Reinhardt Schwartz was leaning on the hilt of a giant sword whose tip rested upon the ground.

In the other he held the head of Ludovico Mocenigo.

For a moment, Cosimo couldn't understand what was happening. When he did, he cried out in anguish.

At that moment, a hail of arrows came from somewhere to the side of him, mowing down Visconti's men.

Hell had arrived upon the earth.

51

Shame

Cosimo had never seen anything like it. The quarrels rained down from the heavens as though a legion of warrior angels had launched a storm of bolts upon them.

He turned his horse around and sought shelter. Only a fool would remain in the middle of the fray and risk being skewered by a stray missile.

Wave followed wave of quarrels, ceaselessly, slaughtering the Visconti soldiers.

Sheltering further back, Cosimo watched as the Genoese crossbow squads unleashed a storm of steel spikes from the slopes of the Anghiari hill, filling the valley with death.

★

Laura stared at the battlefield as tears streamed down her face. In the midst of the bloodshed she saw Reinhardt fighting like a lion. Instead of running away, it seemed that he actually *sought* death, dancing with it, attempting to seduce it, begging to be taken along with it.

At the end of that accursed story, it was death that he loved more than anyone else.

More than her.

She had hoped to have a chance to speak with him, and find a way to spend those last moments together, because she had sensed that he would not return in one piece from that fateful battle.

It was a foreboding – one which she could not explain but which she felt clearly and desperately. Something that she wished she could have prevented yet which was taking place before her eyes.

And she stood watching helplessly, a profound feeling of guilt growing within her like malignant ivy, its stems stretching out until they stifled her breathing.

When he had told her the truth she had felt overwhelmed. How could he have kept silent about it all that time? She had loved her tormentor and persecuted the wrong people. The Medici were not innocents, but they had become the targets of her hatred for a reason that was false – and even, in its tragic way, comical.

And yet Reinhardt had defended her. In the drama of her life, he had been the only one who had stood by her. He had protected her; he had stayed at her side.

Had he done it out of pity? Out of compassion? Out of lust?

In spite of the questions that tormented her, Laura knew the answer. She harboured it in the bottom of her heart and, in some strange way, she had always known it: there was something so perverse in their relationship that it could only have belonged to two lost souls like them.

And yet it was the most beautiful thing that destiny had offered her.

There were sparks of love, though, she was sure of it, and she missed those moments terribly. Despite his being a violent, black-hearted man, he hadn't been in his right mind when he had done what he had done. His fault lay in the omission, in the lie, in the silence. But were the other men she had known in her life better than him? Rinaldo degli Albizzi? Palla Strozzi? Filippo Maria Visconti? The monsters who had been treating her like a whore since she had first worn the leash of that accursed merchant? And the lords of Florence, who didn't hesitate to bribe and scheme to get their way? Who bought men to get them on their side? How much honour was there in their behaviour?

For this, Laura was now repentant.

Repentant that she had not accepted that broken love. Repentant that she had hated a man for his silence and his fears. Repentant that she had not known how to take back her choices.

She looked at the battlefield and felt her bitterness grow.

She wept then, because she realized she had thrown the better part of her life away. She cared not whether it had been a lot or a little – as far as she was concerned, it had been too much.

And now she didn't even have him any more, and she never would again.

She stared at the steel glinting in the sunlight. Reinhardt swung his sword, ending the lives of his opponents. She didn't care – let him kill a hundred more. That was the way things had gone. She had chosen to go up against the Medici, and now the Medici were killing her lover.

Was that what she wanted?

To stand there and watch?

She was sick of it.

Sick of being the courtesan of a man she despised.

Albizzi stood with the duke's commissaries, well protected among the supplies and careful to keep as far away from the battlefield as possible. Lying in the bed of a nearby cart was a stack of swords. Laura took one, slipped it into a scabbard, secured it to her belt and then, turning her back on that gang of cowards who stood there watching, she ran towards the battlefield.

Towards her lover.

And towards the dream of being a different woman.

Lorenzo watched as the hail of missiles filled the heavens, a dark cloud that blotted out the blue of the sky before it rained down upon the battlefield, mowing down their enemies.

It had been a worthwhile attack. Under the aerial barrage, the ranks of the enemy were thinning out.

At that moment, the first bombards – iron cannisters which, once they had been positioned in the ground, were capable of unleashing hell on earth – roared angrily from the rear.

And he saw it.

Hell on earth. He watched the artillerymen loading them and the projectiles flying in a terrible parabola that, after sketching a deadly arc through the blue sky, struck among the ranks of Astorre Manfredi's men.

Upon contact with the ground, they exploded, tearing the soldiers apart, raising red towers of lightning and fire where they fell. Grass, mud and flesh flew through the air, turning it into a tempest of pain.

Lorenzo stood immobile while the deafening roars echoed across the battlefield.

The soldiers faced one another as they tried to take the bridge, fighting in a wild melee, the frightened enemy ranks backing away from the devastating explosions.

The banners were covered with dirt and blood.

Standing with the rearguard and the reserves, Lorenzo fell to his knees. He could not believe what he was seeing, because it was unthinkable.

No plan for hegemony could justify the genocide of these men who were being slaughtered in the name of union.

In the heat of that cursed afternoon, he struggled to breathe.

Seeing death so close at hand was something that could not be described, let alone understood. All they could do was stand there and watch, while Lorenzo's disgust filled him with a burning shame.

He and his brother would found their government on blood. That pain, that massacre, would be an accursed legacy to be reckoned with every day and every night. And they would have to govern with the images of that carnage forever burned in their minds, always aware of an apocalypse that must never again be repeated.

Never again, he said to himself. Never again. And yet in a way he was grateful to God. In witnessing that slaughter he had become aware of a horror that he and his brother had avoided so many times in the past, protecting themselves through the mechanisms of power – unwilling, almost, to get their hands dirty. Now, though, he had seen the blood, and the lives shattered in the mud of the battlefield, and he could no longer ignore it.

He prayed in his heart that the battle would end soon.

His brother had promised that a new unity of kingdoms would emerge from it.

Lorenzo truly hoped that he was right.

July 1440

52

The Hanging

The noise was the first thing that struck Cosimo as he climbed the steps up to the platform. He took his place on one of the wooden benches which had been set up for the Eight of Guard and looked down at the hundreds, perhaps thousands, of people crowded together before him, their angry eyes full of a desire to see blood shed.

The crowd's roar surged when the wagon carrying the prisoner to the gallows entered the square.

'Schwartz! Schwartz! Schwartz!' shouted male and female voices, as if his name were a curse – and perhaps it was.

'Death to the traitor!' cried someone else, and the crowd went wild, others shouting insults and threats, or throwing rotten fruit and vegetables at the man on the wagon.

Cosimo studied Schwartz's face and was surprised to see an expression of profound peace – of bitter calm, as though he had finally surrendered and, in surrendering, had achieved a tranquillity which could be touched by nothing and nobody.

Schwartz cared nothing about dying. His arms were bare and tied to a beam of wood and his long, filthy, reddish-blond hair fell in front of his face like dirty twine. He was on his knees, his ankles in chains, and yet he kept his chest puffed out and his back erect.

He showed incredible strength, given all that he had endured. The gaolers in the dungeons of the Palazzo del Podestà had not spared him punishment and torture: the pale skin of his broad chest was partly covered by a black jacket, now tattered and torn, his face was a mask of cuts and bruises and his lips were swollen and encrusted with congealed blood. His pale-blue eyes had turned dark, like wells whose depths contained the pure essence of pain.

But none of that diminished the dignity and pride with which the soldier faced death, and Cosimo found himself admiring him. He had fought well. He had lost, but there was nothing dishonourable in that. It had taken at least six men to bring him down on the battlefield at Anghiari.

What a pointless waste of talent.

It would have been interesting to have a man like Schwartz in his service, he said to himself. But that was no longer possible.

He was shocked, though, by the cynicism and indifference he saw in himself. Had he become someone upon whom the death of a soldier made no impression at all?

When he had climbed the steps to the platform, he had thought he would feel pity and horror but it was as if all the politics, power, suffering and reversals of fortune had changed him more deeply than he had been willing to admit.

Had he so exercised the art of compromise and calculation that he was no longer even capable of recognizing the value of human life? He, who had known the humiliation of imprisonment and who, in order to escape the death which now awaited the man before him, had not hesitated to bribe his enemies?

He was not proud of himself, and the courage that Schwartz so brazenly displayed was the keenest humiliation he had ever endured.

But he was a leader, the lord of Florence, and he must do his duty for the good of his city. Perhaps he was not the best man of his day, but he would have time to expiate his faults and accept the good and the evil that governing Florence imposed on him. He would not shirk his destiny.

Not now that he had reached that point.

But he could not allow the execution to turn into a lynching either. For the last few days, Piazza della Signoria had been dominated by a colossal wooden structure: a black gallows it had taken a team of carpenters over a week to build. The platform was almost ten feet high and the gallows itself measured at least eight more and towered, sinister and terrible, over the ocean of people that crowded the square. Ravens perched upon it as though they too wanted to see the show. A long, thick rope ending in a noose hung threateningly from the crossbeam.

The executioner was a tall man who wore dark leather armour dotted with studs.

Schwartz deserved a proper execution, and Cosimo would grant him one. Hangings were a ritual celebration of being liberated from fear, but all too often they were also an occasion for the crowd to unleash its basest instincts. The Florentines – who had silently watched the many defeats their leaders had endured as they failed to take Lucca and fought long and hard against Volterra and Pisa – now saw in Anghiari the triumph that would open the door to further conquests and, more importantly, to a period of peace and prosperity.

But Cosimo had to govern that human ocean, and could not allow a thirst for revenge to prevail over the concept of justice.

At his side, the other members of the Eight of Guard, the supreme city magistrates in criminal matters, sat upon their benches. Their faces were blank, and they seemed more interested in the rich fabrics of their elegant robes than in what was taking place before them.

It was intensely hot.

The cart had reached the wooden platform and the city guards freed Reinhardt Schwartz's arms from the beam to which they had been tied and slotted them into fetters.

His shackles making a sinister jingling sound, the Swiss mercenary climbed the wooden staircase that led to the gallows.

The executioner pushed Schwartz under the rope and slipped his neck into the noose. He pulled it tight and the crowd roared.

Reinhardt was no longer afraid. He never had been, really, except of revealing the truth to Laura. Despite the shouts of abuse and the rotten fruit hurled at him by the people who filled the square like a heaving ocean, and despite the executioner spitting in his face while he forced Schwartz's head into the noose with his huge hands, Schwartz had not taken his eyes off Cosimo de' Medici. Cosimo was perched on a bench on the raised platform along with the rest of the Eight of Guard and he stared back at Schwartz, but seemed to find it so hard to hold his gaze that in the end he'd had to look away.

It was a ridiculous little victory, but it put a sneer on Schwartz's face that could have been mistaken for a smile.

He knew that Cosimo de' Medici was now lord of Florence and that, with the victory at Anghiari, his dominion over those lands would become absolute. And deep in his heart, Reinhardt Schwartz hoped that power would strangle him.

Gaining power was one thing – keeping hold of it was another thing altogether.

In a sense, bowing out this way was actually a relief for him. He had fought well, he had honoured his ancestors, he had killed many enemies and he had loved a beautiful woman. Few men could dream of a life containing half the wonders his had.

Now that he was leaving it all behind, he realized that fact for the first time.

He had no regrets except for one that pitched on the tempestuous waves of his soul, and he decided to free himself from it.

'I love you, Laura!' he cried out, with all the breath he had in in his lungs.

He felt his throat burning with the beauty of her name. He had finally found the courage to utter the four words that he had denied himself his entire life.

Then he closed his eyes and waited for everything to vanish.

He heard the trapdoor open beneath his feet and his legs suddenly trod empty air while the rope jerked like a whip cracking.

The roar of the crowd filled the square.

He did not die immediately. It took some time. Seemingly endless moments, during which the rope choked his breathing and the air became heavy. Finally a storm of invisible needles filled his lungs.

He suffered, but in a last, desperate breath, while his body fought against death, his mind and his heart reached towards Laura.

He hoped that wherever she was, she was thinking about him.

And after that last moment of consciousness, he ceased to breathe.

53

Pity and Vendetta

Cosimo had shown no pity for Reinhardt in life, so he had therefore wanted to concede it to him in death. He had given the captain of the city guard instructions to hand the corpse over to the woman named Laura Ricci who would arrive to claim it that night.

He wasn't certain that she would come, but if she did, he wanted her to have the man's mortal remains. Friend or lover, he had certainly been important to her. At that point, Cosimo wanted one thing and one thing only: peace. And showing mercy to their enemies was a good way to begin pursuing that end.

The captain of the city guard hadn't understood his intentions but had promised upon his honour that he would enforce the unusual order, and Cosimo had thanked him before setting off for home.

Over the past few days, there had been one execution after another. It had been a bloodbath, and he was certain that with every hanging, with every beheading, the people in the square had lost some of their remaining humanity.

He repeated to himself that this would be the last execution, that the city must now leave behind it that season of horrors and think only of enjoying peace.

It would be upon that principle that he would found the government of the Republic.

His brother had had enough of it all and had taken refuge in the villa in Careggi. After all the madness Lorenzo had vowed to himself that he would gradually abandon the running of the bank as well as political life. Cosimo had asked him to reconsider, but he knew that it was hopeless.

It wasn't fair, he thought with a sigh as he approached his home.

He prayed that his wife and children would be merciful to him.

Laura wasn't satisfied.

The Medici had allowed her to have Reinhardt's corpse, but that night the hatred she already felt for them took on the colour of truth.

They held the city in the palm of their hand, and to get their way, they had destroyed lives on the battlefield and in the streets, hiding all the while behind the screen of justice.

After grabbing the sword and setting off at a run towards the battlefield of Anghiari, Laura had watched as men were thrown into the air by the explosions from the artillery, while others lay slumped on the ground in agony, bristling with crossbow bolts or lying wounded and mutilated.

Horrified, she had looked desperately around her for Reinhardt, hoping to catch sight of him somewhere, but had soon been overrun by the chaotic retreat of what was left of Piccinino's forces. She had received a blow to the head and fallen to the ground, covered in blood and dust.

When she had eventually come round, she had wandered the battlefield like a ghost. Schwartz did not seem to be among the dead. The smell was unbearable and the heat intensified the odours until they overwhelmed her senses. She had found a horse grazing on the dry yellow grass, far from the site of the battle along the road to Sansepolcro, had climbed into its saddle and had ridden away. And a week later, she was there, at the foot of the gallows. She had come with a small escort – guards that Filippo Maria Visconti had put at her disposal for when she travelled. They were Venetian traitors, so they would be mistaken for allies of Florence. They had hired a local gravedigger who, for a few ducats, had provided a wagon to transport the body.

When they had arrived, the captain of the city guard queried if she was Laura Ricci, as he had received orders from Cosimo de' Medici himself that she could take the body.

For a moment, Laura had thought it must be a trap, but then she had decided to trust the man. After all, what more did she have to lose?

Assisted by the Venetians, the gravedigger laid Schwartz's body on the cart.

The captain of the city guard had escorted Laura and the Venetians to the Porta di San Giorgio. After that, they had continued on their own, stopping in the middle of the night at a country villa whose owner had been well paid.

Laura had ordered Reinhardt's body carried into her room and laid upon a dark wooden table.

And there it was.

She looked at it, and now that she was finally alone, allowed herself to cry. Tears of forgiveness, for Reinhardt and for herself, and tears of guilt at having abandoned him.

When she could weep no more, she washed her face and hands and set about her work.

She went over to Reinhardt's body and began cleaning his mouth, nose, eyes and other orifices with a mixture of vinegar, lemon and marigold that she had prepared. It was difficult but she did a scrupulous job.

After applying a layer of olive oil soap she shaved him, so as to make his skin as smooth as possible to the touch; then, with soft sponges and wet linen cloths, she washed Reinhardt's powerful limbs.

He was as cold as marble and his skin, already pale in life, was almost blue, but she didn't care. He was still beautiful. For the washing she used iced water scented with rose petals. Next she massaged the body until her own muscles ached. It was exhausting, but it gave her infinite pleasure: she wanted to erase all signs of death.

After closing his magnificent blue eyes forever, she anointed his body with perfumed ointments and oils, so as to hide the odour that lingered in the air despite the size of the room, then sewed his lips shut with fine thread.

She wanted to do for him everything she had not been able to over that last year. She wanted to take care of his mortal remains as no other could. It was to be her ultimate declaration of love.

She would expiate her guilt and betrayal and nurture her obsession and, one day, her revenge.

When she had finished, she wrapped his body in bandages and linen cloths perfumed with mint and nettle.

By the time she was done, the sun was already high in the sky. She closed the curtains, letting only a faint ray of light filter through and returning the room to darkness, then sat down in a damask velvet armchair and tried to sleep.

But she could not.

Her mind was consumed by an overwhelming desire for vengeance. After the concentration and physical fatigue of the night, her imagination now wandered wildly in the darkest recesses of her soul.

She would dedicate herself to a single project.

All of the progeny of the Medici would be slaughtered. She would become for them as the eighth plague of Egypt. She would give birth to children and raise *them* in hatred for the Medici, and those children would one day be murderers and traitors, men capable of executing the descendants of Cosimo and Lorenzo.

She was still beautiful, she was fertile and she was shrewd, and her ruthlessness would know no limits. Her revenge was postponed, but it would come down upon the Medici and leave their still-beating hearts skewered upon the tips of the pikes, dripping red blood.

She swore it to Reinhardt.

She vowed it to herself.

And only then did she finally fall asleep.

September 1440

54

The Death of Lorenzo

It had all happened so quickly that Cosimo could scarcely believe it. Not even a month ago he had been fighting alongside his brother in Anghiari and now Lorenzo was sitting in the chair opposite him, fighting death.

He had little time left to live.

Cosimo had just arrived at Careggi. When he had gone home after Reinhardt Schwartz's hanging, he had found a servant waiting for him outside the door. The woman looked beside herself, and told him that the family had left for Careggi because Lorenzo had been taken ill that morning.

Cosimo had immediately raced on horseback to the villa to which Lorenzo had retired. After the blood and pain of Anghiari, he had devoted himself to his favourite pastime: hunting.

And now he was there.

'It's not fair, it's not fair...' murmured Ginevra as she looked at her husband.

Lorenzo was sitting in his favourite old armchair in the portico opposite the courtyard, despite the intense heat.

He loved the garden so much: if his life had to end, it might as well end in the open air, he had said.

Tearfully, Ginevra embraced Cosimo before letting him approach his brother.

Lorenzo struggled to speak. He looked as though he had aged ten years in a single night. His beautiful green eyes were dull and faded and his hair, once a glossy brown, was now streaked with white.

'My brother,' he said, 'the moment has arrived. In faith, I didn't expect it so soon, but I accept what God has planned for me.'

Cosimo squeezed Lorenzo's hands in his.

'Don't say that even in jest, Lorenzo.'

'Cosimo, I have only a few hours left. I feel a great pain in my chest and the doctors say I shan't see the sun rise tomorrow, so let us waste no time...' Lorenzo wanted nothing to be left unsaid, so he measured out his remaining energies as he spoke. 'My first thought is for my family. Look after Ginevra and my two boys

Francesco and Pierfrancesco. No one is better able to do that than you.'

'You know how much I love them,' he replied in a whisper. 'I will continue to love them just as I love Giovanni and Piero.'

'I thank you. It has been an honour to be your brother... I still think about the time we rode together to warn Niccolò da Uzzano... And then... And then to Francesco Sforza's camp... do you remember?'

'Of course I remember, Lorenzo – how could I forget?'

His brother nodded and made to continue, as though wanting, in those last moments, to relive all that they had done together. Cosimo understood perfectly and, so as not to let him tire himself, he continued in his place.

Around them it seemed that time had stopped. Wives, children and grandchildren held their breath, silent witnesses of the end of an era.

'And then the sentence, and the Alberghetto cell. You gathering that army and going to the gates of Florence when you learned that they'd decided to exile us...' continued Cosimo. 'And then Venice, that damn woman, the attack...'

But at that point the emotion became too great and his voice broke. He felt he was losing a piece of his own heart and he began to weep.

'Y-yes...' Lorenzo interrupted, grabbing his arm. '... and then the return to Florence... the league, the council... Ferrara, Florence and then Anghiari...'

And as he murmured those words, his grip grew weaker and his hand fell from Cosimo's arm. His voice faded into a whisper and then disappeared. His eyes, always so lively and vivacious, were now as dull as stones that had suddenly lost their natural brightness.

Cosimo embraced him and held him to his chest. He wept.

Lorenzo was gone.

He would miss his courage, his profound sense of justice, his nobility of spirit and the generosity of his heart. He would no longer hear his kind, steady voice, his laughter, his reassuring advice.

And as hard as he tried, Cosimo could not find the words to tell the others: Ginevra, who was staring at him, and Lorenzo, eyes red from weeping, Francesco and Pierfrancesco, Contessina, Giovanni, Piero. He had run out of words. He thought about how unjust it was of death to call Lorenzo to him first. Lorenzo was the youngest, the best, the most just. The one who had never conspired or plotted to obtain advantages through government and official positions; the one who had never tried to undermine others and who had only ever defended himself.

Cosimo was overcome with intense pain. Life meant nothing if it was to be spent without his brother. How would he manage? Lorenzo, who had been the soul of that family, always there when he, Cosimo, was too busy dealing with politics and handing out official positions. Lorenzo who, more than any other, had, together with Giovanni de' Benci, developed and extended the bank, making sure that its stewards were loyal administrators of the various branches and always trying to ensure that they ran well. Lorenzo who, instead of wasting time in chit-chat, dealt in facts.

Cosimo laid his brother against the back of the beautiful velvet armchair and then went over to Ginevra and the others. He embraced them all, because they were his family. From now on, it would be he and he alone who would have to look after them. Of course, he had guaranteed them a future and had fought for the peace and security of the city, but now it was time for affection and calm – for teaching and listening.

No more infighting and corruption, no more secret alliances and councils, no more appointments and machinations.

He would live inside his family. He would retreat gradually from political life and let his children ensure that the Medici enjoyed a prosperous life. The task had occupied him for so long that little by little it had erased his existence as a man. He must stop before it was too late. He must do it for his brother. To honour his unjust death.

He would do everything in his power for his family, of course, not only to preserve its assets and property and ensure its financial security, but also because he knew that affection, education, apprenticeships and teachings were as indispensable for his children and grandchildren as they had been for him. Now more than ever, Ginevra needed him, and so did his wife Contessina.

The time had come for reflection and for love – for listening and for protection.

That was what Lorenzo had taught him. And that was what he would do.

He broke from the embrace and hurried off to call the servants to help him carry his brother's body to his apartments. They would set up a chapel of rest so that all could come to pay homage to him, then he would have a sumptuous funeral celebrated in his honour in the church of San Lorenzo.

He looked up at the blue sky. The disc of the sun was blazing fiercely down, spreading its rays over the pale blanket of hay that covered the earth.

September 1453

55

Sweet Hopes

My dear Cosimo,

I hope this letter of mine finds you well and healthy, and with your insight and wit enriched by the passing days with experience and patience, virtues which are all the more precious as they are shaped in the gleaming forge of time.

Unfortunately, due to the high esteem in which I hold you and the dark tone of what I am about to tell you, this letter is not one it gives me pleasure to write.

The capture of Constantinople has thrown me into such despair that I struggle to understand the implications of so great a tragedy. In the loss of my beloved city I have lost myself forever, and in a sense I am afraid that I have, because nothing will ever be the same for me again.

When I think of the slavery of so many men and, even worse, of the fortune and happiness from which they have fallen into that gloomy abyss of misery, I can give myself no peace. That I escaped and found shelter some years ago in the Western Roman Church only sharpens a pain which, inevitably, calls me a coward and a traitor for having turned my back forever upon that which I most loved, thinking only of my personal self-interest: a salvation which now feels like a perpetual exile. I know that you will understand me perfectly, having experienced it yourself long before I did, when men who had made an art of betrayal and deception removed you from your beloved Florence and placed you in confinement.

Whenever my thoughts go, even for an moment, to the unspeakable beauty of the churches and palazzos of Byzantium, the magnificent formulas contained in its codes and memorials, the wonder of our language, now lost forever, my heart and my mind inevitably return to those words we exchanged fourteen years ago in Florence. Do you still remember?

We were filled with hope then, and nurtured the dream of a grand reconciliation between the Churches and of a grand union, ready to stand firm against the Muslims, who seemed so invincible. But then events took their course and nothing can ever erase the memories of this wreck of a man who all now accuse of being at least partly responsible.

And when I reflect that, along with the fall of political and spiritual power, my own people fall too, I cannot express to you the downpour of bitter thoughts that overwhelm me. And knowing that the books and language that distinguish us from the barbarians will be lost, my hopes fade into melancholy.

But it is better to endure and, by making ourselves more like God, try to escape from this earth for heaven as soon as possible.

So forgive me for this foolish outburst, my friend. An outburst which is all the more pointless because it cannot turn back the wheel of time or change the course of history. What has happened has already been entered in the great ledger of memory and prepares to crumble into dust. And yet I hope one day to read a letter from you and to be able to draw from your friendly words a comfort that at this moment I can no longer see.

Thanking you again for your generous attentions, I take my leave.

Infinitely grateful, I embrace you,

Basilios Bessarion

Cosimo raised his eyes from the letter and a tear fell on to the parchment, smudging the words. They expressed not only his friend's profound bitterness but also the failure of the plan they had once hoped to realize. In that failure, so clear and evident to all now, were all the errors of a time filled with division and feuds.

He sat in a chair in the library. Rays of pale light penetrated the parted shutters, which shielded the interior of the villa from the September sun. Surprisingly, the morning was cool and a gentle breeze was blowing, occasionally riffling the papers that crowded the large desk at which Cosimo loved to spend most of the day.

After the years spent in politics and banking, Cosimo finally had time for reading and philosophy. He had retired to the Careggi villa, restored by Michelozzo, and there he spent the best part of his time.

For him, that *locus amoenus* was like an artist's impression of a memory – it was the villa where his beloved brother had passed away, and during those disconsolate days Cosimo had resolved to take his leave from political life and dedicate himself to his family. But the place was also a source of the leisure and tranquillity that were crucial for a man of his age. He had only recently handed over the management of the Medici bank to his second son, Giovanni, and had severely reduced the number of his political commitments.

His time was over now. His great enemies, Rinaldo degli Albizzi and Filippo Maria Visconti, had long since died. His most extraordinary ally, Francesco Sforza, had finally managed to conquer the Duchy of Milan, establishing an alliance that, though it had distanced Florence from Venice, had nevertheless confirmed his role as a leader with formidable strength.

Even Pope Eugene IV was dead. That had been a serious loss for Cosimo. The new pontiff, Nicholas V, who was closer to the Albizzi and the Strozzi, did not share the same commonality of purpose and, Cosimo felt, had offered only tepid support to Constantine XI Palaiologos, the *basileus* of Byzantium, in fighting the Turks. The words of condolence expressed by the Pope on the fall of Constantinople had therefore rung particularly false in his ears.

In the light of these considerations, Bessarion's words were even more painful.

It was true that Constantine XI had not formalized the union of the Churches in 1439, but was that enough to justify this lack of interest from the new Pope, which, in hindsight, placed the entire Western world at risk?

Cosimo did not know, but perhaps at that moment, after so many battles and dangers, after exile and conflict, the time had come for him simply to enjoy his long-sought peace with his family.

He pulled aside the curtains and looked out at the magnificent garden that his brother had loved so much. It was already tinged with the yellow and orange of autumn, and there was in that season much of what he had become: an old man, good for giving advice and for playing with the grandchildren. That, at least, was what he aspired to, because the world as he had known it was changed if not gone altogether. What mattered more than anything else in that moment was love for his family, peace and prosperity. The joy of still having Contessina by his side. The joy given him by the children, who would now be responsible for the future of the Medici.

Cosimo was pleased with Giovanni but he worried for Piero: the young man was sick with gout, just as he was, and not very gifted in politics. The position of the Medici in the city was solid, but that was no thanks to Piero.

He was looking again at the colours of the garden before him when his thoughts were disturbed by a melodic voice echoing along the corridor that led to the library, calling his name.

Before he had time to answer, a small, brown-haired fury raced through the half-open door.

'Grandfather! I've found you finally! Where have you been hiding?' asked little Lorenzo. He wore a contagious smile and his eyes sparkled with intelligence.

Cosimo smiled. This was why, despite everything, he had to thank his son Piero: because it had been he who had given Cosimo that wonderful, lively grandson, so full of wit and initiative, who was quite clearly his protégé.

'I've been here all the time, Lorenzo,' he replied indulgently. 'Where did you think I was?'

'Swear you're not lying!' cried the little boy.

The grandfather, who forgave his grandchild any impertinence, nodded. 'I am telling the truth – just as it is the truth that, if you like, we shall go out into the garden.'

'Yes!' shouted the little boy, who couldn't wait to run between the rows of trees in the orchards. 'To the garden!' he repeated triumphantly. 'Let's go to the garden!'

'But if you really want to go, you must make sure you don't tire me out too much. Your grandfather is not as young as he used to be. Will you promise me that you won't tire me out?'

'I promise,' said Lorenzo seriously.

'Very well. Give me a moment and I shall join you.'

'Shall I go on ahead?' the child asked him, assuming a martial-like pose.

'You go on ahead, my brave one. Wait for me at the bottom of the stairs.'

'Hurrah!' shouted Lorenzo, excited again. And then, without another word, he shot out of the library door like a cannonball.

At the sight of him departing with the same haste with which he had arrived, Cosimo couldn't hold back a smile.

'Come now, old fellow,' he said to himself, 'get a move on, or as sure as your name is Cosimo de' Medici, you'll disappoint your grandson.'

And that, he thought, would be a sin he wouldn't be able to live with.

Author's Note

As you can well imagine, the preparation of a historical trilogy like this presupposes manic and desperate study, as Giacomo Leopardi would have put it, because each detail, each scene, each habit and custom must be researched, thought about and reconstructed long before it can be transferred to the page.

It is worth remembering that the story of the Medici involves an arc of time of almost three hundred years: from the beginning of the fifteenth century to the eighteenth century – and this only as regards the period during which the Medici dominated the city of Florence, otherwise the timeframe would be much greater. This fact made some choices inevitable. The first novel is dedicated to the figure of Cosimo the Elder, the second to Lorenzo the Magnificent and the third to Caterina de' Medici, Queen of France: a narrative framework that allowed me to cover a broad period from a historical perspective without of losing continuity.

I chose to shape the backbone of this work through repeated and careful readings of the *Florentine Histories* by Niccolò Machiavelli and *The History of Italy* by Francesco Guicciardini. I did so because I wanted to base the book upon those histories that best captured the spirit of the times in their language and description. For this initial approach, I also undertook some Florentine 'pilgrimages', so as to incorporate into my ideas images of the city's squares, domes, cathedrals and palazzos: because the place is history itself.

And speaking of domes: the first chapter alone, which introduces the work carried out by Filippo Brunelleschi on the construction of the imposing dome of Santa Maria del Fiore, required considerable study. Among the many monographs I consulted, I should mention at least those by Eugenio Battisti (*Filippo Brunelleschi*, New York 1981) and Ross King (*Brunelleschi's Dome: The Story of the Great Cathedral in Florence*, New York 2000).

I could say the same for the battle of Anghiari, another very important passage in this first book about the rise of the House of Medici. Here I will confess that I took a few liberties. It is down to you to discover what they are, but that shouldn't be particularly difficult and they are, perhaps, the only real liberties that I have taken with historical fact. A novelist, though, has to invent and it is in the mixture of fact and *invention* that the particular reaction proper to the historical novel occurs.

In any case, the techniques of war and the individual phases of the battle of Anghiari are reconstructed with care and loyalty to the sources. Among the monographs consulted, I would like to mention Massimo Predonzani's *Anghiari 29 Giugno 1440: La Battaglia, l'Iconografia, le Compagnie di Ventura, l'Araldica* (San Marino 2010).

Another key issue was the study of the mercenary troops and the particular relationship that existed between Renaissance lords and soldiers of fortunes. The profession of arms, to quote film director Ermanno Olmi, was particularly widespread and profitable during the Renaissance, at least for those courageous and unscrupulous enough to change sides when necessary. In this regard, the reading of Ghimel Adar (*Storie di Mercenari e di Capitani di Ventura*, Geneva 1972) proved to be fundamental. Furthermore, I could not have handled the duels and battle sequences satisfactorily without the help of historical fencing manuals, in particular those of Giacomo di Grassi (*Ragione di adoprar sicuramente l'Arme sì da offesa, come da difesa; con un Trattato dell'inganno, et con un modo di esercitarsi da se stesso, per acquistare forsa, giudizio, et prestezza* – translated into English as *Di Grassi, His True Arte of Defence*, Venice 1570) and Francesco di Sandro Altoni (*Monomachia: Trattato dell'arte di scherma*, edited by Alessandro Battistini,

Marco Rubboli, Iacopo Venni, San Marino 2007). None of which prevented me from adding to the traditional the odd hint of modernity, so the terms are not always used strictly as they should be. I trust you will be forgiving.

As regards food and the timing of meals, I have opted for readability and clarity over strict accuracy... but these, I hope, are sins of little importance.

Acknowledgements

This novel is the first of a trilogy. In a sense it is, at least for me, the story of stories, because it tells the saga of the most powerful family of the Renaissance: the Medici. I confess that it was a daunting challenge for a novelist, but I had the perfect publisher for a project like this and when that is the case, an irresistible kind of magic is triggered in my mind.

I had wanted to publish a trilogy for Newton Compton for a long time. I grew up with the novels of Emilio Salgari, a giant of Italian literature and creator of series such as those about Sandokan and the Black Corsair, whose adventures I read in the magnificent Newton Ragazzi series. My father brought home those wonderful books for me, with their white covers edged in red, and I haven't stopped reading since.

And so meeting Vittorio Avanzini, one of the great fathers of Italian publishing, thirty years later was a dream come true. Discovering that I would be published by Newton Compton gave me so much joy that... well, I can still hardly believe it. And that wasn't all: thanks to his profound knowledge of the Italian Renaissance and genuine love of the Medici, Mr Avanzini was a reference point during the drafting of this novel, providing me with many suggestions and ideas. I owe him my deepest gratitude.

Another very big thank you goes to Raffaello Avanzini for his courage, intelligence and energy, as well as his intuition and conviction that a story like that of the Medici and the Renaissance absolutely needed to be told. The trust he placed in my work is a precious gift and his words of encouragement would spur on even the laziest of authors. Every discussion with him leaves me a richer man. I am amazed to see how deeply he believes in publishing and in the book and with what determination he sees every detail as a new opportunity. So thank you, my captain, for this wonderful adventure.

As well as the publishers, I want to thank my agents: Monica Malatesta and Simone Marchi who, as always, made the difference. They worked, and worked, and worked incessantly. Since I met them, my life as a novelist has changed dramatically. I hope that all authors have the opportunity to work with extraordinary professionals like them.

Alessandra Penna, my editor: thanks is too small a word. Her patience, her sensitivity, the beauty of the ideas she suggested and I adopted, her teachings, the chats by email, the greetings in German... it was all simply wonderful – so wonderful that I admit I can't wait to start the next...

Thanks to Martina Donati for her comments and for the precision and the attention offered with generosity and infinite competence.

Thanks to Antonella Sarandrea for having devised effective strategies, for her inventiveness and for her rare ability to handle press coverage and event organization in the best possible way for this trilogy.

Thanks to Carmen Prestia and Raffaello Avanzini (again) for their incredible work with foreign markets.

Finally, I would like to thank all the rest of Newton Compton Editori's team for their kindness, competence and professionalism. Thanks to Edoardo Rialti, literary critic, translator and profound connoisseur of his city: Florence. Thank you for taking me on walks and for the charming explanations full of wonder you gave me: your suggestions and directions, impeccable and precise, made all the difference. Thanks to Patrizia Debicke van der Noot for listening and resolving in a masterly way several doubts that tormented me.

There are two authors who, more than any other, were the reference point for this saga: Alexandre Dumas and Heinrich von Kleist. Anything I can say about their art is absolutely redundant. The best suggestion I can give is: read their novels.

Naturally, I want to thank Sugarpulp for their support and deep friendship: Giacomo Brunoro, Andrea

Andreetta, Massimo Zammataro, Matteo Bernardi and Piero Maggioni.

Thanks to Lucia and Giorgio Strukul, Leonardo, Chiara, Alice and Greta Strukul, my clan, my gang of loved ones, my safe haven.

Thanks to the Gorgis: Anna and Odino, Lorenzo, Marta, Alessandro and Federico.

Thanks to Marisa, Margherita and Andrea 'the Bull' Camporese: you're a great triad.

Thanks to Caterina whom I adore and to Luciano who is always with me, with all his courage and wisdom.

Thanks to Oddone and Teresa and to that African sea we saw together.

Thanks to Silvia and Angelica. Thank you so much as always to Jacopo Masini & Dusty Eye. Thanks to Marilù Oliva, Marcello Simoni, Francesca Bertuzzi, Francesco Ferracin, Gian Paolo Serino, Simone Sarasso, Giuliano Pasini, Roberto Genovesi, Alessio Romano, Romano de Marco and Mirko Zilahi de Gyurgyokai.

In conclusion: infinite thanks to Victor Gischler, Tim Willocks, Nicolai Lilin, Sarah Pinborough, Jason Starr, Allan Guthrie, Gabriele Macchietto, Elisabetta Zaramella, Lyda Patitucci, Alessandro Zangrando, Francesca Visentin, Anna Sandri, Leandro Barsotti, Sergio Frigo, Massimo Zilio, Chiara Ermolli, Giuliano Ramazzina, Giampietro Spigolon, Erika Vanuzzo, Marco Accordi Rickards, Daniele Cutali, Stefania Baracco, Piero Ferrante, Tatjana Giorcelli, Gabriella

Ziraldo, Marco Piva a.k.a. il Gran Balivo, Alessia Padula, Enrico Barison, Federica Fanzago, Nausica Scarparo, Luca Finzi Contini, Anna Mantovani, Laura Ester Ruffino, Renato Umberto Ruffino, Claudia Julia Catalano, Piero Melati, Cecilia Serafini, Tiziana Virgili, Diego Loreggian, Andrea Fabris, Sara Boero, Laura Campion Zagato, Elena Rama, Gianluca Morozzi, Alessandra Costa, Và Twin, Eleonora Forno, Davide De Felicis, Simone Martinello, Attilio Bruno, Chicca Rosa Casalini, Fabio Migneco, Stefano Zattera, Marianna Bonelli, Andrea Giuseppe Castriotta, Patrizia Seghezzi, Eleonora Aracri, Mauro Falciani, Federica Belleri, Monica Conserotti, Roberta Camerlengo, Agnese Meneghel, Marco Tavanti, Pasquale Ruju, Marisa Negrato, Serena Baccarin, Martina De Rossi, Silvana Battaglioli, Fabio Chiesa, Andrea Tralli, Susy Valpreda Micelli, Tiziana Battaiuoli, Valentina Bertuzzi, Valter Ocule, Lucia Garaio, Chiara Calò, Marcello Bernardi, Paola Ranzato, Davide Gianella, Anna Piva, Enrico 'Ozzy' Rossi, Cristina Cecchini, Iaia Bruni, Marco 'Killer Mantovano' Piva, Buddy Giovinazzo, Gesine Giovinazzo Todt, Carlo Scarabello, Elena Crescentini, Simone Piva & i Viola Velluto, Anna Cavaliere, AnnCleire Pi, Franci Karou Cat, Paola Rambaldi, Alessandro Berselli, Danilo Villani, Marco Busatta, Irene Lodi, Matteo Bianchi, Patrizia Oliva, Margherita Corradin, Alberto Botton, Alberto Amorelli, Carlo Vanin, Valentina Gambarini, Alexandra Fischer, Thomas Tono, Ilaria de Togni,

Massimo Candotti, Martina Sartor, Giorgio Picarone, Rossella Scarso, Federica Bellon, Laino Mary, Gianluca Marinelli, Cormac Cor, Laura Mura, Giovanni Cagnoni, Gilberto Moretti, Beatrice Biondi, Fabio Niciarelli, Jakub Walczak, Lorenzo Scano, Diana Severati, Marta Ricci, Anna Lorefice, Carla VMar, Davide Avanzo, Sachi Alexandra Osti, Emanuela Maria Quinto Ferro, Vèramones Cooper, Alberto Vedovato, Diana Albertin, Elisabetta Convento, Mauro Ratti, Mauro Biasi, Giulio Nicolazzi, Nicola Giraldi, Alessia Menin, Michele di Marco, Sara Tagliente, Vy Lydia Andersen, Elena Bigoni, Corrado Artale, Marco Guglielmi and Martina Mezzadri.

I'll certainly have forgotten someone. As I've said before... you'll be in the next book, that's a promise!

A big hug and infinite thanks to all the readers, booksellers and promoters who put their faith in my historical trilogy and its romance, intrigue, duels and betrayals.

I dedicate this novel and the entire trilogy to my wife Silvia: because she has made me happier than I could ever have dreamed of being in this life and because she is the most beautiful woman and human being I have ever met.

About the author

Matteo Strukul was born in Padua in 1973 and has a Ph.D. in European law. His novels are published in twenty countries. He writes for the cultural section of *Venerdì di Repubblica* and lives with his wife in Padua, Berlin and Transylvania.